Not the End

by

Kate Vane

One

No blood, vomit or faeces. No stain working its way across the bed or the sofa or the living-room carpet. No flies buzzing at the window. Maud Smith, aged eighty-eight, may have died leaving no one to bury her, but she had at least done him the favour of not dying at home.

'This is allowed, isn't it?' Trevor hovered in the doorway like a vicar unwillingly called to perform an exorcism, thin fingers worrying at the worst comb-over in Christendom. All because Neil had forgotten his council ID.

Neil scanned the room. Not the usual stuff. No photographs or old lady knick-knacks. Some people filled the gaps left by people with things – china figurines, hard-core pornography, stacks of old newspapers which threatened to crush the unwary cemetery manager under their weight. He'd seen them all.

This was calm and minimal. Free of the detritus of family life. Walls painted landlord magnolia. A couple of abstracts on the wall adding a splash of colour. Newish kitchen which was clean. Nice location too, right on the prom. Not far from the cemetery, he'd have walked if he didn't have stuff to take back.

'Do you know if she wanted to be buried or cremated?'

Trevor looked alarmed. 'Me? Not the sort of thing you talk about, is it?'

'It's my job to talk about it. I take it you didn't know her very well.'

'She paid the rent by standing order. I only met her when she moved in, and once when I came for the quarterly inspection.'

'Nice lady was she?'

Trevor looked blank. 'I suppose so. Didn't offer me a cup of tea. But the flat was clean.'

'Any of the neighbours know her?'

'Doubt it. They're mostly young in this house. Arty types.' He shook his head, mystified. 'It's not really a pensioner's flat, with the steps and the noise from the seafront. I offered to introduce her to a mate who owns a development for the over fifty-fives. Lovely it is, with a lift and a communal lounge. I thought she was going to hit me. What are you after?'

'First I want to see if there's a will or a funeral plan. Anything to indicate her wishes. Letters, address books. The names of any relatives.' Unlikely. The coroner's office had already made enquiries but they weren't always the most conscientious. Not like him. 'And then I want to see if there are any financial papers or other valuables. Anything that will help cover the cost of the funeral.'

'I thought the council were doing the funeral.'

'We'll organise it if there's no one else, but if we can recover our costs, we will. It's public money after all.' And we need every penny, Neil thought. He couldn't even order paperclips since the last round of cuts.

'And when you've finished, you'll clear the flat? Because I can't have it standing empty much longer.'

'Sorry, mate, that's your responsibility. Once I've taken what I need, the rest is down to you.'

Trevor looked around, bewildered. 'I saw them do it on *Grimebusters*.'

'Maybe it was a council flat. Like I said, landlord's responsibility.'

'But how am I going to –?' Neil thought he was going to cry. He stroked his hair again. Trevor's phone rang. He went out into the hall. Neil could hear him speaking in a whine. Sounded like someone wanted to view one of his properties and Trevor was finding it just too difficult to decide on a suitable time. Maybe he didn't want to miss his egg-and-soldiers tea. All hail the small businessman, the backbone of the British economy.

Made Neil wonder, sometimes, how people ended up in jobs that didn't suit them. Thought about the way it must eat at your gut, getting up every day, knowing you had to do something you hated. He was lucky. Maybe no one ever said they wanted to manage a cemetery when they grew up, but he'd found himself in the right place.

Okay, he'd taken a few detours along the way, like the two-week package in Crete that turned into two years doing building work between benders, and a spell on the Enterprise Allowance as a performance poet, though a timely bout of writer's block meant he never actually got a gig.

Eventually he'd drifted into a job with a London parks department and surprised himself by liking it. Physical work was good for him and he learned to love everything about horticulture, from the power and noise of cutting down trees with big machines to the delicate mysteries of propagation. Nurturing life. Cemeteries seemed a natural progression.

There were clothes on the bed, neatly folded. Presumably what she'd been wearing before she went out. A sunhat with a big brim on the chair beside the bed. He opened the wardrobe. Some clothes had been rolled up in a ball at the bottom of the wardrobe. Maybe she'd been struggling more than she let on. Or maybe she'd chucked them in there after a night on the shandies.

He moved the clothes cautiously. He'd once found a turd in a heap of clothes. He wished he'd remembered the latex gloves. Still he had to look, there might be a shoebox full of papers or even cash, but he found nothing.

His phone went. He pulled it out of his pocket. Text from Lisa 2. He put it straight back again. Lisa 2 was his wife. His ex-wife, also called Lisa, was in as Lisa 1.

He'd set this up a year or so ago after he'd popped round to Phil's to pick Tom up from Phil's kid's birthday party. The party was still in full swing, with a giggly, excitable atmosphere coming less from the four-year-old birthday boy and his friends than from the 'grown-up pop' and 'big people's brownies' which Phil was surreptitiously distributing.

Neil found himself joining in a game of musical statues while the host randomly turned the volume up and down on 'Anarchy in the UK'. Tom was first out and his face crumpled. Neil wondered if he should move so he could go and comfort him but he was seized by a sudden overwhelming urge to win that was not diminished by the fact that everyone else playing was either under five or completely slaughtered.

The music stopped again. He stood, one leg in the air. His mobile rang. A woman who'd just been introduced to him as Charlotte, with bright eyes and startling red lipstick, fumbled in his pocket for his phone, showed him the display that said 'Lisa' was calling and then held it to his ear.

He had to listen to a call about his failings as a father, his financial fecklessness and his general unwillingness to take life seriously, while keeping one leg in the air. All while giving the impression of being grateful to Charlotte for her help but not in the least aroused by her breathless, tipsy swaying against him.

Finally, Phil turned up the music and Neil said he was hanging up because his ego needed emergency first aid. As he took the phone from Charlotte their fingers touched and she played at refusing to let go and they both laughed. Neil won the game and by the time the party finished Tom was smiling. He held his cake and present and sang about being an antichrist in a sweet, tuneless voice.

'No that's me,' said Neil, and it was only then he realised he had no idea which Lisa he'd been speaking to.

Lisa 2 objected to her styling. 'I'm your wife,' she said. 'I'm Lisa. She's the past.' He'd said the numbers were just about chronology, he wasn't assigning merit, but Lisa was unmoved. One of the gravediggers had put 'The Wife' and 'The Ex' on his phone, but Neil didn't think Lisa would like that much either.

He went to the window. Sea view and everything. Blue sky above a calm sea. The occasional fluffy cloud like *The Simpsons*. Life seemingly simple and happy in the double-glazed distance.

He found a drawer full of paperwork in the chest by the window. There were bank books, bills and assorted financial papers but he couldn't see an address book. No sign of a mobile or a computer either. Easiest just to take the lot, sort it when he got back. He'd stop by the coroner's office, they said they had her birth and marriage certificates.

He relented and checked the text. Lisa was taking Tom swimming at the Lido. Reminding him that he'd have to tidy 'all that crap' in Martha's room in time for her visit. Lisa thought it was important that they maintain the fiction that Martha had a room of her own waiting for her at any moment, although she only came about once a month. When he was a kid he didn't even get one bedroom to himself, now they were expected to have two.

Martha didn't care anyway. She was nearly sixteen, at the stage where she was happy kipping on floors after a party or in tents at a festival. She wasn't as big on that territory thing as Lisa made out. But then he and Lisa seemed to have conflicting views on just about everything these days.

The kitchen was decent enough. Dishes washed on the draining board. A bad smell turned out only to be the kitchen bin needing emptying.

Maybe he should jump before he was pushed. Spare room for Martha, near enough to pick up Tom. A dream, of course. Renting involved upfront payments and he'd already committed most of next month's salary to paying the last three months' child support to Lisa 1.

There was another door off the hall but it was locked. He picked up Trevor's keys from the hall table and tried them until it opened. He stumbled into another world. Canvases, brushes, paint. An easel. Maybe the old lady had taken up a hobby. A packing case with the address of a Birmingham storage facility. So maybe she'd been a collector.

There was also a row of dolls on the mantelpiece. What did she want with them? They weren't collectors' items, just cheap plastic. Some looked new, the hideous pink-princess type.

There was a whole energy in this one room, different from the rest of the flat, which might as well have been a hotel room. He was intrigued. He often felt this, when he was going through someone's possessions. They were telling him a story. What was Maud Smith telling him? What was she holding back? He felt a chill down the back of his neck. He turned quickly. Trevor was hovering.

'I thought you were a ghost,' said Neil. Trevor paled. A few strands of comb-over quivered and fell over his ear.

'It's gonna take me some time to go through that room,' said Neil.

Trevor stuck his head round the door and then recoiled.

'You didn't see it before? On your quarterly inspection?'

'It was locked. She said she was just using it for storage. I didn't like to push –'

'What about the coroner's officers?'

'I just gave them the keys and left them to it.'

Bet they didn't touch it, thought Neil.

'I suppose you'll take most of it?' asked Trevor, quivering with hope like a virgin at a dance in a Victoria Wood parody of a Jane Austen adaptation.

Neil looked dubious. 'I'll come back and take a proper look. But I can't think there's much of value in there. The paintings in the living room, that's about it. I don't know what you'd do with the rest. There are a lot of personal things in there. Things she probably used, handled, just before she died.'

He wondered if he was laying it on a bit but Trevor was sweating, the stains spreading from his armpits like a BBC2 documentary of the British Empire taking over the globe. 'I expect you normally want a bond for this place,' Neil continued.

'A month's rent. But it's all genuine, goes in a third-party account –'

'I've got a deal for you. I'll rent this place off you, and I'll clear it myself, if you let me off the bond.'

'I suppose I should ask if you'd jump in her grave as quick.'

'Only if the shoring meets British Standards,' quipped Neil.

Trevor wasn't smiling. 'You don't mind? A dead woman's bed?'

What a salesman. 'It's not as if she died in it. And I'll take good care of the place. Not like renting to the art groupies.'

Trevor looked perplexed. The stains under his arms would soon meet in the middle. He'd be a walking Venn diagram. This would require a show of initiative. But then he looked around the room again. So would that.

'Call me.' Neil picked up the folder with the bank details in it. He winked at the dolls as he left. Maud Smith was smiling down on him, he could tell.

Two

Brenda was in a room off the A&E, sitting on the leatherette couch that looked like a sunlounger, swinging her legs. A nurse had shown her in here and told her to sit down. He'd realised there wasn't a chair, so had hastily pulled the big tissue roll down the length of the thing. Like a toilet roll for a giant's backside. Maybe Brenda had shrunk. Maybe that was why everything seemed far away.

He'd hurried out, looking tired, sweaty, his glasses smeared with fingerprints and maybe something worse. She knew he was a nurse because he was wearing blue scrubs. They were all colour-coded, like Paula's knives and chopping boards. Paula's boyfriend Callum was a chef.

Raw meat, cooked meat, vegetables, dairy – what was the other one? There was a poster on the wall, next to one that told you how you knew if someone was having a stroke, and a yellowing one about deadlines for timesheets for Christmas 2011, that said what all the different-coloured scrubs meant.

There was a desk in the room although there were no chairs. There were folders on the desk, one chewed biro, a stapler with the name 'Sheila' tippexed on it, a pile of notepads with 'Gromycitin' on a logo in the bottom right-hand corner of each page.

Someone in green scrubs – that meant junior doctor – with a laptop under her arm, opened the door. Brenda sat up straight.

'Sorry,' said a voice, and the place where the doctor and the laptop had been was already empty air, but the door wasn't shut. It bounced on its hinges. Brenda could hear waves of noise from outside, the rise and fall of voices, wheels on trolleys, paper being turned over, squeaking feet on polished floors.

She waited for someone to come and shut the door. The tissue roll objected as she shifted. The door bounced. Maybe they had forgotten her. Maybe she would be in this room forever. Perhaps she should shut the door. Or open it. Look for someone in pink scrubs (administration) who might have a piece of paper that might say what was meant to happen next. Brenda sat.

A woman stopped the bouncing door with her foot and looked around the room.

'No chairs,' she said, as if it were Brenda's fault. Brenda wondered if she should follow but then the woman came back with two plastic chairs, one stacked on the other.

She said she was a nurse. She told Brenda her name. Brenda forgot it. Brenda asked her why she wasn't wearing scrubs. Blue scrubs. The woman moved her hand slowly to point to her ID badge, all the time keeping her eyes on Brenda. She saw a picture of a younger, happier version of the woman in front of her. Her name was written underneath. Brenda read it and forgot it again.

'I'm a mental health nurse. We don't wear scrubs.'

Brenda asked why. She said she didn't know, they just didn't. She said some people didn't like it, said they didn't know who was a nurse and who was a patient. She started to laugh. Brenda looked at her, confused. She stopped.

The nurse asked Brenda some questions. She looked to be in her forties but was wearing a print dress meant for someone much younger, which only made her look older. She was wearing flip-flops. Brenda didn't think that was a good idea. Flip-flops were for the beach, not for work. They weren't allowed at her work. What if someone dropped something on your foot? What if a patient collapsed and you had to run to help them? What if a patient went crazy and you had to run away. Mental health nurse. That was who Brenda was seeing now.

The nurse wanted to know what happened that morning.

'I was walking Prince – our Alsatian – on the beach. I felt funny. It got worse as I was coming up the hill.'

'Like what?'

'I don't know. Like I couldn't breathe. Tight in my chest. Hot.'

The nurse never looked up, just made a nodding movement with her head as she made notes. She asked Brenda lots more questions.

Brenda told her she was married with two grown-up kids, both in work, thinking how impressed the nurse would be with how normal it all was. Brenda, Bob, Robbie and Paula.

'Robbie brought me in. I told him not to bother but he insisted. He would have waited but I said he should get to work. He's self-employed, you see. Like his dad.'

'On the beach,' said the nurse, 'did anything happen? To upset you?'

'Maybe I should have had breakfast,' said Brenda. 'But it was early. Just gone five.'

'You always up at that time?'

'I am lately.'

The nurse asked if anything had happened to her, 'lately'. Out of the ordinary. That might have upset her, even if she didn't think so at the time. Brenda said she couldn't think of anything, except –

'I found this old woman who'd drowned. On the beach. A couple of weeks ago. When I was walking Prince.'

The nurse's face lit up like she'd been searching for her car keys all morning and had suddenly remembered where they were. She scribbled some more notes. Brenda didn't interrupt. Then she looked up.

'It sounds like a panic attack,' she said.

'A panic attack?' said Brenda, then felt foolish.

The nurse said reactions to trauma or shock were normal. She described a list of symptoms and Brenda said yes to some of them – palpitations, choking, chest pain...

'Panic attacks don't have serious health effects, but they are very frightening and distressing to the person who experiences them.'

'I know,' said Brenda.

As the traumatic event was recent, the nurse said they wouldn't recommend a mental health intervention at this stage. She would write to Brenda's GP. Brenda should make an appointment as soon as possible. In the meantime she would give her a leaflet on relaxation and breathing techniques.

'What will the GP do?'

'Well.' The nurse looked at her notes but didn't seem to find the answer there and looked up again. 'Anti-anxiety medication can help during an attack but that's really just a short-term solution. We often prescribe antidepressants for people who have repeated attacks. Or there's CBT but you know, with the cutbacks.'

She looked suddenly very tired. Brenda thought she probably had a queue of properly mad people all waiting for her help, for a cure which she didn't have. While Brenda was keeping her talking and there wasn't really anything wrong with Brenda, just her heart thumping in her chest and in her ears and the way her skin tingled like pins and needles and the room kept going further and further away.

They smiled at each other, two people agreeing that they both had more important places to be. Brenda wanted to apologise for wasting her time as the nurse got to her feet

'What is CBT?' Brenda blurted out.

'Sorry, that's cognitive-behavioural therapy,' said the nurse as she put her lid on her pen. 'Speak to your GP. If they can't offer you an appointment, there are self- help materials available. Library books. The internet.' Her voice faded again.

'Is that it?' asked Brenda, more to herself, as the nurse got up to walk away.

The nurse turned back, the door already open, holding onto the doorknob. Brenda could see blue scrubs and chrome and sickly yellow light.

'There are other approaches. Meditation. Yoga.' The nurse frowned. 'I was reading something about knitting. There's been some research.' Her voice died and with a shrug of the shoulders she vanished.

'Fish!' Brenda said suddenly. That was the missing chopping board. She laughed at the thought. A woman in grey scrubs (domestic and ancillary) stuck her head round the door, raised her eyebrows, then pulled the door shut behind her.

Three

Jim couldn't help but smile as he walked along the prom, enjoying the late afternoon sun, agreeably jostled by the crowds. Good-natured whining from tired toddlers. Pensioners taking one more turn along the prom before their coach arrived. Sand on the pavement, plastic windmills turning lazily in the breeze.

He felt a generic nostalgia for the great British bucket-and-spade holiday, even though he'd never actually been on one. His family had gone from camping in the New Forest or Normandy when they were small to European city breaks, striding earnestly round the cultural highlights of Paris and Rome. Until the year after GCSEs when their final family holiday had been cancelled and he'd learnt, later than most, that just because your parents promised you something, it didn't mean it would happen.

He found the house in a row of Georgian – or at least Georgian-style – terraces. Wedding-cake frontages, some neat and bright, others grey. One painted a defiantly drab mustard, breaking up the row like a bad tooth. The one he wanted was one of the older white ones. Sash windows in need of restoration. Neither pristine period nor shiny uPVC.

He didn't like cold calls. Roisin laughingly referred to his boyish charm but he hated that look of mistrust in people's eyes when they were convinced he was trying to sell them something (often he was) or even rip them off. Sometimes the friendly ones were worse, the ones who took him straight into their living room and told him lengthy stories while plying him with tea.

Roisin had called to say she'd got a tip from the Dormouth cemetery manager about an estate that might be worth a bit.

'Maud Smith, née Williams,' Roisin had said, not bothering to mention that Williams and Smith respectively were the two most common surnames in Devon. Because she assumed he already knew, or because she thought he didn't?

He'd counted to five and then she'd said the inevitable words, 'I have a hunch about this one.' Of course the words were largely said in self-parody, but still the belief lay buried somewhere in there.

'Did she own the house?' asked Jim, mechanically.

'Flat. And no. But there's some art.'

'That's it?'

'Neil left me a voicemail and when I've tried to call back there's no reply.'

It was one of Roisin's bright ideas to cultivate cemetery managers and environmental health officers. They were responsible for public health funerals, which meant they often knew about estates with no known heirs before everyone else. Once the information was published by the Treasury Solicitor, any probate researcher, professional or amateur, could chase it. A tip-off allowed them to get ahead of the competition.

He hoped this one would be a quick knock at the door, a gruff yes or ideally no and then on his way. He could of course tell Roisin no one had been in but he had a pathetic inability to lie, especially when Roisin was his interrogator.

Four flats. The first floor still labelled 'Smith'. He tried the others from the ground up. No response till he reached the top floor. Got a warm 'hello' through the crackle of the intercom. She must be expecting someone. He spluttered an explanation of who he was and the voice asked him to hang on.

He waited to be buzzed in, moving from foot to foot, one hand in his pocket holding onto his ID, keeping the inevitable form of words at the front of his mind. He had them polished to a slick minimum, so he could get the gist out before the door slammed in his face. Maybe the buzzer wasn't working. He was just about to give up when the door swung open.

'Come on up.' Before he could speak she'd turned. He walked up the stairs, disoriented after the bright light of outdoors, following a mass of copper curls, shining out of the gloom.

She closed the door and smiled at him. He looked around. It was a studio apartment with a large skylight. Despite being under the eaves it gave the impression of space and light and warmth. His flat looked like the sleeping quarters of a submarine.

'Have a seat,' she said. He sat on a big, stuffed sofa and she took the bed.

There were pictures on the wall, a sequinned dress and a feather boa hanging from a hatstand, puppets dancing beneath the mantelpiece.

'Don't be alarmed,' she said.

'Sorry?'

'The draught from the chimney makes them move.'

'They don't seem to mind. They're smiling.' He was gibbering.

'Shall I take that?' She reached out and took his card from him. She had long fingers, milky-white hands. She was wearing a pale, flowing dress, linen maybe. She looked cool and calm after the livid flesh of the beach people.

'Generation. Probate researchers,' she read.

'We find heirs to estates where there is no will and no next of kin has been identified. You've probably seen *Heir Hunters*.'

'I'm sorry, no.' She gave a smile of polite bemusement and he cursed inwardly. He never said that. Because it really wasn't like it was on the telly, all that faux drama generated by incidental music played over someone frantically cranking up a database or lifting a leather-bound volume off a high shelf. But whenever he said 'probate researcher' normally the first thing anyone said was, yeah, like *Heir Hunters*.

21

He was feeling suddenly absurd with his suit jacket and his salesman's script, like the collision of worlds when you get your first Saturday job in Dixons and your cool mates from the anarchist thrash metal band come down to have a laugh at you and shoplift batteries. Not that he'd lasted long in his Saturday job. He'd suddenly developed a fierce ambition, had thrown himself into studying like it was a drug, and his parents had said he didn't need to work, on top of everything else.

He wanted to say, this isn't really me, but since he was here, now, he supposed it must be. He saw a whole other life rush before him. Catching a glimpse of her in the refectory at a conference in a distant university. Falling into a country pub, aching and exhausted and exhilarated after a day's fieldwork, still a mess of grass and mud and feathers, to see her waiting with a smile. Walking through a forest on a spring day, alive to the wildflowers and the rich decay of leaves, her beside him...He felt breathless. Was he dying? Before he'd even had a bucket-and-spade holiday?

'Would you like to put that down?'

Was she amused or unnerved? He was gripping his neoprene laptop bag tight to his chest. He snapped back to banality.

'Actually I don't know too much about the deceased. I just got the call from my boss. She got the details from the cemetery manager.'

'Neil?' she said.

'You know him?'

'He's moving in.' Jim's heart sank. 'To Maud's

flat,' she clarified, with a smile that made him think she must have seen his face drop, did she?

'You knew Maud Smith?'

'Yes.' Her face lit up.

He hadn't expected that. 'You were close?'

She looked at the puppets, as if waiting for them to prompt her. 'I'm not sure anyone was close to Maud. But we talked. About art and – well, everything.'

He wanted to know about that everything, wanted to stay here all day but he thought regretfully of his ID and his paperwork and the questions he had to ask. At least she wasn't an heir. At least he didn't have to get his clipboard out and give her the spiel and get her to sign, playing the absurd but exhausting game of chess where he had to get the information out of her but not tell her who the heir was, in case she decided to pursue the claim by herself.

'Do you know if she had any relatives?'

'She never mentioned anyone. Her husband was dead.'

'She didn't have children?'

'No.'

'Friends?'

'She didn't really see anyone. She hadn't been here long. She lived in Portugal after she retired, came back when her husband died.'

'Can you think of anyone who might be able to help?'

'I – I don't know.' She was thinking about whether she could trust him. Not that he blamed her, he'd do the same. Maybe she'd think about it and then she'd call him and then –

'I was away when she died. I almost missed the funeral. Then I got back and Neil said it was all arranged. It was such a shock. Sorry, that sounds silly when she was nearly ninety.'

'Did she often swim in the sea?' he asked, just for something to say.

'She swam in Portugal every day and when she moved here she did the same.'

The silence lengthened. He hadn't written much in his notebook to take back to Roisin. He should try some of the other flats.

She was still smiling. He was still here. Then the smile faltered and he noticed tears glistening in her eyes. The whole effect was like sun trying to break through after a shower, even though it should have been the other way round.

He had to go, of course. There was a hotel off a motorway interchange where the guest soap was waiting to be released from its wrapping, where a weary waitress was wiping ketchup from a laminated menu in a dimly lit bar, where a TV remote would bring the illusion of life into an empty room.

'Maybe we could go for a drink – or to eat or –' Cursing his clumsiness.

'I'm going back to the pub,' she said. 'It's the wake –'

'Wake? You don't mean the funeral was today? Now I feel even more of an arse –'

She laughed. 'Come with me,' she said. 'Then we'll talk.'

Four

Jim was drunk and he had gatecrashed a wake. He had walked through long narrow streets to this long narrow bar, with its low nicotine-coloured ceiling and shabby wallpaper. He didn't know if he would ever find his way back again. Or if he wanted to.

Her name was Elizabeth. He guessed that was her name as that's what everyone called her. If asked (hardly anyone asked) he told them his. He was glad people liked her. He liked her, why wouldn't they? But he'd just wanted to be with her. And now here was a man who said he was Neil, just when he'd thought they might be alone.

Neil was the only person wearing black. He'd taken off his suit jacket and thrown it on the table with the handwritten sign that said 'Private function' and foil trays of curling sandwiches and sweaty eclairs. Someone had spilt a pint on it but he'd only laughed.

'I can always suck on it later if I get desperate,' he said.

Jim was aware that cemetery managers sometimes attended the public health funerals they had organised, especially if they were likely to be the only mourner. However, this was the first time he'd come across a manager who attended the wake.

Jim was drinking one of those local ales, he forgot the name, something about badger's breath or humping an alpaca, and hadn't eaten. The sandwiches were definitely unappealing. And he wasn't sure, but he thought that Neil glanced wistfully at Elizabeth from time to time. Was that so, or did he think that everyone must be as enchanted by her as he was?

Had he really spent half the morning in a register office where they'd assured him a marriage certificate would be ready to collect only to get there and have them insist it had never been requested? Sat in the cat-piss-smelling living room of a woman who, rather than being pleased that ten thousand pounds was about to fall into her lap, was unhappy that her cousin in Mevagissey, who lived with a man half her age and never sent a Christmas card, was to get the same amount?

'I should have called you guys sooner,' said Neil. 'Only thought of it this morning. Roisin's done us a few favours so –' He took out a cigarette and held it between his fingers.

'You see much of her?'

'Yes,' said Jim. 'Generation's only a small company so –'

'She's something else, isn't she? Took me to lunch once. Drank me under the table.'

As Neil spoke, Jim looked across at Elizabeth who was talking to someone. It didn't matter who.

She'd told him she was an artist, in one of their brief interludes alone, but then gave a self-deprecating laugh, explaining that she also worked part-time in a shop and gave private lessons to kids and invigilated at exams and worked for Royal Mail at Christmas and anything else she could get between commissions. He had listened to her words but was also intensely aware of the sound of her voice, the light in her eyes, the pumping of his own heart –

'Wasn't sure organising the wake was quite within my remit.' Neil was still burbling. 'But Dave – that's the landlord – said he'd do the buffet for free. Course I didn't know who she was at first. Colin from the paper tipped me off when I put the death notice in. Recognised her maiden name. Then I started getting calls. Wasn't sure this was the best place for the do, it being the home of Hugh's legendary Monday night sessions but – doing a favour for Dave, to be honest. He'd love to get the arty crowd back here again. You know how they drink.'

Neil waved his unlit cigarette around the room, then headed for the door, calling out, 'Charlotte!'

Jim had no idea what he was talking about.

'Who's Hugh?' he asked Elizabeth, when they were finally alone, but then someone else appeared at her elbow. Casual linen jacket, lilac shirt.

'Saw you at the funeral,' he said to Elizabeth. 'I was hoping we'd have a chance to speak.'

Elizabeth tensed. Jim felt it. She smiled and turned towards the man but she wasn't happy.

'Hi Fraser,' she said.

'I can't believe she's died,' said Fraser. Jim was searching for some conventional words of condolence when Fraser continued, 'before I could get something out of her.'

Elizabeth continued as if he hadn't spoken, introducing the two men. Fraser McKendrie was an art historian, it seemed.

'Heir hunter, eh?'

He handed Jim a card and Jim felt obliged to reciprocate. 'Let me know if you get anything I can use.'

'Use for?'

'I'm writing a biography of Hugh Bonnington. We're bound to be covering some of the same ground, if you're researching Maud.'

Jim was about to ask what he meant but Fraser was quicker.

'You don't know?' His eyes were mocking.

'Jim's just got here,' said Elizabeth. 'I was going to tell him.'

Fraser gave a world-weary sigh and then began in lecture mode. 'Hugh Bonnington was an artist. He was a working-class boy who would probably have ended up in a factory if it wasn't for World War Two. But he learnt to paint in a POW camp. After the war he came here, looking for somewhere cheap to live while he developed his craft. He gave lessons – mostly to the local girls,' he said, with a knowing look, 'generally tried to scrape together a living. He and Maud had a liaison.'

'More than that,' said Elizabeth. There was an edge to her voice.

'She was his protégée, muse, mistress, call it what you will. However, he became infatuated with his housekeeper, a chirpy Cockney by the name of Olive. Maud left, running into the arms of one Mr Smith, who she apparently met when he was holidaying in the area. She disappeared into obscurity and never painted again. Incomprehensible, but there you are.'

'Perhaps she was happy,' said Jim.

'Oh, *happy*,' said Fraser. 'I expect you'll be talking to Olive. She's of no use to me, but she might oblige you.'

'Sorry?'

'Hugh Bonnington's widow. She's still going strong, much to the chagrin of the Hugh Bonnington Trust. Whatever's left when she goes reverts to them, but she's allowed to take "reasonable expenses" for the remainder of her life. And dear Olive won't be scrimping and scraping on their behalf. That home she's in is an art deco palace. No wipe-clean chairs and broken custard creams for Olive.'

He turned to Elizabeth.

'You'll let me know if anything turns up, won't you?'

Elizabeth turned away. Jim watched Fraser smirk and go.

'What is he looking for?' asked Jim.

'When Maud left Hugh, he was working on a painting of her. The painting had caught the eye of a London dealer before it was even finished. It would have been Hugh's big sale. But after she left, so the story goes, he was so heartbroken that he burnt it.'

'He destroyed his one chance of success?'

Elizabeth laughed. 'The story was the making of him. Suddenly everyone was interested in this tortured soul.'

'So what's Fraser after?'

'There have always been people who doubted the story. It was said that Maud hated posing. That she agreed to model for Hugh only because he told her he wanted the picture for himself. That he would never sell it. When he agreed the sale, she was furious. Some people suggest that she may have destroyed it before she left. Or even taken it with her.'

'And Fraser thinks she might still have had it.'

'Hopes.'

'What do you think?' asked Jim.

'I don't know.'

'Did you ever ask?'

'I thought she'd tell me if she wanted to.'

'Fraser would have asked,' he said.

'Exactly,' she said. 'He's passionate about Hugh. So much so that he can lose perspective.'

Her voice sounded cool when she said it but there was heat in her face. What did Fraser mean to her?

'It's good to be passionate about your work,' he said.

'I'm guessing you're not,' she said.

'I used to be. I was an academic too, an ecologist. I was doing post-doctoral research. Short-term contracts. Then no contract. So this job, in theory, is temporary, although it's a permanent post, while the job I loved was temporary, though in my heart it was my life's work, but I've been out of it for a couple of years now –'

I'm rambling, he thought. I must shut up. Roisin always said he became earnest when he was drunk.

'What were you working on?'

Neil had sidled up to them again.

'I've always loved birds,' Jim said. 'My specialism was urban ecology. Most recently, how breeding patterns are affected by changes to food sources in –'

'Like urban seagulls,' said Neil. 'I've been reading about that. And my daughter's into conservation. Made me watch *Springwatch* – '

A man grabbed Neil's arm. 'Your round, mate,' he said. He winked at Jim as he led Neil away.

He waited for her to say, but you can go birdwatching at weekends (hardly the same thing). Or something will turn up (statistically unlikely). Or why don't you start a blog (not even worth explaining)?

'You're bereaved,' she said.

'That's it. Exactly!' he said. Finally someone got it. She'd put into words something that he couldn't fully explain himself. His hand, seemingly of its own accord, held hers, and suddenly they were kissing.

'Oh God!' he said, moving back.

'What?' She seemed amused.

'I feel so selfish. You're the one who's bereaved. Literally.'

'We have a lot of seagulls nesting on the roofs near us,' said Elizabeth. 'Wake you up at dawn. You should hear them.'

She smiled and sipped her drink. He was about to say he'd never actually done any work on seagulls but then she kissed him again and he thought better of it.

Five

'Brenda, there's someone wants to see you.'

People were always popping in, saying they wanted building work done. Even people who didn't know her. They'd smirk and ask for Bob the Builder's wife. Bob didn't mind, he always said, 'I don't care if they laugh, as long as they remember me.'

She put down the box she was shifting. They'd had a rush on disposable barbecues so there was an empty display at the end of the aisle. The manager had told her to fill it up with soup cans because no one would buy them in a heatwave.

A man said, 'Brenda?' and she frowned.

'Do I know you?'

But of course, Brenda didn't know people like him, with his floppy blond hair and his clothes which were somehow scruffy and yet expensive – why buy linen if you can't be bothered ironing? – and his battered satchel like one she'd had at school.

He wasn't the type that came here with the kids. He was the type that rented a caravan in a campsite on a farm, miles from the beach, and swam in a lake that looked like a sewer and bought eggs from the farmer with the chicken shit still on them and thought that was real Devon life.

And paid twice what they would at Dawlish Warren for a lovely beach and an indoor pool and a train line that took you all along the estuary, and still thought they were clever.

'Fraser. Fraser McKendrie.' He held his hand out for her to shake. She put her hand limply into his.

'Can we talk in private?' he asked.

'I can't take long,' she said, looking over her shoulder. That was her afternoon tea break gone.

'Oh. Okay.' They went out to the car park and sat on the wall which surrounded the bed of tightly trimmed hebes and chunky bark peppered with fag butts. She was on rota to come and pick them out later.

'If it's building work you're after I can give you his mobile –'

'Me? I'm staying at a friend's place. Inherited it from some mad uncle. Not that it couldn't do with some work but that's why I got it cheap. Not fit for tenants.'

She wasn't sure if that was a yes or a no. She waited.

'I'm writing a book on Hugh Bonnington. I'm an academic, but a publisher has asked me to do a biography. It will be ten years since his death in two years time so she's thinking there'll be the usual – op-ed pieces, documentaries, souvenir tea towels. Only I'm struggling to get the tone for the ordinary person – you know – someone who listens to Radio Four, maybe takes in the odd book festival, watches an Andrew Graham-Dixon documentary a year while balancing their Marks and Spencer meal deal on their lap and thinks they're an expert –'

'What's this got to do with me?'

'You found her, didn't you?'

'Who?' But she felt a thud in her belly. Like a stone dropping into a pond. You could hear it. Thud. It vibrated through her, right up to her ears.

'Maud. Maud Smith. Maud Williams as was. His muse. Until the untimely intervention of Olive, later Mrs Bonnington.'

Brenda knew Olive Bonnington alright. 'How did you find me?'

'Saw the article in the local paper.'

'It never mentioned that I work here.'

'That's the beauty of a close-knit community, isn't it? So we hear. Everybody knows everybody's business, the rules are clear, anyone who doesn't conform is ostracised until they succumb –'

He sounded angry but she didn't know why.

'Anyway, I just thought it would add a bit of colour. That's what these biographies do, according to my editor – I never read them myself. She suggested I start with a vignette, then go back to the beginning.' He sighed. 'I suppose there's a subversion of the pathetic fallacy, perhaps a poignant counterpoint in the early morning sun, the promise of a new day and then –'

'It wasn't sunny,' she said. She was thinking about what it said on the leaflet from the hospital.

Breathe. She'd have laughed a month ago. Anyone can breathe. Unless they're drowning.

'Perhaps not,' he conceded. 'It was early, wasn't it? Five thirty, it said in the paper.'

That was when the world started misbehaving. She'd seen a woman on the beach, in a costume. A sunbather. And yet the sun was hardly up. Sunbathing, she was, foolish woman, thought Brenda, and then she got closer and she thought, why is she on her front, head out to sea? But there were always plenty like that, sitting with their shirt off in a gale, turning their legs to one side to brown the pale stripe down their inner thigh, desperate to take their tan home with them.

And then she saw her head was in the water and she thought – why? And then she touched her and she was cold, like marble and she stepped away and then she phoned and –

'I'm taping this,' said Fraser. 'That's okay, isn't it? And I can quote you? I should have asked before but I didn't want to interrupt. I need an image. What was her expression? Peaceful? Tinged with regret? Agonised?'

'I never saw her face,' said Brenda.

'Oh. Then there's not much point –'

'Bob left me,' she said. 'I took Prince for a walk and when I got back, Bob was gone.'

Fraser turned to face her, as they sat side by side on the wall. Their eyes met, briefly. He had blue eyes, or maybe grey. Like the sea when the sun goes in. She suddenly thought he might be considered good-looking, by a certain kind of person.

He looked thoughtfully into the distance. Or at the new toilet block, she wasn't sure which. 'Maybe – no. Doesn't work,' he said. 'I mean there's no thematic link, is there? Two endings, I suppose, but it's a bit trite.'

'Sorry,' said Brenda.

'I'm not sure it would have worked anyway,' said Fraser. 'I need a Hugh anecdote, not a Maud one. She's just a footnote, really. Except my editor doesn't want referencing. Just a bibliography. Apparently the so-called "intelligent general reader" doesn't like too much page furniture. She actually said that! I'm to think of the page as a cool, minimalist space. Don't you find that absurd?'

'S'pose so,' said Brenda.

He sighed. 'Is it really worth it? Do you know how little authors make? It would raise my profile. But do I want it to be raised? Do I want to shout my wares in the middlebrow market, shoving elbows with Waldemar Januszczak and Alastair Sooke?'

'I've got to go,' said Brenda. 'I'm making up a display.'

'Oh yes? Carnival? Country fair?'

'It's for the food bank. There's a raffle too. Win a hamper.'

'That's in rather poor taste, isn't it? Instead of singing for your supper you have to gamble for it. Or perhaps it's an apt metaphor.'

He got up, frowned. 'Actually, Delia might be interested. She's coming down soon.'

'You can buy tickets at the checkout.'

'No – I meant – can you give me the number for that builder?'

Six

'Obama's come to see me?'

'Olive!' said the care assistant.

'He doesn't mind, do you lovey?'

'I've been called worse,' Jim said.

'We'll have tea please, Kasia,' said Olive imperiously.

Kasia did a mock-curtsey and winked at Jim.

'Lovely girl,' said Olive. 'Plays the piano beautifully. Such a shame for her to be shut away with all these old people.'

She held court in an armchair in an airy conservatory. She had her back to the garden with its beds stuffed with perennials and looked imperiously towards the door from the hallway. A few people sat limply in the other chairs placed in small groups. All eyes were drawn to her when she spoke.

Her face was pale apart from a slash of red across her lips but her eyes had a sparkle in them. She was smartly dressed in a navy trouser suit with a scarf tied jauntily round her thin neck.

She smiled at him. Coquettishly, he supposed you could say. A word his dad had made him learn once, when he came across it in a book, which he had never since had occasion to use. One of the hazards of having an English teacher for a father. Perhaps there were no coquettish women any more. He certainly didn't know any.

'I had a black boyfriend back in London. Just after the war. Nigerian he was.'

'My dad's from Trinidad,' said Jim.

'My dad said if I came home with a darkie baby he'd see me in hell.' She laughed. 'And then I got sent here. Might as well have been hell. I was a city girl. You can take notes if you want. What is it, a book?'

'No,' said Jim.

'A thesis, then.' She managed to make 'thesis' sound like faeces.

'Actually, I've come about Maud Smith – Maud Williams as was.'

'It's normally women who come about Maud. Doing faeces on women's studies, whatever that is. They never have books out. Or telly. I've done telly a few times. About Hugh. They'd never make a programme about Maud,' she said, with a look of triumph.

He felt a little stab of resentment. Elizabeth had cared about Maud, and he was a little in love with Elizabeth (just the thought made him tingle!) and so therefore any disparagement of Maud felt like something he should take personally.

'You'll want to know about *Woman Baking Bread* I expect. That's the one she did of me. Of course I wasn't an experienced model then, as I was when I posed for *Spring Tide,* but then of course Hugh was able to put me at ease –'

'I'm a little at sea myself,' said Jim.

'You probably know it as the mermaid picture, my dear,' she said, with warm condescension. 'Hugh's most famous work, as I'm sure you're aware. A runner are you? I think it's terrible, the way they treat the unpaid interns. Just because they want to be in telly. It's not all it's cracked up to be. I should know, I've done a lot –'

'I'm trying to trace her heirs,' said Jim. 'You – you know she's dead?'

'Of course I do,' she said scornfully. 'Just because I'm in here it doesn't mean I don't know what's going on. *Heir Hunters*, is it?'

'Something like that,' he said.

She looked away for a moment and he thought she might be upset but when she turned back she was grinning.

'You'd think she'd have made a will. I've made a will. Not that I've got much. Hugh had most of the money. I've got a life interest in the house, then it goes to the Trust. The vultures would like to have it now but I'm hanging on. Just because I can't live there any more, doesn't mean I might not want to visit. Did she leave much?'

Jim knew more thanks to a string of texts from Roisin. A hungover Neil had returned her calls and had given them information including her previous UK address. 'It seems she still owned a house in Birmingham. She and her husband had been living in Portugal. When he died, she came back here.'

'Hugh never married her, of course,' said Olive,

sitting up a little straighter. 'He chose me.'

'Was Maud local?' he asked.

'Oh yes,' she said.

'So I suppose you knew her family.'

'Yes. She was an only child. So that won't take much research. I expect you'll have to pad the show out with stories of the old days. Pictures of Hugh and his paintings. There's plenty of archive of Hugh and me. None of her, of course –'

He was listening, and yet he was still there, in her room. Her hair, the taste of her lips, her skin smooth against his...

'Actually I'm just interested in the family history –'

'I was staying at my aunty's. She was a land girl who'd married a farmer. Had two young kids. Needed some help around the house. I think my dad hoped I'd marry a farmer too, at least I'd have enough to eat. He died in 1947 of cancer. His last wish was that I should go to Aunty Jean's.

'For two years I thought I'd die of boredom. I had boyfriends, of course, but I wanted to get back to the city. It was like real life was happening somewhere else. But how could I? Dad was gone, there wasn't anyone – Two years is a long time when you're young. I thought it was going to be forever. It just shows you how things can change.'

Waking and her smile as she said he'd have to get up because she was going to work. If he didn't come now he'd be locked in. Him thinking, lock me in, let me stay.

'I found out he needed a housekeeper and I went for the job. She was there too. I found myself wondering, why can't she do the housework, if she's always here? And him – I had never seen a man like him.'

Olive was different from the people he normally spoke to. They were struggling to rake up memories of people they hadn't thought about in years. Olive, by contrast, was working through a well-rehearsed script. How much had it changed in the telling? Did she remember the events at all, or just the story she'd told so many times about them? And that accent. It was London, but not the London he heard every day. It was like a voice from a newsreel or an Ealing comedy.

None of this was relevant and he didn't have much time. Roisin wanted him in Swindon that afternoon. But there was something compelling about the performance. Fraser would love him to pursue this, he thought, which made him all the more determined to stick to the point.

'What about her parents? Did they have family?'

'I think her mother was an only child as well. But her father had a brother who worked in the shipyards in Plymouth. I remember people talking about it because it was a reserved occupation. They used to say he'd been sent upcountry. That used to make me laugh. Upcountry.' She chuckled to herself. 'Like the world ended at Exeter.'

'What was his name?'

'John Williams. Her father was Harold and his brother was John. He was a couple of years older.'

'Did he come back?'

'Not that I know of. I think he ended up in

Liverpool or one of those places.'

'Those places?'

'Places that did shipbuilding. Of course, Maud's parents weren't exactly friendly with me after she left. I don't know if she was close to them anyway. Or if she came back to see them. She certainly never came here.'

'Until recently.'

'Yes,' said Olive.

'She didn't try to see you?'

Olive sat up a little straighter in her chair and tilted her head towards a woman who was standing nearby, looking out at the garden but somehow not seeing it, muttering to herself.

'Know what's wrong with her? Constipation. Makes them confused. A lot of them have got it in here. That or the other. While I'm regular. I have my cup of tea in the morning and then I'm off!' Her eyes lit up with malicious glee, then she slapped the wrist of the other woman as she attempted to take one of their biscuits.

'You don't know where that hand's been. The staff here do their best but when you see what some of them are like...'

'She didn't try to see you?' asked Jim again.

Olive daintily laid down her cup. 'Do you remember *This is Your Life*? Or are you too young?'

'I just about remember it.'

'They'd say, "And now, your long-lost friend who you haven't seen for thirty years", and I'd think, if you haven't spoken to someone for that long, it's probably because you don't want to.'

'Did you want to?'

'You will come back, won't you lovey? I don't get many gentleman visitors. Not young handsome ones. There was one the other day. Looked like he'd slept in his clothes but spoke all lah-di-dah. No manners. Said he interviewed Hugh when he was alive but I certainly don't remember him. Didn't tell him a thing.' She chuckled maliciously.

'What would you have told him? If you had liked him?'

Olive looked at him shrewdly. 'People think anyone can be a model. That it's like being a bowl of fruit. But it's a skill. You have to give the artist something, then you have to let him think he found it by himself. Maud couldn't do that.'

'Which?' asked Jim.

Olive closed her eyes, as if to doze or as if to make him go.

Then she opened her eyes suddenly and said, 'Of course, you also have to hold back what you don't want him to see.'

'I think Fraser already knows that story,' he said.

'But it's a good one,' she said, with a twinkle.

Seven

Now Martha was fifteen she was allowed to take the train down on her own. No more of those awkward handovers in a service station car park, with Neil feeling like he was doing a hostage exchange with a mutely furious agent at the Berlin Wall who had realised, too late, that he had reneged on his side of the deal.

Lisa 1 was safely in London. She did insist on sending Martha midweek though. No doubt a ploy to cause him maximum inconvenience, although she had rattled off a list of school-holiday activities to Lisa (she always called the landline and avoided speaking to Neil if she could help it) which meant these were the only days when it was convenient.

So he'd taken the day off and he and Martha were going to move his stuff into his new flat. Doing it midweek also meant he didn't have to have Lisa and Tom 'helping'.

Lisa had been round to see the flat, tutted at the lack of sockets, wondered where he'd put his laundry, like she was a parent sending a child off to university. She had finally pronounced it adequate and agreed they could find the money for the non-existent bond if they went overdrawn for this month, which had helped him out of a spot.

She had already discussed the financial implications of the split with some guy who did benefits advice at the hospital where she worked, even though it was, of course, only temporary. He didn't know whether to feel pleased or disappointed that she wasn't more aggrieved.

At least it was all very civilised. Unlike Lisa 1. After doing the obligatory thing of throwing his clothes out the window, she had poured his part-fermented parsnip wine on the glossy green avocado plant he'd lovingly nurtured from a stone and topped up the demijohn with urine. Or so she later claimed. He couldn't say it had tasted noticeably different.

Martha went ahead of him, her Doc Martens clopping up the stairs, or maybe it was the banging in his head.

When he opened the door and led the way in, she stood for a moment in the hall, as if sensing the atmosphere. In the living room her shoulders slumped.

'Not much here, is there? For a whole life.'

He dumped his bags in the living room.

'The auctioneers have got the good stuff.'

He'd wondered whether the paintings on the wall might be worth a bit but they'd said not, they were recent works by a local artist. In any case, he'd put a stop on the instruction to sell until he heard from Roisin about whether they'd found an heir. Any heir might want to keep Maud's possessions. As long as the council got paid, they could do what they wanted. So he just had to take what was left down to the skip which was already waiting for them on the street.

He showed Martha the second bedroom. 'This will be your room. Well, yours and Tom's.'

He'd barely touched it. It was a mess of artists' materials and props.

'Wow. Old lady and dolls, that's spooky,' she said. 'But amazing, to think she was still creating art at that age.'

She leaned over and looked a doll straight in the eye. Had she ever played with dolls? He couldn't remember, which probably told its own story. Lisa 1 would hardly have approved of Barbie and friends, but she might have thought that Martha should make her own choices.

'I'll start in here,' she said.

Her messed-up hair was sticking out of her Castro cap. When he complimented here on it, she looked blank. As if Castro was a brand, like Superdry.

'Your mum used to wear those boots,' he said, but she had her head in a cupboard and didn't reply.

He took a couple of bags down to the skip, old clothes and bedding mostly. Decided to keep the books and the couple of classical CDs, even though he probably wouldn't listen to them.

Martha came out of the bathroom. 'I felt a bit strange using the old lady's bog roll,' she said.

'It's what she would have wanted,' he said. He put his hand to the back of the cupboard and came out with a pack of tablets.

'Look what I found.'

'Give them here. I want to see if you can get blasted on them.'

'Go for it,' he said, in his best amiable-dad voice, but really he was thinking, they're mine.

'Not for me,' she said, 'so I know whether it's safe to leave them with you.'

'Give them to me. I'll pass them onto the coroner's officers.' He wouldn't. He sensed that the game old girl had left them for him.

Martha hesitated, then handed over the pills. 'Dad, do you think I could take some of the art stuff?'

'Don't see why not. It's only going in the skip.'

'Just thought, I could use it for my coursework. Not sure how yet.' She frowned. 'Sculptors use found objects. Why not found materials? It's weird though. This stuff looks like it hasn't been used. Why would she buy all this?'

Probably for the same reason he had a pristine breadmaker and a premium subscription to a photo-editing service for which he couldn't even remember his username.

'You think if you use her brush you'll be infused by the old lady's spirit? Anyway, I thought she was just the mistress of Hugh Bonnington.'

'She was an artist in her own right till she moved away. She never showed or sold a painting after that. Maybe she was trying to get back to where she was. Both physically, by moving here, and creatively.'

He decided to clear out the kitchen. He should have done it earlier. Now mould was growing at speed under the cling film on a piece of cheddar in the fridge. How did it grow? Would it do you any harm? What about Stilton, and that cheese in Sicily that had maggots in it and was considered a delicacy –

'Dad, you know there are some canvases that she started work on?'

'Yeah?' Didn't mouldy cheese have hallucinogenic properties? He seemed to remember something about the Romantics eating it before bed to make their dreams more exciting.

'I can use them but do you need them? For the estate?'

He thought about it. For about a second. Thought about how he'd have to take them to the auctioneer, amend the inventory. Rewrite his paperwork, the document he'd formatted and reformatted to just get it to fit on two pages (he hated it when one line went over) before classifying it and saving it on the incomprehensible electronic storage and retrieval system which meant it could never be destroyed, so if he produced an updated version, there was the potential for endless confusion and hilarious misunderstanding.

Just as happened with his 'Dormouth Cemetery Grass Cutting and Environmental Sustainability Policy FINAL 3' at a full council meeting, where a simple typo about broken ceramic and glass memorial vases and their impact on ass cutting had passed into council myth and had even been used as a cautionary tale in the training course entitled 'Report Writing for Impact', before the latest round of cuts meant that nobody got training in anything any more.

'Just take what you want,' he said.

'Maybe I'll put them in the car,' she said, 'so we don't get mixed up and put them in the skip. We can drop them at Lisa's later. Give us some space.'

'That's what she says.' He laughed as he took a carton of milk out of the fridge and waved it in her face. 'Want some yogurt?'

'Gross. You got any dusters?'

'Huh? Oh, we'll pick some up later.'

'Lisa will have some,' she said.

After what seemed like years, Martha said, 'I reckon we need food. Chips maybe.'

He checked his watch. They'd been here for less than two hours. 'And Irn-Bru. The perfect hangover cure.'

'You too?' She smiled. She was acting so grown-up it came as a shock when he realised he was expected to pay. He just about had enough cash.

'I pay, you go,' he said.

On his next trip to the skip he saw Elizabeth rummaging and his heart briefly thudded.

'Hi,' he said, 'Doing a bit of dumpster diving?'

'I left a couple of things in Maud's flat,' she said. 'I hope you don't mind.'

'Come up and take a look,' he said.

When they got to the flat she headed straight for the second bedroom.

'What are you looking for?' he asked.

'Just the dolls,' she said, picking one up off the mantelpiece, but her eyes continued to cast around the room.

'Was there something else?'

He felt a knot in his chest. Maybe it was love, maybe she was about to mention the canvases and brushes which Martha had set her heart on.

'It's just sad to see it looking so bare. Though I'm sure it won't for long.'

'Everything of value went to the auctioneers,' he said. 'For the estate.'

He knew who she reminded him of. Demelza Poldark in the Sunday night TV series. His first crush. Not one he'd ever have admitted to, when his older brothers had pictures of pop stars and Page 3 models. Doing his homework in front of the telly, pretending to be bored when it was on, his mum engrossed, if you could be engrossed when you were knitting, smoking, chewing a mint and making sure he finished his sums at the same time.

'I wish we'd met sooner. I mean – you could have organised the funeral. It wouldn't have cost you anything. Funeral expenses are the first call on the estate.'

She looked at him with polite incomprehension. He didn't recall Ross wooing Demelza with the finer points of burial law.

Martha came stomping up the stairs. She looked suspiciously at him and Elizabeth.

'This is Elizabeth,' he said. 'This is Martha.'

'I live upstairs,' said Elizabeth.

Martha looked from one to the other. 'I see,' she said.

'Elizabeth was just looking for something she left in Maud's room.'

'Right,' said Martha, sceptically.

'Thanks for this,' said Elizabeth, gesturing at the dolls. She held them to her chest, so he couldn't help looking at their little faces, although then he realised that Martha would think he was staring at her tits.

'No worries,' he said.

'And if you need anything, I mean, I know you're local, but if you – well, I'm up in the attic. Just knock.'

'He will,' said Martha.

After Elizabeth had gone she said, 'You can't let groupies in to ransack the place. Just because you fancy –'

'Elizabeth knew Maud.' Maybe Maud sent her, he thought. Maybe this was why he had positive vibes about the flat from the start. 'Anyway, why would Maud have groupies? I thought she disappeared into obscurity.'

'Some feminists have argued that her work and her influence should be re-evaluated. She might even have worked on some of Hugh's paintings.'

'Like Dick and Mary Francis?'

'Mmm,' she said, as if she knew who he meant, quiet now that she'd exhausted the accumulated knowledge and wisdom of a Wikipedia stub.

They ate the chips out of the paper because Martha said she didn't fancy eating off the dead-old-lady plates until they'd been washed and neither of them had thought of it. It occurred to him that Lisa would have done that first. Martha was quiet for a few mouthfuls, but he knew it couldn't last.

'You can see there's a pattern developing, right?'

'What's that?'

'You met Mum when you were both in your twenties, did the getting pissed and stoned thing, graduated, got jobs – at least she did – had a child, left ten years later, met Lisa when she was in her twenties, did the getting pissed and stoned thing, she graduated, got a job, had a child, you've left her now she's in her thirties – so next you'll be looking for –'

Elizabeth must be about twenty-four, twenty-five, he thought.

'At this rate the next wife but one will be younger than me.'

'I haven't left Lisa. At least, I'm here temporarily, but that's only because she wanted me to go.'

'That's not what she says.'

'You've been speaking to her? You should be on my side.'

'I phoned up to speak to Tom. And so we had a bit of a chat.'

'I think I prefer the wicked stepmother paradigm. Now you get on better with her than you do with me.'

'Not at all. You're a mate to get wrecked with.

She's a parent and an authority figure. Someone to rely on.'

'Thanks, I feel so much better.' He lit a cigarette.

'What are you doing?' she said, aghast, as if he'd done a Nazi salute.

'I thought you were smoking these days.'

'Not tobacco. Not in the house. Not when other people are eating. I hope you don't do that in front of Tom. If you do you deserve to be thrown out.'

'I thought she didn't throw me out.' He took a final drag then stubbed the cigarette out on the polystyrene chip tray. It gave a half-hearted fizz.

'Shall we go to the Kebab and Calculator for one?' he asked. He could smoke it on the way.

'What?' asked Martha.

'The pub.'

'It's the White Horse, for fuck's sake.'

'I know but –'

'It's not funny when you call it that. It's just a sad old man joke.'

'That's me. With only a beautiful daughter to redeem me.'

Eight

Paula came as soon as she heard.

She swung the car into the drive, stepped out, slammed the door behind her, pushed her big sunglasses up her nose and flung out her arm to set the alarm as she walked up to the front door. Brenda came away from the window. As Paula jiggled the key expertly in the lock – the barrel was loose and Bob hadn't got round to fixing it – then strode through the hall, Brenda thought she felt the house shift on its foundations, just a little.

Strappy sandals, painted toes, a dress she said looked like Victoria Beckham but was actually in the sale at H&M, full make-up when she finally took her sunglasses off. The metallic eye shadow matched the paintwork on her car. Paula thought of everything.

Paula nodded at Brenda as she lifted the kettle and, satisfied with its weight – Brenda always filled it up while Paula only put in what she needed – flicked it on.

Robbie came in, his hair still wet from the shower. He sat down, although he'd said he was going out. Turned his van keys in his hand.

Slowly, over and over. Like it had to be done a certain way which only he understood.

Paula glared at him and brought the drinks over and sat down, turning her chair towards Prince so he could jump up and put his paws in her lap.

'How's my baby?' she crooned, stroking between his pointy Alsatian ears. She'd get hair all over her and she was so fussy about her clothes but she didn't seem to care, when it was Prince. Something else Brenda didn't get about her daughter.

Then suddenly Paula stood up, marched over to the far wall.

'It's right along the join with the extension,' said Paula.

'I know,' said Robbie.

Brenda turned round slowly, as if not to surprise it. She could see it. Running from floor to ceiling.

She'd never even wanted the extension. What was the point when the kids were grown up and moving on? Paula anyway. Because Bob wanted it. Added value, he'd said.

The extension could go. Float free. They still had the house.

Robbie kept watching the crack. Did he think he could see it grow? Or that if he kept watching, it would stop it growing? She watched too. She tried to imagine what it was like inside the crack. Thought about when they bought the house, did it up themselves, peeled back layers of wallpaper. All those other people's lives, layer upon layer. But there was no life in the extension. Just smooth plaster, pale emulsion. No one's dreams.

Robbie sat still and quiet. But then he surprised her. 'If he's not done proper footings –'

He. Bob. Bob the Builder. Does everyone else's house, never got time for his own. Except he'd done it. In the winter, when things were quieter. So the weather was always bad and he was always moaning. Standing water in the excavation. Mud being walked through the house. Fridge and microwave in the living room. And when there was a decent day he went off and did another job. Left the work to a couple of casual workers who he said were good lads.

But Bob always did a good job, didn't he? Before he got a mobile, she took all his calls on the landline. They'd had the odd one complaining, sloppy work, needs sorting, will go to the Federation, or Trading Standards, or the papers. He said it was nothing, you'd always get that. Sometimes he'd ignore them, sometimes he'd go back to make some changes, just for the goodwill, he said. She didn't know if it still happened now he had the mobile.

'This place probably needs underpinning,' said Paula. 'They've all been done round here. It's the drains.'

'What do you mean, the drains?' asked Brenda.

'They go, the water's swimming round the foundations, next thing –'

Water doesn't swim, thought Brenda. Does it?

'They're all pitch fibre,' said Robbie. 'This house is older than the others. It was built before they started using it.'

Paula looked at him doubtfully. 'They say if you can get a 10p piece in a crack then it needs looking at.'

'Who are *they*?' asked Robbie.

'I saw it on a documentary.'

'Never mind what I think,' said Robbie. I'm just a time-served plasterer, what do I know?'

'Can you get a 10p piece in it?' asked Brenda.

'Dunno,' said Robbie, but Paula was already in her bag, searching for a coin.

She stood at the wall, like a kid with a moneybox, then like a kid trying to force a square peg into a round hole.

'Push a bit harder,' said Robbie. 'Maybe the coin will go through and take you with it.'

Where would she go? Brenda wondered. She had a vision of Paula, falling through space, dragged by a 10p piece, and she couldn't shake it.

'So what can we do?' asked Paula.

'I'm gonna fit a movement gauge,' said Robbie.

'I think we should get a structural engineer,' said Paula.

'You mean a surveyor,' said Robbie.

'No,' said Paula.

'I'll monitor it,' said Robbie.

'But if –'

'Leave me the coin and I promise I'll try and post it every day.'

'Get your own coin.' She turned to Brenda. 'Mum?'

'Your dad will sort it,' said Brenda.

They were both quiet. They looked at her.

Paula spoke, very slowly, like she was talking to a small child. 'Mum. You know he's left, don't you?'

Left? 'Of course I do,' she said calmly. 'But it's still his house.'

'Well, do you know why?' she said, an edge to her voice. 'Because I don't.'

Robbie was concentrating really hard on a small spot on the floor.

'I mean, has he met someone else? Is that it? Have you even tried to talk to him?'

Someone else? Bob?

Nine

Roisin Desouza was of Goan-Portuguese-Irish-Liverpudlian descent. People often said, you must have a fascinating family history, I expect you've researched that. If they were clients, she'd murmur something non-committal and move on. If they were in the pub on a Friday night, she'd be a little more forthright. Roisin was her own creation, as far as she was concerned. No one else deserved the credit or the blame.

Eight o'clock and she was already in full flow in the open plan – she had an office but rarely spent any time in it – pacing while speaking on her phone headset, leaning momentarily over a trainee who was turning the microfiche like a kitchen boy roasting a hog, sweat on his top lip, as she cried out in exasperation.

She had the sleekest, shiniest black bob Jim had ever seen but she claimed it was the result of luck rather than any effort on her part. Her fiercely cut designery suit (she got them from her brother who got them from somewhere undivulgeable at a huge discount) was struggling to keep up with her. On a desk behind her were several sheets of paper sellotaped in a strip with a printed family tree scrawled with handwritten notes. Jim assumed she was using the eyes in the back of her head to refer to it.

'Sunita, try Preston. We've got an Emily Louise Clapperton born on the right date. Yes, I know we're looking for Emily Lindsay but you haven't found her, have you? And if the competition get there first we're all going to bed without any supper so you'd better be standing outside the register office when they open...No, I don't know if she's the one. That's why I need to see the birth certificate...Call it a hunch.'

Jim turned away with a sigh and faced his monitor. Watching Roisin's energy lifted him for a moment, but now he was back to the grim reality of office life. Lamenting the artificial light, the dry sticky feel of the air as he breathed. The office was in a basement, small dark and cramped, chosen because it was on the shabby outskirts of a prestigious postcode, not for the comfort of its staff. Jim sat a long way from the open window, which was in any case mainly covered with Roman blinds in an off-white colour, spotted here and there with splashed coffee and dead flies.

Jim had come here as a temp to create a bespoke database. Roisin liked what he did and asked him to stay on, finding him other work to do, which mostly involved liaising with the hosting service for their main database.

In his previous life, his *real* life, he'd designed databases to help analyse bird populations and breeding patterns. Then the database had been a means to an end. Now the databases *were* the end. He was quite good at it. He hated it.

He was supposed to have a meeting with Roisin but she was still busy. This was normal. There was always something she deemed more urgent coming up.

Elizabeth. He could feel the euphoria fading. He'd thought the excitement, the way his body tingled, the memory of her face, her body next to his, would help him get through the day. Here, in the subterranean gloom, he was beginning to wonder if it was all a dream.

He thought about Fraser. He wondered how much he'd published. Googled his name. Various university-related pages and networking sites came up first. Added 'Hugh Bonnington' to the search. There was a full biography on Wikipedia with numerous references. Many of them to articles by Fraser McKendrie.

'This the guy you met in Devon?'

Roisin's whisper made him tingle. She was so loud normally but she could do quiet, just to disorientate you. She was leaning over him, looking at his screen, speaking softly in his ear. He suspected she was short-sighted and didn't want to admit it. He didn't know why. She'd look good in glasses. Roisin looked good whatever she wore.

'He probably wrote the page himself, to big up his area of research.'

She laughed, stood up straight. Roisin was never still. He swivelled in his chair. His eyes couldn't help but follow her.

'Is that what you used to do?' she said.

'I may have contributed to relevant articles. To share my knowledge for the common good.'

'I forget, how did you meet this guy?'

'I was introduced to him by the – neighbour.' Jim turned quickly back to the screen, but he could still feel Roisin exposing him to the full force of her forensic stare.

'What aren't you telling me?'

'Nothing.'

'You got laid, didn't you?'

'How can you possibly know that?'

'You've got that post-coital flush. Actually I was only guessing but you've admitted it now. Shit – I've got a call coming in. You'll have to tell me over lunch. My office.'

Roisin was eating takeaway sushi. He had his home-made cheese and pickle.

'So you've been sharking in work time.' She stayed behind her laptop and he sat across from her, which made it feel less like lunch and more like a disciplinary. 'No more jollies for you.'

Their agent in the south west had left recently and not yet been replaced. Since Jim had family down that way, Roisin occasionally let him loose with the pool car. He was unclear whether this was kindness masquerading as a business decision or the other way round.

'It wasn't like that, it was just...'

Roisin was sending an email. She looked up. 'Relax. She's not a client, after all. Unless she turns out to be Maud Smith's secret long-lost grandchild.'

'She *is* an artist,' Jim said.

'Oh God, you've got the wonders.'

'The wonders?'

'Where you're fascinated by every little detail about someone just because you've shagged them.'

'Right.' Jim waited for Roisin to ask more about Elizabeth but she looked around, restless now.

'Anyway, yer woman Olive was wrong about Liverpool so we started on other northern shipbuilding towns. We found a death certificate for a John Williams in Sunderland, the right date of birth. He had one daughter, dead, she had two kids, only one still living. We spoke to her. She lives in Whitley Bay. She confirmed her grandad worked on the docks and the dates tie up. We couldn't find anyone on the mother's side. Not much fertility in either line.'

Jim drifted off. It was supposed to be lunchtime after all. But Roisin didn't see her job as something that interfered with her life. To her work *was* life. She was the kind of person who dragged herself in with flu. Who got bored on holiday and phoned up to see how things were going. Of course, when he'd been on holiday from the uni he would have taken his binoculars and scheduled some casual birdwatching, but it hardly seemed the same.

He thought idly about Elizabeth. Being an artist was hardly a little detail, it was who she was. So that didn't count as the wonders. He wondered (so maybe it *was* the wonders) what she was doing now, if she was thinking about him at all.

'Should I ring her tonight? Or maybe wait a bit?' he asked, out of the blue, and then blushed.

'Ring her?' Roisin asked. 'Are you mad?'

'What do you mean?'

'You can't ring a one-night stand. You'll look sad and needy and very naïve.'

'I will?'

'Look. She's slept with someone, knowing he's from London, on business, will never pass that way again, it's cool, like a holiday romance, ships that pass in the night etc. And then he calls and says, "do you want to go the pictures some time?" Even if she says yes, you've got to chat like you hardly know each other, which you don't, although you've already jumped each other's bones, and it'll be totally embarrassing and cringey and you'll both regret it. Which is why she'll probably tactfully make something up, like she's already got a boyfriend or she's emigrating to Antarctica.'

He thought about it. 'So you don't think I should ring?'

'No! Now I've just bought a list of Empty Homes Officers. I'm going to offer them the same deal as cemetery managers – we'll trace owners and their heirs for free as long as we get to contact them first. Can you upload them or import them or whatever it is you do?'

Elizabeth began to recede. Maybe it had just been a dream. There was something ethereal about her while Roisin was vital and solid. And here. With work for him to do.

She'd finished speaking and was putting her headset back on and dialling. Jim gulped down his last bit of sandwich and shuffled back to his desk.

Ten

Lisa asked to bring Tom round, so, she said, he could see his parents interacting normally. Once round, she seemed to want to stay. Next thing, she was telling Neil the place wanted decorating and was appalled by the state of the kitchen.

She was scrubbing out the black gunk from the bottom of the oven. Neil stayed in the living room to keep an eye on Tom. He was quite happily playing with a big empty cardboard box left over from when Neil was packing up.

He got in it, tried to close the lid on himself, spoke to himself in different voices. He took the box under the table and turned it on its side. Crawled in again and was perfectly still.

Perhaps he thinks it's a coffin, thought Neil. Perhaps he's playing cemeteries. Maybe he wants to be just like his dad when he grows up.

Lisa was saying something about how it was the landlord's responsibility to get the place clean before he moved in. He couldn't tell her about his arrangement with Trevor, since he'd trousered the 'bond' money. And he wasn't going to decorate. It was the calm neutrality of the place that had attracted him, though she said it was like a soulless holiday let and had brought a sample card with colours that she described as 'warmer' though they didn't look much different to him.

She was an occupational therapist, specialising in people with brain injuries. He imagined her at work, talking people through their exercises and adaptations with her relentless competence and empathy.

She was wearing a sundress, a pretty thing that made her look almost girlish and was at odds with her long-suffering maturity. He wondered if she'd worn it for him. But now she had her arms in rubber gloves and her head in the oven, acting the drudge.

She was saying something but he wasn't listening, he was watching her bottom swing and her body vibrate as she scrubbed at a particularly stubborn stain, feeling aroused. If Tom wasn't there, he could pull her out of the oven, have a quickie on the kitchen floor, hike up her dress, she could keep the rubber gloves on – She used to like that, spontaneity.

That was what he'd loved about her, that intriguing mix of sensible and crazy. She'd been a mature student, had worked in residential care before doing her occupational therapy degree. She was only a few years older than the rest but she despised their laziness, their inability to get up before midday, their financial incompetence. She'd made a point of doing all her work, taking a part-time job and still getting as hammered as the rest of them. He'd admired that. She'd been up for anything then, had loved his unpredictability. Not now.

'I'm thinking a feature wall in your room.' Her head had emerged from the oven. She had removed the rubber gloves which were thick with brown-tinged suds and had lost their erotic charge. She had a black smudge on her face. He went to wipe it away and she flinched, just a little.

'We could do Martha's as well but I don't want to invade her privacy.' Martha, it seemed, was an adult and able to make up her own mind. Lisa liked Martha, always had, 'in spite of her parentage'. He had said, whatever you say about my ex, she's a good mother. She'd said, I wasn't talking about her mother.

I'll have to stall her, he thought. I can't go through this hassle. I'll let Martha paint her room purple if she wants and the rest can stay as it is.

She was dusting the chest of drawers, then she was opening the drawers. Was she really going to fold his underpants? Or was she looking for something? Most of them were empty. He hadn't brought much. After all, it was 'only temporary' until he'd 'sorted his head out'.

'What are the neighbours like?' she asked casually. Too casually.

'I haven't met most of them.'

'Martha said –'

'Oh yes,' he said, as if just remembering, 'we met the woman from the top flat. Seems nice enough. I expect Martha mentioned the tablets as well.'

'Did you –'

'I took care of it.'

'You gave them to the coroner's officers?'

'No, I binned them.'

'But there's still an inquest to be held. They might have been significant.'

'Sure. The laxatives could prove crucial in the case. Perhaps the weight of her unevacuated stool was what pulled her under.'

She shushed him. 'Tom might hear you.'

'He's going to have to learn the facts of life one day. "Daddy, what's constipation?" he'll ask. And I'll have to sit down and find the words to tell him –'

'I meant, joking about it. The poor woman's dead. Drowned. Hardly a laughing matter.'

'Of course the last thing we should do is talk to children about death. I mean it's not like it's something they'll ever have to face, is it? And if they do you'll have a full-colour pamphlet about it with lots of drawings and activities and balloons and details of a support group. Which is far better for them than a normal conversation –'

Neil was starting to sweat. This weather! He heard a shuffling sound. The sound of walking cardboard. He could feel two eyes burning into the back of his head. Uncannily like the two in front of him.

He laughed. 'You've got what you wanted for Tom. Mummy and Daddy interacting just like they always do.'

'Perhaps we should go,' said Lisa.

'No, I'll go,' said Neil. 'After all, you've made

the place your own. It's me who's in the way.'

'Hardly,' she said. 'All I've done is pay the rent!'

And they left. Lisa said Tom should leave the box so he would at least have one special toy when he came to Daddy's but Tom dragged it mournfully behind him.

Eleven

Jim was walking home from work when he passed Finn at the end of his road, looking chilled in shorts and baseball boots. He was a session musician who lived in the flat above Jim's. He liked practising his bass at four in the morning but was otherwise okay.

'There's a woman for you,' said Finn. 'I said she could wait in my place but she said she'd rather wait outside. She's sitting on your steps.'

It's her, thought Jim, and his heart jumped a little, as it always did when he thought of Elizabeth. He almost skipped round the corner, like a kid at the end of school, then felt ridiculous. How would she even know where he lived?

He still thought about her. Found himself daydreaming (he'd have been looking out the window if they had one worthy of the name). It had been a week now, surely he should be over it?

He could see a silhouette. A bright summer dress, a broad-brimmed straw hat. Even at a distance he knew who it was. 'Edie,' he said, smiling. He looked closely at her. She was smiling too. He relaxed.

He let her in the front door then twisted round to open the sliding door into the lounge before falling in onto the sofa. Edie tried to follow but her hat got stuck. She removed it, stepped forward, fell on him. He lifted her over to sit next to him.

'Am I delusional or is this place getting smaller?'

She smiled again. He smiled back. That was enough.

She had bleached her hair. It was short, urchin-like, framing her face. Green eyes staring dramatically out of light-brown skin.

'So how are you?' asked Edie. 'Still in love with Roisin?'

'Roisin is in love with a six-foot-tall blond barrister and former downhill-skiing champion. Called Melissa.'

'I never said Roisin was in love with you.'

She was teasing him. He didn't care. He thought about Elizabeth and felt an overwhelming urge to say her name. Like he just had to tell. And who could he tell if not Edie? His twin.

'I met someone. Her name's Elizabeth. But it was just a one-night stand.'

'You don't do one-night stands.'

'I can learn.'

'You're still thinking about her.'

'Maybe.'

'Doesn't she want to know?'

'I haven't asked her.'

'Why not?'

'I thought it would be spooky and stalkerish.'

'Why?'

'Roisin – well, she implied it.'

'If you're still thinking about her you have to at least try. If it doesn't work out, then move on.'

'I've never done that before. Before it's just happened.'

'You mean your over-achieving exes made all the moves and you fell into place, oblivious. Now, let's go out for dinner. I'll pay. Can we have Lebanese? It's ages since I've had Lebanese. Or how about Moroccan. Something with couscous. Or what about Egyptian? Know any Egyptian places?'

He was used to these sudden switches. Edie did that. 'Lebanese sounds good. Let's go to our usual. I'll just get changed.'

'Keep the suit on, it's cool.'

'Roisin chose it,' he called from the bedroom.

'Her brother still doing fake designer?'

'It's not fake, it's "discounted surplus stock",' he said, with a laugh.

'Of course,' said Edie, 'otherwise Roisin's suits wouldn't really be Armani and that would be impossible. Roisin has only to say a thing and it is so.'

He walked back in and she assessed his cargoes and crumpled T-shirt, his hiking boots. 'You look like you're going on a field trip. In fact you always look like you're going on a field trip.'

'So I am,' he said. He felt light-headed and giddy now, perhaps because Edie's good mood was infecting him, or perhaps because she'd told him it would be alright to call Elizabeth. Not that he would, but just the thought of the possibility raised his mood. Life was – could be – one big field trip.

They walked through the summer streets, and what felt like urban sprawl most of the time seemed alive and exciting with Edie there. People strolling to bars and restaurants, cafés with people sitting outside, music playing from open windows as people sat on their doorsteps.

Maybe life isn't over, just because I can't do the work I love. There's a whole other world I haven't noticed. Maybe there are other ways to be happy after all.

The restaurant looked the same as ever when they approached, older Middle Eastern men sitting on chairs piled with cushions smoking shisha, a mixed group of young tourists trying it for a laugh, but inside it had been transformed. The walls were now plain, the furniture spare and clean-lined, the lighting subtle. The waiters were taking orders on tablets.

'Wow,' said Edie.

Jim thought he'd preferred it before when it was a little down-at-heel with faded pictures on the wall and geometric wallpaper. But he had to admit it gave the place a sense of space. Or maybe it was just the contrast to his flat.

Edie ordered for them – plates of hummus and fuul and something gorgeous with aubergine and falafel and salads and round flatbread. Edie couldn't decide whether to take her hat off or not. Their waiter joined in the pantomime of looking for a place to leave it safely, before finally bringing the hat a chair of its own. Edie was grateful, he was charmed.

By the end of this encounter Edie had established that he was a postgraduate engineer from Jordan, that he missed his wife who was a doctor at home, and that his younger brother wanted to move to Canada, but he was determined to make a life in Jordan, despite the economic problems there. Jim had been coming in here for a couple of years but had never got beyond a tentative few words about the weather.

As she shovelled food down magnificently, Edie said, 'Henny, I have to ask a favour.'

Only Edie dared to call him that. His parents – or really his father – had decided to celebrate his love of American literature by naming him Henry James Jackson. At the age of nine he'd announced to them that he no longer wished to be known as Henry, or Harry, and that even his mother's last ditch compromise of Hal was not acceptable. He would take his middle name and be called Jim.

They'd assumed it was a phase but he'd stood firm. He'd even managed to persuade his primary school teacher to amend his name on the register. It was his first act of rebellion. And his last, Edie said. People asked her if she'd been named after Edith Piaf or Edie Sedgwick, either would have been cool, but she was happy to tell them that it was actually a tribute to Edith Wharton.

'What's that favour?'

'Can I stay with you?'

'Sure, I'll make up a suite in the west wing. I'd

assumed you'd stay tonight anyway.'

'I mean a bit longer. I've found this great place in a really cool shared house but the guy's not moving out for a couple of days. He's flying out to Guatemala to do aid work. How exciting is –'

'You're moving back to London?'

'I've got a job down here. For a charity.'

'What happened in Manchester?'

'You know, funding ran out.'

It sounded plausible so he left it. Edie worked in PR, mostly for arts organisations. Lots of short-term contracts, moving on, so the gaps in her CV weren't a problem. She could sell herself on her personality, and when Edie was on form, she was pretty hard to resist.

'You're welcome,' he said. 'But I'm not sure there's room for the hat.'

'Let's have dessert,' she said. 'Halva. Or do I mean baklava? I always get them mixed up.' She smiled at the waiter who immediately came over. Jim would have been waving his arms like a windmill for a week. After they'd ordered she said, 'Maybe you should just marry Roisin. Her family would be happy. You'd have a strong woman taking charge. She could see Melissa on the side.'

'I'm not a Catholic.'

'Is that the best you can come up with?'

'Nothing less would satisfy her family.'

'A Catholic and a man. So does she still call herself bisexual?'

Roisin told the story, when drunk, of how her only boyfriend had gone on to become a priest.

The details varied in the telling. Sometimes she said he was her first boyfriend, or her last. Of course, all three could be true.

'I think she just says that to torture Melissa.'

'Or you. So, her parents are still not speaking to her?'

'No.'

'She should have lied,' said Edie. 'Hasn't she got a sister who says her boyfriend is her flatmate? And they fell for it?'

'Roisin reckons they know it's not true, but it allows them to appear to believe it's true.'

'So her sister's lying, their parents know she's lying, she knows they know she's lying, but it's outwardly acceptable in the eyes of the Lord so they all just carry on?'

'Roisin says they can accept her and Melissa for what they are or go fuck themselves. That's the cleaned up version. It's a matter of principle.'

'Roisin's not principled, she's just stubborn. Which actually makes her just like her parents. Which means –'

Edie had been at the pop psychology again. He made the expected response and she continued with her stream of consciousness. He was happy. Edie was on fine form, the food was great, and his mind was free to wander. To Elizabeth.

Twelve

Bob's van went by and her arm went up. Like it always did. Brenda didn't do it. The arm moved by itself.

She could see the 'boy', as he always called the latest lad he had working for him. Not one she'd met before. They came and went because he said he couldn't afford to offer them an apprenticeship. The boy turned his head when she waved and looked blankly at the place where her hand had been. She couldn't see Bob. Maybe just the way the sun fell on the windscreen but it was as if the van was driving itself.

The arm returned to her side but her legs were frozen now, as she stood in the middle of the pavement, a wave of tourists moving towards her dejectedly from the seafront, looking to buy something so they'd know they'd had fun. She was swept along, as desperate as them to eat up time but with no prospect of a coach to take her away.

Passing the fudge shop and the tattoo parlour and the discount store with its camping chairs and fishing nets, she saw the woolshop and thought again of the shattered nurse and her sentences that never ended.

The shop seemed dark after the sun outside. She stood by the door and breathed slowly and immediately was carried away by the woolshop smell. The smell made her think of coming in with her mum when she was a kid.

As her eyes adjusted, she saw Dora Micklethwaite move from behind the counter and head towards her like a battleship.

Dora had seemed old back then but now she didn't seem any older. She still had a golden bowl of hair which she must spray into submission every morning. Her eyebrows were plucked to nothing then put back with a pencil. She had moved here years before Brenda knew her, but she still talked longingly of Yorkshire.

Brenda hadn't been in here for many years but Dora was a fixture in the town and impossible to avoid. She was a prime mover on the carnival committee and something in the Dormouth Wives, although she'd never been known to have a husband, and for one glorious year had glared out of the front page of the *Dormouth Informer* almost weekly as the mayor's official consort.

'Brenda,' said Dora, crinkling her foundation in an expression of sympathy. 'How art, lass?'

'Alright,' mumbled Brenda.

'There's many as say you never know a man till you divorce him.'

Brenda wondered if she was talking about her own mysterious past then realised Dora was talking about her. She wasn't getting divorced though. Was she? She looked around for something else to say.

'Lovely day. For the tourists. Kids.' Her words tailed off as her thoughts refused to make sense.

'Happen,' said Dora. 'But it's not a patch on Scarborough.'

A phone rang from the back of the shop.

'That'll be t'wholesaler,' said Dora as she went to get it.

A girl with red hair about the same age as Paula was standing at the counter looking perplexed.

'I'm trying to work this out,' she said.

The girl – woman, Paula would say - was wearing a green paisley silk thing that looked like a dressing gown to Brenda. She was probably one of the so-called artists that hung around the White Horse.

She had a doll-sized dressmaker's dummy in front of her. The proper kind, with adjustable parts so you could get the size right. Except its torso was in pieces on the counter.

'I've been struggling with it all morning,' she said happily.

Paula would have looked for it on YouTube and fixed it in no time.

Brenda shrugged. 'Why would you need a dressmaker's dummy shaped like a doll? Why not just use the doll?'

'That's what I thought!' She smiled. She had little neat teeth that made you think of a child.

'Although,' she continued, 'dolls can be very unstable. While this would stand firm.'

Best to humour her, thought Brenda. 'You could put it in a dolls' house.'

'Yes.'

'If you had a doll that made clothes. Perhaps the doll could work out how to fix it. Maybe the doll would look it up on YouTube.'

She looked at Brenda for a moment and then laughed. 'That's brilliant.'

Dora came gliding back out, like an ocean liner coming into shore.

'Elizabeth, this is Brenda. Her as found your friend.'

Friend? thought Brenda. I haven't found anyone. Only –

'You found Maud?' said Elizabeth. 'I'm glad it was you. Someone kind.'

Brenda thought it didn't really matter who had found Maud, given that she was long dead by then, and she didn't see how a young girl like this could be friends with an old woman. Maybe the old woman was a witch, and she was her apprentice, weaving spells in her dressing gown, talking nonsense to Brenda and Brenda somehow being charmed. Maybe the witch had given Dora the secret of eternal middle age.

But that couldn't be right, could it? Because witches didn't drown.

Elizabeth had changed her expression under the watchful gaze of Dora, and was asking, with a serious face but somehow a little twinkle too, 'How can I help?'

Brenda looked around the shop. 'I just fancied

doing some knitting,' she said. But what? 'I'll browse,' she said.

There were patterns on display next to balls of wool. Some of them had little doll-sized versions of the garments next to the pattern. She could guess who'd made them. Not Dora. She couldn't recall ever having seen Dora knit.

She took one down and looked closely at it. Imagined it created on doll-sized needles by a doll-sized knitter, though of course it wouldn't have been.

What did she want to knit? A house, thought Brenda. Not a whole one. She would like to stitch up the crack in the kitchen, neat as a raglan sleeve. If dolls could be dressmakers, why couldn't she fix a house?

She chose a pattern for a scarf. Not too big but with a bit of an Aran detail in it. So she'd have to concentrate. Not throw an arm up in the air for no good reason.

She bought the recommended wool. She didn't swap for a cheaper one like Mum always did, so the tension was never quite right and you were always going up a size or down a size. And the needles, including the little Aran needle with a point at either end, even though she'd probably have some at home if she knew where to look. The attic? There was years' worth of stuff up there.

Could she afford it? All she knew was she put her card in the machine and money came out.

As she went to pay, she found herself saying, 'My dad had a shop around here. A greengrocer's. I used to help him sometimes on a Saturday.'

'Did you like it?'

Cold winter mornings, driving through the dark to the wholesaler. It seemed like the whole world was asleep. Filling up the shelves, the smell of a bag of sprouts when you cut the thick brown paper with a knife. Or the sweet scent of apples as she stacked them. She sometimes did the veg at the supermarket but she'd never noticed it smell of anything.

'It was alright.'

Just her and Dad. Their special time. She'd disappear when the shop opened, she was too young to work and Dad always liked to do things right, for all the good it did him.

Elizabeth took her money and put her things in a bag. She said shyly, 'I've got an exhibition soon, at the Boatshed, maybe you'd like to come?'

She gave Brenda a postcard. Brenda couldn't read it without her glasses so she put it in the pink carrier bag with the 'A-Dora-Balls, Wools and Haberdashery' logo on it.

'Thanks,' she said, although she knew she'd never go.

Elizabeth was looking at the doll's dummy again. 'It's so sad,' she said. 'She never gets to wear her own clothes.'

Thirteen

Teri (or as she always said, 'Teri like the one from *Desperate Housewives*') was waiting outside the disused chapel that housed their office, talking to a man. That meant she'd forgotten her keys again. It meant he was late. Or perhaps it meant she was pretending to have forgotten her keys to highlight the fact that he was late.

She was throwing back her hair and laughing. No doubt she'd had a successful outing last night to New Beginnings, the singles club she went to in Paignton, even though she was married to an ex-marine. Her husband was somewhere off the coast of Somalia doing private security, blissfully unaware that while he was laying down his life, she was laying down his wife.

The guy was playing along. Boden man. As he drew nearer he thought he recognised him.

'This is Fraser McKendrie. He's an art historian,' enunciated Teri, like a four-year-old saying ambulance for the first time.

'You'll be looking for Hugh Bonnington's grave, I expect.'

'No,' he said.

Neil had a headache, a bit of a dry mouth, a vague sense of unease. Must be the weather. Everyone was supposed to love the sun but he'd had enough of it already. He preferred autumn. Mellow fruitfulness and all that.

He waited for the man to elaborate but he didn't so he decided to play nice. He laughed. 'Well, you show some taste then. Come on in.'

As they sat down, Teri said, 'Fraser wants to ask you about the Section 46.' She nodded meaningfully at Maud's ashes on a high shelf, as if she was communicating in some secret code. Section 46 was just the section of the Act under which councils carried out public health funerals. She wasn't forewarning Neil. She wanted Fraser to think that she was forewarning Neil. No, she wanted Fraser to think that Neil needed forewarning.

'Coffee?' she asked, in the sing-song voice she used with visitors. Like a bag of rusty nails drenched in syrup.

'Yes please,' said Fraser.

'Tea,' said Neil.

Teri hated him. Teri was the kind of woman who needed every man on the planet to fancy her, from the visiting chaplain at the local hospice to the guy hassling you for spare change with the dripping nose and the piss-stained shoes. And Neil didn't. He felt repelled by her sub-Cheryl Cole big hair, her obsessive cuticle-tweaking, her endless raw food diets and Galaxy binges. Teri was merciless. If you didn't play, you had to pay.

As she put the mugs down it came to him. 'You

were at Maud Smith's funeral,' he said to Fraser. He didn't add, ingratiating yourself with Elizabeth. 'So how can I help?'

'As I'm sure you know, Maud Smith was formerly Maud Williams, a minor local artist in the post-war years and sometime mistress of Hugh Bonnington. I'm writing a biography of him. I'm aware that Maud still owned a small number of paintings when she died and I would like to see them all.'

Maud was on the shelf above the index cards that predated the database, along with flyers from a company that turned ashes to diamonds, a broken granite vase awaiting collection by a stonemason and a spare printer cartridge. The shelves were all on one side of the chapel because the other side was damp. The windows were small and leaded so they had to keep the lights on even on the sunniest day. It wasn't much of an office. Teri was always lamenting that they weren't in the main council building in Dormouth but he liked being hidden away here.

Neil was clenching and unclenching his jaw. He had downed his tea in one go, must have been thirsty, never mind he'd burnt his tongue, and Fraser was looking at him quizzically, was that the word, or did he just mean like a smug shit in a pastel shirt?

'Everything of value went to the auctioneer.'

'Everything of value?' Fraser echoed. 'According to?'

Neil sighed. What was it he disliked about this guy? A certain arrogance, but also an underlying sense of desperation. That he really wanted something and could be dangerous if he didn't get it. Teri had it, this guy had it.

We were all supposed to want something these days. To strive. Or to pay overpriced subscription packages so we could sit, beer resting on belly, watching men – and occasionally women - in brightly coloured corporate-sponsored clothing do it for us.

Neil, he didn't want anything. Just a bit of peace and quiet. And perhaps the cool hand of Elizabeth soothing his fevered brow.

He looked up at Maud for inspiration. A sturdy presence in a plastic container shaped like a sweet jar but a little nipped in at the waist. Earth-coloured, bearing the legend 'Amber Coast Crematorium', although it was ten miles inland and past an industrial estate. Teri said it was disrespectful leaving Maud there but he still hadn't made a decision. Responsibility. He hated it.

'Like I said, speak to the auctioneer.'

'I already have.' Fraser smiled, conciliatory now. 'I have a description here of the picture. Perhaps you can look again, in case you missed it before.'

Neil looked at the photocopy. 'What's this?'

'An extract from the diary of the dealer who agreed to buy the painting.'

'When was that?'

'1952.'

'So what makes you think Maud had it?'

'An intuition.'

Neil felt something stir in his brain. Apart from whisky-flavoured nausea. Something that might have lodged during a half-watched documentary that Lisa wanted to see on BBC4 or an article in *Devon Life* he flicked through at the dentist. Or the incessant scratchy-papered ravings of the Dormouth Local History Society, fiercely trying to stake their claim to a local hero in the face of the high-gloss, Twitter-trailed musings of the better-funded Hugh Bonnington Trust.

'This is about the famous painting of Maud that Hugh Bonnington was supposed to have destroyed!'

He was quite excited for a moment to be part of such a story, forgetting that his role in it was destined to be fool or minor villain.

Fraser looked put out. He clearly hadn't wanted to share that information. He looked across at Teri but she was typing rapidly.

'That's why it's important that all items are accounted for. I'm sure your team did a very thorough job –'

Teri harrumphed and arched her back to highlight her waistline. 'He doesn't have a team. He did it by himself. And then moved in there.'

'You've moved in to Maud Smith's flat?'

'It was available for rent, I'm paying the going rate –'

Fraser smiled sardonically.

'I'll go back to the auctioneer,' said Neil. 'And recheck the inventory for the items Maud had in storage.'

'Can't check the skip though, can you?' said Teri.

Fraser looked downcast. 'And what about her papers? Are you sure she didn't leave a will? I would have thought she would. She was an intelligent woman –'

'We see it all the time,' said Teri, turning from the desk and crossing her legs emphatically to draw attention to her fake-tanned calves. 'The most unlikely people. It's as if they think if they make a will they're acknowledging they're going to die. Which is irrational of course.'

This particular nugget was one of Neil's own and he didn't like hearing it from someone else. It was obvious Teri would never have come up with such profundity on her own.

'Look at him, for example,' she said, gesturing at Neil. 'Ex-wives and kids all over the place. Can you imagine the mess there'd be if he went under a hearse? But has he made a will? Thinks he'll live forever. That he's got nine lives. Or nine wives, anyway.'

She cackled to herself at this particular witticism. The only consolation was that Fraser looked as unamused as he was.

'If you could give me a ring,' said Fraser, 'By the end of the week. My card.'

A steely look, as it would say in one of Teri's 'erotic-historical – it's not porn you know' romances.

'I'll add you to our contacts,' said Teri, practically snatching the card from Fraser's hand as he left.

Neil looked up again at the sweet jar.

'She can't help you,' said Teri, fingers pounding the keys like they were the eyeballs of every man who'd ever rejected her.

Fourteen

'You're late,' she said, as he walked into the flat.

A mannequin in the corner – was it there before, Jim couldn't remember – was wearing a macramé bikini and a fedora over her eyes. Even so, she – it – looked unimpressed.

Elizabeth was standing at the counter which separated the kitchen from the rest of the room, arranging salad on two plates. Beautifully. Oh God, it is the wonders, he thought. I'm even infatuated by her lollo biondo.

He didn't know what to say. It had taken the last shred of his nerves to turn off the motorway, drive to the same car park as before, set off striding manfully, remember he hadn't bought a ticket, stride back to the pay and display, hesitate and wonder if it was a sign, set off again while ignoring the pied wagtail pecking at the tarmac, walk past the house several times wondering if he was an idiot, as Roisin, who obviously had more experience of the world than him had said – and finally, nervously, ring the bell.

Elizabeth's voice had sounded so real, and his so unreal and small and before he'd even finished speaking she'd pressed the buzzer, which he at first took as a rejection, a giant raspberry on his feeble intentions but he'd trudged up the stairs and now – it seemed he was expected, but how could that be?

Two plates. 'Sit,' she said, and he did.

They ate. The food was delicious. He had no idea what it was. His mind was spinning. The portions were small, suggesting that perhaps she hadn't been expecting him after all. He looked to the mannequin but she gave no indication, behind her fedora.

The cucumbers tasted sweet and juicy, almost like melon, quite unlike the ones in the shops. He said that, then realised how banal it sounded. Next he'd be complaining about the traffic on the M5.

She told him she had a friend with an allotment and she sometimes helped him. The salad was all from there. He told her, mournfully, that he was on the waiting list for an allotment in his borough, and at current rates he would be a hundred and four when one became available. She said when he was a hundred and four he'd probably appreciate the exercise.

So many things he'd dreamt of saying to her. He was flailing in a pit of small talk quite unlike the sparkling exchanges he'd imagined between them, and yet somehow infused with a magic of their own. Just because he was here, with her, noticing the shape of her earlobes, the fine down on her arms, the particular colour of her hair. She was both more wonderful and more ordinary than he remembered, but the ordinariness reassured him, the trace of paint under her fingernails, the chickenpox scar on her right cheek. She was real. This was real.

'I'm glad you're here,' she said. 'When you didn't call back, I thought maybe –'

'Call back?'

'I called your work mobile. A woman answered.'

'I leave it on my desk when I'm in the office. What did she sound like?' María José must have forgotten to pass on the message.

'Northern. Liverpool maybe?'

No maybe about it. 'Roisin,' he said.

'I hope there wasn't a problem. I know she's your boss.'

'No problem,' he said.

She cleared the plates when they'd finished and they moved over to the sofa. The dolls in the fireplace were still today. There seemed to be more of them, sitting on the mantelpiece.

'Have your dolls reproduced?'

'They're rescue dolls,' she said. 'They were at Maud's. Neil was about to put them in the skip.'

'Maud had dolls?' he asked innocently.

'I left them there.'

'So you were close?' Maybe she was the long-lost granddaughter after all. He'd have to walk away, like the psychiatrist who falls for a patient, or the detective who suddenly finds out that the witness who they thought was an innocent bystander before they fell in love is now a murder suspect. He should go.

'Maud had a spare room. She used to let me work up there.'

'Close,' he said, disconsolately. Should he ask to see her birth certificate? What if Maud had a secret love-child who was adopted at birth and she grew up to –

'I always admired her work, and then I ended up living in the same house as her,' smiled Elizabeth. 'It was fate!'

Of course the scientist in him knew that was nonsense. She was looking from the wrong end of the telescope. Maud had rented a flat in an artist's community, spawned in large part by the Hugh Bonnington connection. It was highly likely that one of the people living in her house would be an artist with an awareness, if not an interest in his work. Still, he was charmed.

'So you knew her well?' Roisin would kill him.

'I'm glad you're here. And that not even the traffic on the M5 could deter you.'

Thinking, has she just read my mind? And all that was in there was the M5? And why hadn't she answered his question?

She went to top up his wineglass. 'I'd better not,' he said, 'I have to drive tonight.'

'You don't,' she said with a smile. Mind-reading again.

Lying beside her, the evening through the skylight muted now, the freckles like a dusting of cinnamon on her shoulder.

'I'm glad you came back,' she murmured.

'My sister told me to see you. Well actually she told me to ring you but I lost my nerve.'

'She sounds very sensible.'

He laughed. 'That isn't exactly how I'd describe her.'

'What's she like?'

'Like? Clever, funny, charming, impetuous, demanding, self-destructive...' He sighed. 'At the moment, she's great. But she's –I don't know how to explain it. The doctors don't even know. She's had a bewildering number of diagnoses. ADHD, schizoaffective disorder. They seem to have settled on bipolar. But she's fine. At the moment. But I worry –'

'You feel responsible?'

'I suppose I've felt I had to look out for her over the years. We're twins. I've always thought that was a special bond. Roisin said it just means we shared antenatal accommodation. She said she had years sharing bunk beds with her sister and they don't have a mystical connection.'

Did she move away a little? Move away, then give a little compensatory smile and move back again? Why was he talking about Roisin?

'When you're a twin you go through everything together. The first day of school, exams. Birthdays, obviously. She first got ill just before our 'A' Levels. Or that's when we first knew for sure she was ill, not just acting up or being a teenager or going a bit too far.'

'What happened?'

'I went to university and she went to hospital. Then she came out. I went home when I could. At the end of my first year I had the chance to go to New Zealand and work on a conservation project for the summer but I thought it was too far. I went to a nature reserve in Norfolk instead. She got to uni a couple of years later, then dropped out, but it doesn't seem to have mattered. When she's well she can do anything, charm anyone. But when she's not –'

He sighed. 'Mum told me once that when she went into labour I was in position to be born first. But I moved aside at the last minute. I told Roisin that story, she said it's been like that ever since.'

She didn't say anything but she was close, and her very closeness made him calm.

'So that's my family. What about you?'

'My dad's a solicitor. And my mum's a Methodist minister.'

'Oh,' he said, taking his hand off her breast.

She laughed and put it back. 'I was a little surprise, I think. My sisters were twelve and ten when I was born. So I was left to my own devices. I suppose they'd already done the baby thing and they were older, and tired. But that was good. It left me to work things out for myself. I spent a lot of time drawing and making things and in my own world. Now I just have to work out how I can do that for the rest of my life.'

She said it with a wry smile but still with such certainty. Was she naïve, or was he defeatist? What if you can't, he half-thought, half-whispered. How will you feel if this is still your life when you're thirty? Forty?

*

The next morning, they had breakfast in bed though, since the kitchen was in the same room, that was as much practical as decadent.

'Your flat feels like a home,' he said. 'It's so much nicer than mine.'

'Do you share?'

'No, it's just me. It's mine.' He said it, but it didn't feel like it. Not in the way this place felt like hers. 'What I mean is I own it, well, I've got a mortgage on it.'

'Right,' she said, as if it didn't really matter.

If someone had told Roisin that, she'd have demanded the postcode and date of purchase and looked up what it cost compared to their salary and demanded to know how they'd managed to swing that. Which is exactly what had happened when he'd told her. If someone had told Edie she'd have been massively excited for them. Which wasn't exactly how it had been with him, but there were complications.

'Mum and Dad said they'd guarantee the mortgage, and they lent me the deposit and it made sense because what I'm paying actually compares favourably with when I used to rent – It's a flat,' he said, 'a very small, dark, basement flat.' He thought, when Dad wasn't much older than me, he could support a wife, two kids and a three-bed-semi on a teacher's salary. Why do I feel I have to apologise because I'm twenty-nine and I've got a mortgage?

'I've been lucky,' he said miserably. Then, 'I knew I'd seen it before!'

'What?'

'That painting.' It was a picture of a woman kneading bread, looking up as if she'd been interrupted. 'It's one of Maud's, isn't it? And that's Olive Bonnington.'

'Just a copy, I'm afraid. By me.'

'I saw it on Wikipedia. It said it was in a private collection.'

'Yes. But it was in an exhibition in Plymouth when I was a student. I copied it. I copied a lot of work during my degree. It's a great way to learn. You develop your technical skills, but you also try and get into the mind of the artist.'

'It's very good.'

'It's not bad. The brushwork isn't quite right. I don't think I quite understood the painting when I did it. I'm not sure I do now. That's what makes it a good painting.'

'How do you mean?'

'It's a classic domestic setting, the hearth, the breadmaking. And there's a look in her eyes. It's been interpreted as a feminist challenge. Look – I'm capable or more than this. But equally, it could be sexual. And once you know it's Olive, and that it's painted by Maud – some have said it was Maud she was challenging, saying, I can have all this. Home and hearth and the man besides.'

'Olive looks so flirtatious.'

'But who's it for? Of course male artists paint sexualised women, but what was Maud's intention? Is it her intention that we're seeing or Olive's? It's hard to know who's in control, the artist or the model. Or if they were complicit.'

'Is that why you work with dolls?'

'Oh, they can impose their will as well.'

'What happened to Maud after she left?'

'I'm glad you asked. Most people assume her life was over because she left Hugh. Her husband was an engineer. She was a housewife for a while, then she did voluntary work. Somehow got involved with what were then called battered wives. Did a law degree at the Open University. Worked at a law centre in the Seventies. Quite a radical in her way.'

'But she didn't paint any more?'

'Not as far as we know.'

'So there is life after art,' he said.

'For Maud there was,' said Elizabeth.

Fifteen

'I swear the hot weather sends people loopy,' said Paula. She was pulling the chocolate chips from a cookie one by one and sucking on them. 'Either that or it's a full moon.'

Brenda had found herself pacing on the beach before dawn, Prince at her side, so she knew it wasn't a full moon. Paula had put the cookie down and was speaking.

'First the customer is upset because they've had two different letters with the same date, one saying their refund is being processed and one saying they can't have a refund. Well, we can't help that, those letters are computer generated.'

'But you're customer service –' said Brenda tentatively.

'So he told her, you can have the refund but the credit agreement stands.' Most of the cookie was in pieces on her plate. There was one chocolate chip left. Brenda watched it, wondered why Paula had left it, whether she would stop speaking soon to swoop on it.

'And then she starts bleating about why would she want the credit agreement when she's already taken back the laptop.'

But wasn't that right? Maybe Brenda wasn't paying attention. 'They took out a credit agreement to pay for the laptop, but now they don't have the laptop. Isn't that what you said?'

'And then she asked to speak to a supervisor so I said, right, I'll talk to her,' she drew herself up to her full height in her chair, 'and then I said they're two separate agreements, if Madam had read the small print before she signed she'd be aware of that. The contracts are fully legal and comply with all regulatory requirements.'

'Even so,' said Brenda tentatively, 'it does seem a bit unfair –'

'Anyone who signs an in-store credit agreement is either desperate or stupid. I mean, the rates they charge. I'd never do it. Why don't they get a bank loan or take out a credit card with zero per cent on purchases and save the money and then pay it off at the end of the interest-free period?'

'You shouldn't get into debt,' said Brenda. The words helped her breathe. She no longer had to feel sorry for the woman with the laptop, or anyone else.

'Meanwhile, on planet earth,' said Paula.

'It sounds like you're doing well, anyway. Since the promotion.'

'Yes,' said Paula. 'So how are you?' Paula looked her mum in the eye, put a hand on her arm.

'I'm fine, why wouldn't I be?' she said and pulled her arm away. Next Paula would be saying, 'Love you'. She heard it all the time, people on their mobiles, on the street, in the shops. What do you want for tea, love you. I dropped your keys down the back of the dresser, love you. I've got to go to Granny's, the nurse says she's backed up again, love you.

When did it start? And how did Paula know before she did? Like fashions, she'd see Paula wearing something but by the time Brenda had caught on to where to buy it Paula would tell her it was on the way out.

'What does it feel like?'

'What?'

She felt like Paula was leaning in too close, her face suddenly looking bigger than it was, the gleam in her eyes too bright. That was how things looked now. Too close, and yet too far away. She thought of trying to put that into words for Paula and imagined Paula's eyes getting ever wider.

'Robbie says you've not been well again.'

'I'm fine. It's just you lot who are acting strange.'

She'd never said 'Love you,' to anyone. Not even her mum when she was dying in that bed in the home. 'I love you,' perhaps, a long time ago, but that meant something else.

'Just tell me,' said Paula.

'Like butterflies, that's all.' Only with butterflies you knew what they were for – a job interview or going on the rollercoaster but with this –

'Stomach cramps?' asked Paula. 'Anxiety?'

'Well –'

'Going too much, or not enough?'

'Isn't everyone?'

'I knew it!' said Paula. 'Irritable bowel. It's all in here, listen.' She pulled a magazine from her bag. 'It says your gut is the "primitive brain". So it's reacting to stress. Well that makes sense, after what he did to you.'

Brenda wanted to interrupt but her stomach churned. She wanted to go to the toilet but not now. Not while Paula was here.

'Avoid wholemeal bread, alcohol –' Brenda didn't tell her she couldn't eat anything except rice pudding and plain crisps. White foods. Why white? Robbie had brought her Complan. Not said anything, just brought it. That was white too.

White, like a clean toilet bowl. Think of something else. There was Paula, so bright and shiny, just like a white toilet bowl. She'd read a thing in the paper that your toilet bowl was probably cleaner than your kitchen sink. Because the ceramic was smooth but the stainless steel was all tiny scratches. That's me she thought. I'm all tiny scratches. There's a Brillo pad scouring the inside of my belly. While Paula's clean and flawless. Shit just bounces off her. She almost laughed. Paula was still talking. She looked at her, alarmed.

'And I suppose finding that body didn't help. It's just selfish. If people want to kill themselves that's fine but they shouldn't leave other people to clean up the mess.'

'It's always a mess when people die,' said Brenda quietly.

'You did everything you could for Gran,' said Paula, touching her arm. Brenda moved away.

Paula must have got that from her magazine as well.

'Anyway,' said Brenda. 'I don't think anyone said she killed herself.'

'Might as well. Swimming at that age.'

'I didn't know there was an age limit.'

Paula didn't reply. She gestured at the crack. 'I think it looks worse. Don't you?'

'The gauge says not.'

'Has Robbie got the surveyor in yet?'

'I think he's phoned them.'

'Have you spoken to Dad yet?'

'No.' It sounded firm when she said it, like Paula in Customer Services mode. Like Paula full stop.

'I don't blame you,' said Paula. 'I won't either. I bet him and Robbie are thick as thieves, but he won't get any support from me slinking off to his bedsit in Starcross.'

He's in Starcross? thought Brenda. That somehow made it real, when his phone was ringing out, or going to voicemail. She could picture the phone, sitting in the bedsit in Starcross. Just not him.

'I don't want you to take sides, Paula. He's still your dad.'

Bob's voice on his voicemail sounded just the same. Except she listened to it now in a way she hadn't needed to before. As if there might be a clue in there. The pause that went on a little too long after he said his name. As if he was waiting for you to speak. He sounded awkward but genuine. A man you'd trust with your patio or your retaining wall.

'I mean, you don't have to speak speak. There's no reason why you should. But there are things that have to be resolved.'

Resolved. Like a complaint. 'Once you've got the surveyor's report, you can get the work done. You don't want it losing value. Not now.'

They had to take care of the house. They'd gone without all sorts for nearly thirty years, just so they could know, we'll always have the house. She couldn't tell Paula that although there was more house now, it was less hers.

'Are you going to tell me what this is all about?'

'What?'

'You and Dad.'

Brenda didn't answer.

'Is he having an affair? Are you?'

But she said the last bit as if she knew it was impossible.

'It's okay,' said Paula, looking into her eyes again, 'I can see you're not ready to talk.'

She put her magazine away, took her coffee mug to the sink, put the remains of the cookie in the recycling. 'I'd best be off, Mum. Callum's gone to B&Q and he won't know where to put anything.'

She walked into the hall, looked at herself in the mirror, got out her lipstick, except it wasn't a stick, it went on with a brush. Brenda watched, fascinated. Paula finished and glanced at the letters on the shelf.

'Water rates. You paid it?'

'Your dad's still paying the bills.'

She opened her mouth as if about to speak. Brenda pointed at the flyer she'd left on the side.

'Have you seen this?'

'No,' said Paula.

'Something Dora Mickelthwaite's involved in.'

'There's nothing that woman isn't involved in.' Paula skimmed the flyer. 'Art? She's more bring and buy.'

'Probably not your sort of thing,' said Brenda.

Paula looked dubious then put on a smile. 'You want to go?'

'It's your night.' Paula always came round on Thursday nights.

Paula looked again at the flyer. 'Why not? It'll be a laugh. And you need cheering up.'

Paula put an arm round her and kissed her on the cheek. Brenda was afraid she might tell her she loved her.

Sixteen

Let Teri think he was worried. Okay, he had certain logistical difficulties to overcome, but that was alright. He just needed to think about it methodically. He went to the fridge, then remembered his earlier pledge not to drink alone.

Thinking was not something that could be done in the pub very easily, in his experience. He'd seen plenty of films where people – usually men – sat alone and ponderous at a bar, contemplating some life-changing moment. Usually at the point where an enigmatic woman sat beside them and turned the story. He hadn't seen too many enigmatic women in the Kebab and Calculator, nor too many introspective loners.

Besides, when he'd made that pledge, he hadn't envisaged that there would be so much time to eat up between work and bed. He never seemed to have any at home, what with dinner and bath time and putting Tom to bed and Tom getting up again. He looked at his watch. Five to seven. If he ran he would just make it to the Inconvenience Store on the corner before it shut.

He got back, still breathless from the sprint, and opened his bottle of red. If Lisa saw it he'd tell her it was for cooking. Not that he was sure what you'd use red wine for. A splash in a pasta sauce perhaps? Liven up gravy? Did people still eat gravy? He had a moment's nostalgia for the meat, mash and veg paradigm of his childhood, which had seemed monotonous then, as he'd left home and run with open arms to the sunny uplands of pasta, rice and even couscous. Anyway, what did it matter what Lisa thought? Wasn't that the whole point of leaving? He couldn't quite remember what the point had been, but he had weightier issues to consider now.

In honour of his no-drinking rule, there were no wine glasses, but he thought there was a certain earthy appeal in drinking it from a tumbler. Like a French peasant coming in after a day's toil. Well, his was almost an outdoor life, with much time spent pacing the cemetery, not least to escape the charms of Teri, looking for vandalism and unauthorised memorials, sure, but also noting the subtle changes of the seasons.

And listening to the comments and complaints of the passers-by that they cut the grass too often (destroying vital habitats) or not enough (disrespecting the dead). Or that their restrictions on memorials were too strict (heartlessly disallowing glass beer bottles and plastic windmills) or not strict enough (allowing tacky teddy bears and photo memorials).

Fraser's picture. Focus. He wished he'd bought something to accompany the wine. The French peasant would probably have freshly baked bread and cloves of raw garlic. The Inconvenience Store only ran to hot pasties, misshapen cakes and paracetamol. And rows and rows of booze. And fags. And presumably condoms, although he hadn't looked. This was the sort of thing he should be researching, now he was back on the market.

He thought Martha might have left behind some crisps. Frittata and Mediterranean olive. What other kind of olive was there? He was going to bring out a brand. Tautology and pisstakalata. With red wine one should only eat ready salted crisps, he thought. But he would make do.

The picture. First thing – no one knew for sure if there even was a picture. Apart from that old witch Olive Bonnington, and she wasn't telling. He didn't blame her, might as well milk it for all she could. Being Hugh's consort probably hadn't been a barrel of laughs, what with his artist's ego and his well-documented infidelities.

Martha had taken some canvases. That was the insistent thought that kept coming back, accompanied by a low but profound drum roll in his belly. He did his best to mask it by pouring wine on it but it was still there. She'd said she was going to take some stuff and he'd just said yeah, because she was a sensible girl, wasn't she?

So maybe Martha had it. If there was an 'it'. So he could just leave it there, in far away London. But if Martha was studying art might she not realise what she had at some point? And as her mother had instilled in her a social conscience, would she not feel obliged to reveal it? Or perhaps she'd be torn apart by her conflicting desires to give art to the world and protect her feckless father. He didn't want her to suffer because of an accident of birth.

And there was something else. It was like when he found a batch of index cards for the old closed churchyard out at Diddlescombe where no one had been buried for at least a hundred years and no one much visited, apart from heroin addicts and goth student filmmakers. He could have binned them, but he was aware that this was a piece of history.

So he'd had Teri add them to the database and she'd complained that the dust provoked her allergies – she'd had a test done by some online charlatan and now had a whole range of 'triggers' that she hadn't had before. He'd told her it was nothing to worry about, just hundred-year-old dandruff and snot particles. When she'd finished, he'd put them away again in a cupboard. But at least they were still there. Them and their story.

He tried to call Martha's mobile but she wasn't accepting messages. He'd have to text her. He hated texting. The predictive text, like his Lisas, didn't understand him. He managed a couple of sentences. She was a bright girl. She'd see through the typos.

He poured another glass of wine. The crisps were better than he'd expected. He tried to come up with some more flavours. Maybe they should be less literal. First date and pheromone. Fallen tear and broken dreams. He liked that. It had a mournful, minor key quality. Maybe not what crisp marketers were looking for, but it worked for music, why not for food? Otherwise everyone would be eating chocolate cake and no one would eat capers or blue cheese.

To his surprise she came back quickly. 'Hv p8ntngs. Will uz 4 plmpsst.'

Plmpsst. He said it aloud. 'Plmpsst.' He knew how it felt but not exactly what it meant. Plmpsst. Like if he went upstairs to Elizabeth's flat now, he could say, please excuse me, I'm a little bit plmpsst, take pity on me and let me lie on your couch. In your arms. Stroking your beautiful -

Palimpsest! He knew what that meant. It meant creating a work of art in the style of another. They did it in films all the time, though then they called it an *hommage*. No worries then.

He sent another text to Martha. 'Pls send p8ntngs bk. No hurry.'

Now he could relax.

Seventeen

Generation's computers were down. Everyone sat back in their chairs for a moment, like prisoners who'd been held in solitary confinement in the dark for years whose cell doors had suddenly been thrown open. They blinked as if blinded by the light. Then they began to fidget and complain.

The old timers shook their heads and said that was the trouble with computers, before ambling off to the library to dig out the archive boxes or take one of the dusty leather-bound volumes of the *London Gazette* off the shelf. Everyone else got their phones out, desperately needing to know that someone out there was still alive and sending spam.

Jim was happy to muse about the weekend. He'd stayed in Dormouth till Sunday afternoon, wanted to stay forever, hoped this was the beginning of something. As he left, Elizabeth had shyly mentioned the opening of her exhibition and asked if he might want to come. Of course he did! Okay he'd have to miss the junior moth safari with the urban wildlife group, but they'd understand.

His reverie was interrupted by Roisin who was pacing the office, issuing death threats and shouting, a more restrained, 'Don't give me that server bollocks!' into her wireless headset at regular intervals.

Liaising with IT providers was strictly his responsibility, but Roisin couldn't resist an opportunity to shout at someone and he was happy to let her.

'They say it'll be at least an hour,' said Roisin incredulously. 'What do we pay them for if –' She was too furious to even finish her sentence. Roisin was always surprised anew on the rare occasions when the world didn't bend to her will. If there was an earthquake and central London was riven in two she'd take it as a personal affront.

'Let's go and grab a coffee,' said Jim, knowing otherwise she'd be calling the engineers every five minutes to give them abuse, thereby stopping them from actually doing any work. She stomped to her empty office, looked at her desk, which was bare apart from her laptop, tablet and mobile, and presumably realised there was nothing she could do.

'Okay.' She stopped to shout across the room at María José, who had a Masters degree in Applied Linguistics, was fluent in five languages and would have a go in several others, and was currently working as their receptionist.

'If those fuckers call back I'm on my mobile!'

They went to a place with the ambience of a Provençal patisserie, between a bookie and a cheque-cashing place. Roisin automatically went to the counter.

'I thought we could try the novel experience of sitting down while drinking a coffee,' said Jim.

'Is that what these tables are for,' said Roisin, but she took a seat by the window, leaving him to sit by the doorway, where people would continually push past him. As the waitress approached she continued loudly, 'They probably spent hours assembling all these mismatched stripped pine tables and rickety old chairs. That one's more woodworm than wood. Krish knows a guy who sources this stuff. Mainly closed down institutions. He says most of it reeks of piss when he gets it.'

Krish was the brother who dealt in designer-ish clothes. He knew someone for everything. He had been christened Christopher Cormac but decided somewhere along the line that an Asian-sounding name made him seem more entrepreneurial.

'So how was your weekend? Good, I hope, since you stood me up.'

Melissa had invited her touch rugby team round for a session. They were a mixed team who Jim had once encountered at a party. The men had been determined to work their way through the whole gamut of obnoxious drunken rugby player stereotypes and the women were determined to outperform the men.

'So what did you do? Join in the piss drinking, testicle waxing and other jolly japes?'

'I went clubbing with Joolz on Saturday. Then Sunday I babysat for Krish. Did I ever tell you how much I like fishfingers mashed into my hair?'

'You'd probably have got the same from the rugby team.'

'So you had a good weekend?' she asked again, as she cut into her hazelnut croissant with the grim concentration of a barber-surgeon.

'Good,' he said. 'Great.'

'You've gone all dreamy and mushy. Can you be more specific?'

How could he put into words what he felt? 'Everything seems easy with Elizabeth.' As if he'd known her forever? As if it was meant to be? But that was fate and he didn't believe in fate. 'Even though we haven't known each other long I feel comfortable –'

'Sounds really exciting,' said Roisin. 'So, where'd you go?'

'Go?'

'Did you eat out, or hang out at some beachfront bar or what?'

'I don't think you've quite grasped the concept of Dormouth,' he said. 'We went for walks on the beach and there was this really cool farmers market where we bought some stuff to cook and –'

Roisin got her phone out. 'Just checking in with the office. And you spent half the day shagging, it's okay, I remember those days. Before it got grown up.'

Roisin thought he was boring. Or rather she thought his relationship was boring. Her relationship with Melissa was constant drama. Class war in the kitchen, blazing rows in the living room, elaborate sexual games in the bedroom (and kitchen and hall...). She told him snippets from time to time. He wasn't sure if she did it to arouse or embarrass him (it did both). And he was excited about ewe's milk cheese and beetroot with the mud still on it and –

'Did I tell you Elizabeth upholstered her own sofa?'

'Wonders,' she said, without looking up.

But that was the thing about Elizabeth. Life was new and exciting when he was with her. Domestic details seemed endlessly fascinating. And making a meal seemed inseparable from the lemony scent as he kissed the back of her neck which led to her turning her face to kiss him which led to – to things that were too precious to share with Roisin.

'Melissa has many wonderful qualities,' he said. 'But I'm not sure inviting the touch rugby team over for a mass nude Twister party counts as grown up.'

The massacre of the hazelnut croissant had not, apparently, been a prelude to eating it. She pushed it around the plate like a cat torturing a mouse.

Something was bothering Roisin. Something more than the ever-present hurt that she refused to admit, that her family wanted nothing to do with her, not the real her. She'd once joked that even if she renounced hot lesbian sex and took the veil they wouldn't take her back, but he knew that wasn't the point. She wanted them to love her as she was, and they couldn't. Apart from Krish, who was firmly on her side, and two sisters who kept in touch on the sly, the big argumentative family she'd grown up in had fallen silent as far as she was concerned.

But that was always true. This must be something else.

Roisin put down her knife. 'Melissa wants to put my name on the mortgage.'

'Oh. Well, that's good, isn't it?'

'It's not mine. I haven't worked for it.'

Nor has she, thought Jim. She'd inherited a significant amount from some convoluted family trust.

'You're a couple. You help each other. She may have more money, but you bring other things to the partnership. Shouldn't that be recognised?'

Roisin grunted. 'We should get back.'

'María José would have called if we were needed. Go on.'

'There's nothing else to say.' Her face was closed.

'Okay. So tell me about Maud Smith's heir instead,' he said.

'Why? It's not your case any more.'

'I don't want the name, I just want to know –'

'That Rover's going to a loving home? You're the one who abandoned him after Christmas when your new love interest appeared on the scene.'

'I'm just curious.'

'John Williams' granddaughter lives in a bungalow in Whitley Bay, has no idea who Maud Smith was, or Hugh Bonnington, didn't even pretend to care, and is planning to use the windfall to buy a conservatory. Probably a hideous uPVC one.'

He let it go. 'It doesn't seem right,' he said.

'Okay. I lied. She's a devoted amateur watercolourist, a patron of her local gallery, and she's going to use the money to set up a benevolent fund for destitute painters. Is that better?'

When he thought about it, which he generally tried not to, none of it seemed right. But there was no point in saying that to Roisin.

Which made him wonder why he found himself saying to Roisin, 'Don't you ever wonder about the ethics of what we do?'

'Eh?' Roisin looked at him like he was speaking Mandarin.

'I mean, maybe it would be fairer if it went to no one at all.'

'You mean the taxman?' She sneered incredulously.

'I mean,' he retorted. 'Why should people inherit large amounts of money, tax free? They haven't worked for it, they don't in any sense deserve it.'

'You know they've identified a gene for liberalism?' said Roisin. 'If you're lucky, one day they might find a cure.'

'You think I'm wrong?'

'Wrong question. It's just the way it is. You've got to take what you can get in life.'

'And you call yourself a socialist?'

'That's enlightened self-interest. The working class might stab each other in the back but we know that the ruling class will shit on us even more.'

'We? You're living in splendour with a minor member of the gentry.'

'Don't worry, I make the bitch pay,' she twinkled. 'Every night.'

'But,' he blustered. 'Your job, your suit – you're not working class.'

She finished her coffee and got to her feet. 'Of course I am. It's hereditary.'

Eighteen

Life wasn't getting any simpler. The morning after he'd seen Fraser, Neil had woken with a vague sense of ennui, a mouth like the inside of the abdomen of a corpse that had been left on a body farm in Arkansas, and a sinking sensation that he'd got the wrong definition of 'palimpsest'.

He'd looked it up on his phone. He wasn't concerned about the etymology, only the principle that his daughter was going to, or perhaps already had, painted over a small but career-threatening piece of art history. And Martha was not answering her phone.

He had even resorted to contacting Lisa 1 via the mediation of Lisa 2. He wondered if their previous frosty courtesy would now be replaced by a sisterly solidarity as they discussed his shortcomings, ex-wife to ex-wife. Lisa 1 said that Martha was at an arts and crafts summer retreat in rural Herefordshire and it was quite likely she would be out of signal. He didn't want to say what it was about and Lisa 1 didn't want to give him the landline number unless he could convince her it was an emergency.

He was sure it would all work out. Martha was a sensible girl. She wouldn't have taken a completed painting, would she? And besides, they didn't even know the thing existed. Fraser's wishful thinking would not magic it into life, any more than Neil could say a few words to Maud's urn and find her sitting at his desk finishing the budget for him.

That reminded him, he should really do something with the ashes. Maybe he'd ask Elizabeth. He could slink up to her flat one night on the pretext of a chat. She'd invite him in for a glass of wine, there might be tears as they talked about Maud, he could offer a sympathetic ear, but then might draw nearer to offer comfort – Maybe take the urn with him. Might heighten the emotion of the evening. Or Maud might play gooseberry.

And he had a meeting first thing. Going straight from home to the Seventies brutalist building that constituted the nerve centre of Dorbridge District Council – or, as the *Dormouth Informer* called it, Drawbridge, due to its defensive approach when challenged on anything from refuse collection to executive pay. He had a headache.

Malcolm Hannon was a man who was in the wrong job. How he'd ever come to be Head of Parks and Cemeteries was a mystery. There were rumours he'd done astrophysics at university. He'd worked his way up in management from a background in accountancy. He was said to be a genius with figures. People fazed him.

He greeted Neil mournfully and shifted a black daysack from the second-best chair. It was open and Neil spied a volume of Schopenhauer and an open packet of mini muffins. Malcolm's tweed jacket hung in a corner of the room. It had been there since the spring, slowly shedding. Neil wondered how long it would take until there were more fibres not in the jacket than in it. He wondered at what point you could no longer call it a jacket. Now he was beginning to understand some of the agony of being Malcolm.

Malcolm had a phone headset tangled in his luxuriant grey hair and two monitors on screen save. He frowned and his voluminous eyebrows appeared to knit.

'Such a difficult situation,' said Malcolm. Neil didn't speak. He was unsure whether this was a reference to the disappearing picture, the accelerating universe or some more esoteric existential hell.

He waited. 'Fraser McKendrie,' said Malcolm.

'Oh.'

'A Scottish name, I believe.'

'He's not, though.'

Malcolm paused to reflect on this. Neil didn't see that it was relevant but in an interconnected universe who can say?

Malcolm licked his lips. His eyebrows coalesced in a frown like two exquisitely choreographed caterpillars. 'He referred to a picture.'

'We don't even know if the painting exists.'

'How can we be said to objectively know anything?' said Malcolm.

'Right,' said Neil.

'Is the situation irredeemable?'

'Can one prove a negative?' asked Neil, hopefully.

Malcolm put his hands together. 'One might consider all the places where the hypothetical painting could hypothetically have been.'

'I'll have a word with the auctioneers,' said Neil. 'Could be a cataloguing error.'

Malcolm nodded thoughtfully, his gaze in the middle distance, as if already on higher things.

'There are people who deal only in the world of certainties. Who care nothing for nuance, complexity.'

Neil wasn't sure who he meant. Did he mean the council? 'You can trust me,' said Neil, generically.

'The fourth estate are relentless in their pursuit of me.'

'The *Informer* on about the skatepark again?' asked Neil.

Malcolm shrugged helplessly.

Neil looked over Malcolm's shoulder at a printout of an email, dated from the previous afternoon, flagged urgent and peppered with exclamation marks. It was a request to answer a media enquiry.

'You have to log onto the database to read the enquiry and give your response.'

'I can't look,' said Malcolm.

'It can't be that bad.'

'No, I can't. I'm locked out.'

'If you call IT they'll reset your password.'

Malcolm sighed wearily.

'I'll deal with it for you,' said Neil, feeling like a shy, gifted pupil presenting a poem to a demanding but appreciative English teacher.

'You will?'

'Sure. Is there anything else?'

Malcolm waved dismissively. 'I am confident that you have everything in hand.'

Neil smiled. He had already seen the media enquiry. It was a request for information on the council's policy for protecting the common primrose for a nature documentary on Radio Four. He'd written the policy himself. Peasy.

Nineteen

Boredom. There was something pure and dense and physical about it. You could almost feel it between your teeth, at the back of your throat, as you watched the long hand on the office clock, willing it to move from one minute to the next.

Jim realised he hadn't been bored like this since school. Double History, Friday afternoon, sun falling on the desk, the drone of the mower throwing up the smell of freshly cut grass, centuries of human existence compressed into a pre-packed collection of paragraphs, forced down for regurgitation on the day of the exam. Causes of the First World War, that was one. Starting, for reasons he could no longer remember, with the assassination of Archduke Franz Ferdinand and ending with something to do with Belgium.

What must it have been like for the teacher? To them he'd seemed boring, with his mechanical answers, but perhaps he was just bored. He must have studied history. Maybe he was even passionate about the richness and complexity of past lives, the interplay of individuals and events, technology and environment. Jim had never really thought about other people's motivations for work before.

Even now he was none the wiser. Did Bert (who knew that there were still people called Bert?) poring over the football results while he took his daily dump (at 10.34, Jim had learnt through bitter and malodorous experience) think of the emptiness of his life and the monotony? Did he accept it as a trade-off? Was the ritual defecation a form of rebellion? Or did he thrill to the spin of the microfiche?

Or like Jim, did he slide across the surface of the day in a kind of fug, looking neither left nor right, thinking on some unconscious level that this was just a dream and he would soon be back to his real, meaningful life, even as the image of that real, meaningful life became more blurred and distant.

María José was surreptitiously switching between a Polish grammar webpage and updating the meeting room calendar. Polish wasn't one of the languages listed on her CV but she'd made some Polish friends in London and was keen to make the most of the opportunity to learn from them.

Bert was watching the clock. Almost salivating like a dog who was expecting his dinner. Ten thirty. Jim watched the clock almost as assiduously as Bert. He would go to the Gents now. For the next half hour it wouldn't be safe to enter.

Sebastian floated past Jim in the corridor outside the toilet. Jim forgot Sebastian existed most of the time, but then something would happen to remind him that Sebastian owned the company, and that Roisin was just his vicar on earth.

Sebastian floated everywhere. He seemed to be on intravenous ecstasy. Perhaps he'd taken it from the breast. He'd been born in some posh commune in Rajasthan and had then gone to a progressive boarding school in Sussex where kids made all their own rules. In fact his whole life was like that. Perhaps that was why he'd been drawn to Roisin and put her in charge of the business, or hobby, or whatever Generation was to him. She was the authority figure he'd never had.

'Roisin's quiet,' Sebastian said. Which would have immediately put Jim on his guard but Sebastian announced it with joyful acceptance. He knew that the universe was arranged for his benefit.

Jim decided to saunter past her office. The door was open. She was staring into space, not actually doing anything, which was unheard of. He went and stood in her eyeline.

'Go away,' she said. 'I'm thinking.'

'You never think. You act impulsively, emphatically and – some other adverb which I can't think of right now.'

'You'll have to phone your dad.'

'Yeah, he'd like the challenge. So, what are you thinking about?'

'Nothing. How's your love life?'

Constantly in his thoughts. A little thread of gold through the dull, rough weave of his day.

'Oh, you know. Long distance. But we speak on the phone all the time.'

'You speak? On the phone? How retro. Next you'll be saying she's your best friend. I hate it when couples say that.'

'Care to elaborate?'

'No. And is that Fraser feller still hanging around?'

'I don't know. Why?'

'Because you're worried about him.'

'No I'm not.'

'You disliked him on sight. You never dislike anyone.'

'You think I'm jealous because he's a successful academic and I'm a – I'm not?'

'No. I thought you might be jealous cos he was hanging round your girlfriend while you're two hundred miles away but I suppose not all girlfriends are bitches.'

'Roisin, why do you keep not saying the thing you're clearly dying to say?'

'I took your advice. Though why I'd listen to a fuckbrain like you –'

'About the deeds?'

'I told Melissa I was willing to go along with the arrangement, given that we'd been together for a while and we were, I suppose, a "couple". She looked at me like I was an eejit and said she'd already got the papers drawn up. All we need to do is sign.'

'Well, she should have involved you in the decision, I suppose, but since it's what you wanted –'

'She's done a spreadsheet detailing who's put in

what equity, who's paid what each month, and what we've contributed in terms of work on the house – that would be what I've contributed, since she doesn't know a lump hammer from a fish slice.'

'You're made for each other,' Jim said, but then he drew in his grin when he saw that Roisin was not amused. 'What's the matter?'

'She's decided I'm entitled to a third of the property. A fucking third!'

Melissa was truly the bravest woman he had ever met, he thought. 'So before you didn't want anything from her, but now a third is not enough?'

'What does she think I am, the fucking live-in help? French maid plus extras?' Roisin slumped in her chair and for a moment he saw the vulnerability in her. 'This was supposed to be her showing we're a couple, committed to each other, sharing everything. Not divvying up like a works night out at the curry house.'

'Shouldn't you – talk?' But as soon as he'd said it he saw the mask was back in place.

'Talk? It was talking that got us into this mess. We should have stuck to fucking.'

Twenty

Brenda was knitting for Paula. Desk toys which she said she was going to give out to 'incentivise' her team of call-handlers. A dalek, an owl and a cupcake. Like bronze, silver and gold, she'd said. Only one of each. At the end of the week they'd have to give them back so they could be given out again in a little ceremony on Monday morning by the interactive whiteboard.

She heard the door. Barking. Then Robbie came in with another man. He was in clean clothes, not work clothes like Robbie, and she had to call Prince back. The man said he didn't mind and went to stroke Prince. She called him back anyway, held him under his snout, close by her side.

'This is Tony,' said Robbie. 'He's going to take a look at the crack then we're going for a drink.'

She and Tony stared at each other for a moment. Then she offered him a drink. He followed her into the kitchen where she saw she'd left the ironing mid-flow. Brenda never started a job without finishing it.

She put the kettle on. She could hear the shower go on upstairs. He'd be a while then. She waved

Tony towards the kitchen table.

Tony sat down. He looked at the crack, then looked away again, as if it was rude to stare. She put a drink in front of him then went back to stand behind the ironing board.

Robbie had mentioned this Tony but she'd thought he'd be younger. He must be about her age. She'd thought he'd be younger because Robbie said he was going to pick him up. Why would a man of that age need picking up? A builder without a van was like a builder without a right arm. Drink-driving? Messy divorce? Debt?

She wasn't going to talk to him. She hadn't brought him here, why should she have to talk to him? A man who got picked up.

In Dormouth they waited by the Dormouse Café to get picked up for a day's casual work. When she saw them waiting in the morning, if she was out walking Prince, she always smiled and said hello but really she wanted to cross the road. She felt sorry for them and she didn't like feeling sorry. Having someone feel sorry for you was the worst thing of all.

She'd ironed all the T-shirts and there was only underwear left in the basket. She didn't want him looking at hers so she picked up a pair of Robbie's pants and started ironing them. The iron wasn't hot which at least meant she'd hadn't forgotten to turn it off.

Prince got up, turned round, then lay down again by her feet. Tony looked around the room. Like he was pricing up new units. Looked at Robbie's pants. What was taking Robbie so long?

'Nice garden,' he said. At least she thought it was him but she didn't see his lips move. The silence flowed on, as if it had never been broken.

Was it? Brenda never really thought about it. Every spring, after the bulbs had started to die back, Bob got the lawnmower out and complained about it and she went to the garden centre and got some bedding plants and put them in and then forgot about it.

That was how a home should be, wasn't it? You shouldn't have to be running round noticing things, like on holiday where everything was different, even the things that should be the same, like cups of tea. A home and a family should just be there. They shouldn't change.

'The marigolds look good,' he said.

Last year, Paula had asked if she could plant some annuals. Callum was into cooking with edible flowers. Marigolds, nasturtiums, violas, some others she didn't recognise. She'd even grown a few lettuces in the flower beds, lollo rosso, which Brenda thought a bit weird but she'd left her to it. Some of the flowers had self-seeded and come back.

'They're weeds,' she said dismissively.

'Oh no,' he said, 'they're beautiful flowers. Always make me think of sunshine. Keep away pests too. Great companion plants for tomatoes.'

She looked out and saw some other flowers. Purple petunias, red pelargoniums, some sort of dahlia. How had they got there? And the grass was short and neat too. How had that happened? How was the world going on, like nothing had changed?

He was quiet after his outburst.

'So you like gardening,' she said, because she couldn't think of anything else.

'I love it,' he said. 'Though I haven't got a garden now.'

Debt, she thought. Or divorce. Both? People get divorced, they have to sell the house, divide up what they've got, there are legal fees – She felt sick.

Dad lost the shop. There were whispers and tears. She learnt a new word. Bankruptcy. Her mum tried to explain, then gave up, as if she didn't understand herself what had gone wrong. It was a good business, she said, over and over. Dad was at home all day but it wasn't a holiday, he was on the dole.

Breathe. Think of something else. She looked at Tony's shirt. It was white with little blue flowers. They were the thing now, apparently. She could imagine what Robbie would say if someone told him to wear a flowery shirt. Paula had bought one like it for Callum but she'd never seen him wear it. Not that they saw much of Callum, with the hours he worked. Must be a wife. Or a girlfriend. She was sure no man she knew would have bought that shirt.

He was still looking out of the window.

Robbie came in, hair still wet, smelling of shower gel or was it aftershave, wearing a shirt like Tony's but with a black print on it. Not flowers, more like squiggles, but even so. She didn't know where he'd bought that. When.

Robbie walked over to the crack and Tony looked at her like he thought she might bite then followed.

They talked in low tones. Robbie asked Brenda to bring the surveyor's report and his Dad's original plans which he'd left on the side in the hall. When she came back, their heads were close as they both looked at the crack. Tony was laying his hand on it and his cheek was almost resting on the wall, as if he were listening to it or feeling it, rather than just looking. Like the wall was a corpse and he was trying for a heartbeat. Except the corpse would have to be standing up.

They went outside. She waited in the house. They came back in again. She hadn't heard them speak but they seemed to understand each other perfectly.

Tony smiled at her and explained what he was planning to do. She nodded, because Robbie was nodding, although she didn't really follow.

'So it's not going to come down?' That was all she wanted to know.

'No,' he said. He rested a hand on the wall again. She wanted to say, it's not your wall, it's mine.

'The footings are adequate.' He looked thoughtful. 'I might have put a crocodile in but...'

'Cutting corners,' said Robbie, shaking his head sadly, builder to builder, like he was sorry for the wall, rather than criticising his own dad.

Then they were gone, in their matching shirts.

Twenty-one

When he opened the door the light from the kitchen spilt into the hall and he felt a sense of anticipation, as if the scene was set and waiting for the actors to arrive.

'Lisa?' he called. There was no answer. He must have left it on when he went to the pub. Another of his faults. He could hear her weary voice, 'You've left the light on.'

It was years since he'd been to the theatre. Used to go a lot when he was living in Leeds. Experimental stuff in small venues. Social clubs. The studio at the Poly. Had a girlfriend who was an actor before he went out with Lisa 1. Or possibly during. Liked East European Theatre of the Absurd. He saw her a few years later playing an anxious mum on *The Bill*. That was what it said on the credits. Anxious Mum.

He thought of Tom looking through the gap in the box. An improvisation of his own. Except Neil had felt more watched than watching. Now that was experimental.

He couldn't shake the thought that he was being watched now. Felt it in his fingertips. A tingling. Maybe it was the old lady. He was glad Lisa wasn't here. She'd have too much to say. Now if Elizabeth were here…Life would be restful. He thought of her coming down to see the old lady, forming an unlikely friendship. Perhaps he could dress up as grandmother and she could come down in a little red hood...

The room was spinning, just a little. What do you think, Maud? Had he spoken? He wasn't sure. Maybe he should take some of her tablets, get on her wavelength. But perhaps not tonight. Perhaps tonight the drink and the thought of the lovely Elizabeth were enough.

Coffee might be an idea. Or sleep. Elizabeth who had been in the pub. Alone. Well, not alone, but not with Jim. With a couple of female friends. They were all wearing paint-splashed overalls and said they had just come from their studio. They'd smiled indulgently like he was Elizabeth's slightly odd uncle who she insisted was a charming eccentric but who they suspected might be a creep.

He collapsed on the bed in all his clothes, put the TV on, what had they talked about? He'd asked her if she knew anything about the painting, but subtly, he was sure. She said no. He didn't believe her. He liked the laughter in her eyes, as if she knew he knew she was lying and she didn't much care. He thought of her beautiful eyes and the slow, easy way she moved her body, so unlike Lisa's frenetic efficiency – He let go of his limp penis and picked up the more reliable remote with his other hand.

What was the point in leaving Lisa if she was

still there in his head? Did Lisa have his voice in her head? He lay very still as if to hear but all he could make out was the lone scream of a lost young seagull and the poignant counterpoint of a teenager vomiting up their post-pub chips.

Lisa, he imagined, would hear a strident, headmistressy voice. Someone she had always wanted to impress although she wouldn't acknowledge it. That struck him as quite profound. It seemed he had quite a complex and thought-provoking dialogue with the Lisa in his head, as if they were characters in a Poliakoff three-part drama. His relationship with the real Lisa was like a couple in a bad Seventies sitcom.

Of course the Lisa in his head wasn't exactly the real Lisa. The people in your head were always so focused and certain. They only had one interest – you. They didn't have voices in *their* heads knocking them off course. They didn't have good days and bad days. They were constant, like characters in films. They only had to contend with one plot at a time.

Elizabeth didn't have a voice, but she was there in his head, laughing joyously and lying back naked on silk sheets in – in an entirely implausible porn-star pose. He smiled sleepily to himself. He wondered if Lisa wasn't maybe short for Elizabeth. So he'd tried two parts but only Elizabeth offered the whole. He thought about resuming his wank but decided to dream about her instead. It seemed more pure somehow. Wholesome.

He could hear a noise that might be the gurgling of the pipes but he liked to think it was

Maud laughing. But not at him. He lifted his head abruptly from the bed, so abruptly he cricked his neck. More a confirmatory laugh. That was a big word. Maud had been an artist, after all. She'd have got him, he was sure. He saw her as a doughty formidable character, who would take no nonsense but would still appreciate his rebellious sense of fun. Something like Stephanie Cole in *Waiting for God*.

He didn't mind sharing a flat with a dead tenant. Of course if she wanted a grave in his cemetery she'd have to pay, but here there was no charge. Just as long as Trevor didn't get wind of it. He'd accuse him of sub-letting. And then there was always the hope that Maud might bring him a glass of water if she was here, not let him drift into a dehydrated sleep.

Soon be morning. Had he set his phone? Had he got his phone? He'd find out when the alarm went off, or didn't. Sometimes when he couldn't get out of bed in the morning he heard his mum's voice, like she'd been back then, five boys in two bedrooms, first up, best dressed, they used to laugh, but it didn't make them get up any earlier.

She'd be frying bacon, shouting up the stairs, adding fifteen minutes to the time to make them move but of course they all knew she did that, so it had no effect at all. Happy days, lying there in their teenage fug of stale cider and sharp sweat and illicit fags out the window. How simple life had been then!

And as he fell asleep, thinking of his tired, smiling mum who had no words for love but showed it every day in her relentless housekeeping and her rare, startling smiles, he realised something else, that voices never die.

Twenty-two

Jim hadn't heard much from Edie since she moved into her new flat. That was a good thing – probably. If she needed help she'd get in touch, wouldn't she? But what if she thought everything was fine, as she did when she was high, and in fact it wasn't at all?

So he was relieved when she came to pick up the rest of her stuff and announced she'd be coming round again, and bringing a friend from the charity where she was now working, who she described as another survivor of the mental health system. What's – Jim had begun to ask, but then hesitated. He couldn't say, what's wrong with her?

Edie assumed that because he'd been around her for so long, he understood the needs of her friends with mental health problems. She thought he was comfortable with them, didn't have the fears and inhibitions that others had, but the opposite was true. They made him uneasy.

If they appeared well he waited anxiously for something to go wrong. If their behaviour was odd, or erratic, or obviously disturbed he thought, will it set Edie off? Is this what we've got to look forward to?

'What's Kay's diagnosis?' he finally asked.

'Jim, you're not going to label her are you? Diagnoses don't mean anything. There was some research I was reading about just the other day where they ignored the patients' diagnoses on a psychiatric ward and distributed drugs at random. They found they did just as well as the control group.

'Of course it was years ago, they probably couldn't do it now. Like Laing and LSD. I mean think of all the diagnoses I've had. Psychiatrists don't know fuck all. Well apart from Dr Parmar. I loved Dr Parmar. She saved my life –'

'Sorry, I just meant – is there anything I need to be aware of? To make her feel comfortable?' Jim had to interrupt. He couldn't bear to think that when Edie said someone had saved her life it was literally true. And a little bit affronted. It seemed only yesterday she'd been outraged because so many people couldn't get a diagnosis and therefore the support they needed.

'She's fine. She just likes things to be predictable. Quiet and steady –'

'And she's your friend?'

'And she's not keen on confined spaces.'

'She'll love my flat then.'

'This will be a bit of a challenge for her, but she's making progress and I know it'll be fine because you're so sensitive and non-threatening –'

*

'Our ducks live in a bigger house than this,' said Kay, as she walked into the living room and took a seat on the sofa.

'She's not rude, she's just literal,' said Edie, sitting next to her.

Kay shuffled away. 'I didn't know we had to share,' said Kay.

'Now that is rude,' said Edie.

'I know,' said Kay.

Jim sat on the computer chair which he kept in his bedroom. He didn't actually have room for a desk, but the chair was a hangover from his previous flat with Annika, until she left him to take up a place doing postdoctoral research in Astronomy at St Andrews.

'Kay grew up on a farm,' said Edie to Jim. 'Jim loves the countryside,' she said to Kay. 'He's an ecologist.'

'He'll hate farmers then. Naturalists always hate farmers. They think farmers poison the countryside. And kill biodiversity.'

'Well...' said Jim.

'You can say it,' said Kay.

'It's not rude,' smiled Edie mischievously, 'just literal.'

Jim went to fetch drinks. Edie wanted Earl Grey because she said it was about the only stimulant she was allowed to take now and she'd left a box here when she was staying. Kay wanted a mug of hot water.

'He doesn't do farms,' said Edie, 'he does parks and urban gardens. And motorway verges and abandoned buildings and all the places where life bursts forth despite our best efforts.'

'I did,' he said, mournfully. 'Most recently I was looking at how blackbirds adapt to urban ecosystems.'

They were both quiet, perhaps respectfully marking the passing of his career.

The evening passed slowly, Edie and Kay keeping up their to and fro, Jim occasionally joining in. A beer would have helped pass the time but it felt wrong when they weren't drinking. He mused on why Edie would be friends with Kay when they seemed so different.

Kay was apparently doing a placement of some kind at the charity, doing data entry. She'd started a Maths degree but never finished it because she became ill. Her hair looked like she cut it herself and her clothes were shapeless and of no particular colour. Her conversation was mundane and categorical.

He hated to think that maybe the only thing they had in common was a condition or a diagnosis or a – what had Edie said last week? A unique perspective. But she'd said it with a twinkle in her eye. A twinkle to which Kay would be oblivious. Diabetics didn't feel the need to hang out together, or people with ingrowing toenails. And if it really was a unique perspective then didn't that make it – unique?

There was a knock at the door. Jim wondered if Edie had invited anyone else and forgotten to tell him, friends, the guy from the off-licence, someone she'd got chatting to at the bus stop...It wouldn't be the first time. She shrugged, apparently innocent.

It was Roisin. He recoiled in shock. Roisin never turned up. She sent a text like a royal proclamation, announcing her intention of visiting, then punctuated the journey with regular updates on her progress.

'Come in, join the party.'

When she saw Edie and Kay she seemed to shrink back but Edie was already enthusing at her presence.

He offered Roisin the computer chair. Kay nodded to her in acknowledgement before they continued their surreal yet banal banter.

'Do you want coffee?' he whispered to Roisin. 'We're drinking Earl Grey.'

'I'll have booze, the strongest you've got,' she growled. She turned to Edie and Kay who had stopped speaking. 'Coffee keeps me awake.'

'Alcohol does too,' said Kay. 'It may cause initial drowsiness but it stimulates the adrenal glands and causes dehydration, leading to –'

'I know. I'll be awake at three in the morning, howling at the moon,' said Roisin. 'I still want it.'

'I'm not sure I've got any booze,' said Jim.

'I thought you said this was a party,' said Roisin.

Jim found a bottle of beer hiding at the back of the fridge. He handed it to Roisin and perched awkwardly on the edge of the sofa next to Edie.

Jim watched Roisin. She was tense. He'd seen this mood before. When she was hurt. When she had to attack because she felt she'd been attacked. Like when the first she knew of her sister's baby's christening was when she saw the pictures on Facebook.

When her dad published his family tree on a genealogy site and she realised he'd been researching it for years and never once asked her for help. At least her name was on it, she'd said grimly, but of course Melissa's wasn't. She'd sent him an email offering to help with the Portuguese records, and had even briefed María José, but he never replied.

She listened to Edie and Kay without attempting to intervene but he knew she was just biding her time. She couldn't meet his eyes. They've split up, he thought suddenly. And now she's here to tear me limb from limb.

Roisin was staring at Kay. Or perhaps she was staring thoughtfully into space and it just seemed like she was staring at Kay. But Kay had noticed. He had noticed too. He braced himself, waiting for Roisin to say something about the haircut. Even Edie was quiet. He wasn't sure if it was a rare pause for breath or if she too was sensing an atmosphere in the room.

'I can hear your neighbours,' said Kay, arms folded, almost hugging herself.

'Sorry, Finn's a bit noisy. He's a musician. Has a lot of friends round. Jamming sessions.' Not normally at this time, though, normally later. When Jim was trying to sleep.

Jim listened but he couldn't hear anything much. Someone at the front door. Sounded like a pizza delivery. 'They're saying things, bad things.'

'Is she a psycho?' asked Roisin.

Edie laughed. 'People on the autistic spectrum sometimes hear sound as distorted. They think they hear a voice when it's actually something else.'

'Jesus Fucking Christ,' said Roisin, not quite under her breath.

'You hear them too?' asked Kay. She was beginning to be agitated.

'Hang on.' Roisin pretended to listen. 'I think it's a voice from on high saying something about Aunt Florrie left her diamond ring in the teapot on the side. The one that went to the Red Cross Shop.'

Kay looked confused.

'Roisin, you're such a cow,' said Edie, but she laughed.

'Or maybe Mario's is out of garlic bread,' she said.

Jim felt torn by the invisible energies bouncing off the walls of the tiny room. Kay's flat self-assurance seemed to be giving way to distress. Edie was apparently delighting in her role of mentor, reassuring Kay by staring into her eyes like a hypnotist on a cable channel. Roisin the wounded lioness had been goaded into action. Each in their own bubble and only he was being drained of life, like an alien abductee who'd had the blood sucked from him.

'You shouldn't dismiss the voices,' said Edie. 'That's what psychiatry's always done. But increasingly people are learning to live with their voices, to understand what they mean.'

He wished he was with Elizabeth. Where there was tranquillity. And silence.

'Oh come on,' said Roisin. 'I mean, you don't hear voices, do you?'

Or even alone, he thought. In my three-quarter bed, with my eyes shut.

'We all hear voices,' said Edie. 'It's how we interpret them. What we in this culture call hallucinations, others call visions. We're learning to live with the voices rather than suppress them.'

Kay's eyes darted round the room but alighted on no one.

'I don't hear voices,' insisted Roisin.

'Come on, don't tell me that when you're about to get it on with the lovely Melissa you don't hear your mother saying sex is a sin outside marriage.'

Oh no, thought Jim. Don't mention Melissa now.

Kay looked at Roisin. 'You're uncomfortable.'

'You're not wrong.' Roisin held her eyes.

'When Edie mentioned sin.'

Roisin blinked first. She looked at him and then back at Kay. 'So now you're the fucking psychic.' She stood up. 'I'll be off now. Jim, will you walk with me?'

'Since when did you need a male protector?' laughed Edie.

Roisin didn't answer.

It was getting dark. It was still August but the dusk was encroaching more each day. He was used to thinking of autumn as a beginning, anticipating the arrival of winter migrants, or perhaps he was just conditioned to the academic year, but tonight he felt some of that melancholic end-of-summer feeling he'd had when he was a kid.

Roisin was walking fast. He skipped a couple of steps to keep up. Didn't know what to say, so he waited for her to speak.

'Edie's looking well,' she said.

'Do you think so? She seemed a bit high tonight.'

'You worry too much. She's grand.'

'You're sounding all warm and empathetic. You're making me nervous.'

'The friend's a fucking fruitcake.'

He laughed, but said, 'I thought she was quite perceptive.'

Roisin stopped and turned to face him. Was that a tear, or just a trick of the light?

'It's okay,' he said.

She hugged him. One of those non gender-specific, friendly bearhugs. Except she stayed, pressed against him. Her head rested on his chest. He breathed in the coconut scent of her hair and the salt smell of her scalp. Like gorse baking in the sun.

'What is it?' he whispered.

'Why do I have to fight *everything*?' she whispered.

She looked up at him. Their lips brushed briefly, so briefly it might have been an accident.

'There's a cab,' she said.

'Wait!'

But she had already broken away. As she got in she turned to shout, 'I'm marrying Melissa!' and then she was gone.

Twenty-three

Something had happened to the house. Nothing to do with the crack. The house was where she'd left it, the extension still attached. Something else.

It looked like Brenda's house but – Prince hadn't come running. There was a display of chillis and limes in a flat glass bowl on the dining table. A pair of terrifyingly high heels in the hall.

Paula appeared, wearing her good navy suit – she'd be hot under that jacket – and the bunny-rabbit slippers she kept in the cupboard for when she stayed late watching TV.

'What are you doing here?' she asked Brenda.

Was this Paula's house now? 'We were quiet so they told me to finish at lunchtime.'

'You should join a union. If they've offered you a shift and you've come in, it's not fair to send you home. I mean you can't just choose not to turn up, can you?'

Was this the same Paula who said the unions were nothing but trouble at her place and she didn't need anyone to look after her, thank you very much?

Brenda had so many questions but she found

herself blurting out, 'What's that smell?'

'Cinnamon Danish,' said Paula. 'Warm and welcoming but with a more contemporary feel than baking bread. Certainly an improvement on dog.'

'My house doesn't smell of dog,' said Brenda.

Paula smiled sympathetically. What's she done to Prince? thought Brenda.

'I've put Prince in the shed,' said Paula, as if mindreading was now added to what she called her skillset. 'Don't worry, he's got his basket and his bone. I know he likes the squeaky mouse better but I didn't want him making a noise.'

Maybe Paula had been planning a surprise party. Perhaps Brenda had a new extra birthday in this strange dream.

She waited. She didn't want to ask anything that would make her look foolish but finally there seemed no alternative but to say, 'So what are you doing here?'

'I've got a viewing.'

'A viewing?'

'Gemma's a negotiator at Blake Deighton now.'

Brenda had known Gemma since she was paired with Paula in the Year Four three-legged race. They came last and Brenda had the feeling Gemma had been paying for it ever since.

'I was browsing in their window when I saw her.'

Paula and Callum were both working every hour they could to save for a deposit, but it seemed the more they saved, the more they needed.

'I sounded her out, you know, just to get a feel for what you might get for it, and she offered to pop round on Saturday while you and Robbie were both out.'

Brenda was pretty sure it hadn't been Gemma's idea.

'And then she had a couple come in, just this morning, and she thought this would be perfect. So she said she'd send them, even though you haven't signed the paperwork yet, because we're friends.'

'And you just happened to have a day off work.'

'I know. It must be a sign.'

'But it's not for sale.'

'Of course not.' Paula was putting the bunny-rabbits into the cupboard under the stairs and putting on her high heels.

'So these people will be wasting their time.'

'You're missing the summer market. Mugs down from London wanting to live the dream. Houses round here look cheap to them. Even now, there are buyers out there. The photos look great –'

'She's already done photos?'

'I said she might as well, while she was here. And she'll put it on the internet and do the flyers, as soon as you sign. Of course, if they made us an offer before then we could cut the agents out and there'd be nothing they could do. I'm not sure Gemma's cut out for sales.'

'I suppose she thought as you were friends –'

'Mum, it's your future,' Paula said sternly.

'What about your dad?'

'He doesn't need to sign does he?'

'But –'

He didn't need to sign because the house was in her sole name. They'd done it years ago, on the advice of his accountant, because when he first started in business he was a sole trader. Later there was a change in the tax system, or something, and he'd formed a limited company, but they never changed the house back to joint names.

'She said if you decide to go ahead you can pop in one day and sign the forms. But you need to get changed now.'

'What?'

'They'll be here in ten minutes.'

'Who?'

'The couple who want to view.'

'Why do I need to change? You selling me as well?'

'We want them to see the house as aspirational.'

Brenda stood. She didn't understand.

'What do you want me to wear then?'

'Something smart casual. Like if you were meeting a friend for lunch.'

'When have I ever met a friend for lunch?'

'What about the blue dress you got for Gran Canaria?'

'I haven't shaved my legs.'

'Well, something else from the holiday.'

Brenda seemed to remember there'd been a time when she'd told Paula what to wear, rather than the other way round, though it seemed unlikely now. She quickly changed into a pair of white cotton trousers and a blue top. The trousers kept slipping off her waist. She must have lost weight. She couldn't remember the last time she'd gone out in anything other than dog-walking clothes or her work uniform.

'You look good,' said Paula, without looking at her. She went back into the bedroom to make sure Brenda hadn't left anything out and wiped an imaginary speck of dust from the chest of drawers.

When the doorbell rang Paula opened the door. 'You must be Mr and Mrs Walsh.'

'Mr and Ms,' said the man, looking round the hall. They were younger than Brenda had expected. They were both wearing sandals and cargo shorts and she looked tiny in a long skinny vest. Paula showed them round.

In the lounge, they said nothing. Paula tried to keep up a patter about central heating and television sockets but they ignored her and looked around impatiently as if they'd put their keys down and couldn't find them again.

In the kitchen he smirked and said to Brenda, 'So you like Thai food?'

'What?'

'The limes and chillis.'

'Oh.' She looked helplessly for Paula but she was following the woman around the extension telling her about the vacuum-sealed double glazing and the stainless steel one-and-a-half-bowl sink. 'Paula's boyfriend's a chef.'

'Your estate agent's boyfriend dresses your kitchen?'

'Paula's my daughter.'

'Oh. So she actually chose to wear that suit.' He laughed to himself.

The woman had stopped at the crack in the wall. For a moment, they were all silent. Brenda didn't dare so much as twitch. Paula straightened her jacket and stood up tall.

'It's just a movement joint,' she said casually. 'We've got a surveyor's report. And we're getting it repaired. Of course you'd want your surveyor to look at it, if you bought.'

'Of course,' he smirked, as if he was making a clever comment that no one else could possibly understand.

'It's probably just differential settling,' the woman said, turning away. 'It's a common problem with extensions. I saw it on Sarah Beeny.'

'You like Sarah Beeny too?' said Paula enthusiastically.

'She watches all the lifestyle crap,' he said.

'So where are you moving from?' asked Paula.

'Oh, we're not moving,' he said.

She said, 'We're looking for a second home. A weekend place.'

'Well, it's great here. A real family home, near the seaside, lots for kids to do –'

'We don't have kids,' he drawled, 'certainly not together.' He smiled that, I'm-really-funny smile to himself again.

'We're brother and sister,' she said. 'We inherited a bit of money. Not enough to each buy a place, so we thought we'd club together.

Somewhere handy for Dartmoor for me –'

'She's a fell runner,' he said, shuddering delicately.

'And he's a foodie,' she said.

'We like the South Hams but we can't afford it.'

'And we thought this might be an up-and-coming place, with the Hugh Bonnington connection.'

'A sort of low-rent Newlyn or St Ives,' he said, looking round doubtfully.

'The rents aren't low,' muttered Paula.

They continued round the house. Paula kept up her singsong customer-service voice. She never once answered back the smirker. That was the worst of it. Paula, who said she never took crap from anyone, not even at work.

What did it matter? They obviously weren't interested. People like that would want something older, or more contemporary, with a sea view or in a field with a stream at the bottom of the garden (they wouldn't consider the flood risk till it was too late). Brenda relaxed. They didn't want to buy, she didn't want to sell.

When they left, Paula freed Prince and the bunny-rabbits and slumped on the sofa. Prince put his head in her lap and they looked at each other for a moment, both sad-eyed.

'I think that went pretty well,' Paula said, still wearing her customer-service smile.

'What's all this about?'

Paula lay back on the sofa. She suddenly looked very tired. 'I've spoken to Dad,' she said. 'He

won't tell me why, but he says he's not coming
back.'

Twenty-four

Roisin announced, but only after they were out of the office and halfway to their usual greasy spoon, that actually she wanted to go to Noodle Zoo.

Jim objected. 'I hate those places. McDonald's for the middle classes.'

'The food's good.'

Watery bowls of noodles so spiced they took the roof off your mouth. But that wasn't the problem. 'It's the ambience I don't like. The big barn acoustic and the prison-canteen bench seating mean you can't discuss anything you wouldn't want to share with the party of purchase ledger control clerks on the razzle on one side and the fractious four-year-old who's been grabbed from the crèche by a corporate lawyer scheduling quality time on the other. It's all designed to get you out as soon as possible.'

'It's lunch,' said Roisin, 'smash and grab. Not some spiritual communion.'

'Why don't we try the new Italian?'

'Italian. Oh, everybody likes Italian.'

He thought that would have been a recommendation but apparently not. Roisin continued striding towards Noodle Zoo. He followed behind. Nothing had changed, which made him wonder if he'd imagined that whole almost-admission of vulnerability, the kiss that was not a kiss. Except Roisin was being more Roisin than ever.

When they got there the benches were full. They had to sit on high stools at a round table, knees banging the central leg, like elves drawn up to a toadstool.

At least we don't have to share, thought Jim, just as two guys pulled up the other stools. They were red-faced and hearty. They had thighs the size of tree trunks bulging through their pinstripes which they had to spread to accommodate the toadstool. Which meant the guy next to Jim kept bumping knees with him.

'We've a shitload of things to do. I've made a list,' said Roisin.

Or something like that. The two guys were bellowing at each other as if they were both on a rugby field. In adjacent counties.

'I was hoping you'd be my witness.'

'Sure.'

'I mean, I know it's just a civil partnership but Melissa thought it would be good if we each had someone special at our side –'

'A kind of best person?'

'I guess.'

'Has Melissa got someone?'

'Her dad. But he's not giving her away or any of that Medieval shite.'

'Are you sure you wouldn't rather ask Krish?'

'He'll be there but he wants to keep a low profile.'

Doesn't want it filtering back to their parents that he's been. What's he going to do, thought Jim, hide his face every time someone takes a picture? Ask to be pixellated? He sighed. At least Krish kept in touch. He thought how lucky he was. He couldn't imagine having to choose between Edie and his parents.

Roisin was still talking, barely audible above the amplified sound of a waiter dropping a spoon on the other side of the restaurant. 'But he knows this great venue and we're going there this weekend. It's hush-hush and very exclusive so I can't even tell you what it's called.'

'I won't have heard of it anyway.'

Their food arrived. Roisin began eating with chopsticks in one hand, phone in the other.

'I need you to come to the florist with me, sort out the flowers.'

'I'm the wrong person to ask. I hate cut flowers.'

'These aren't hothouse roses, it's all organic and native, sprigs of heather and herbs and that shite.'

He reached for a chunk of tofu and sauce dripped onto his trousers.

'They're still dead,' he said grumpily. 'Anyway, doesn't sound like your kind of thing.'

'It's what Melissa wants.'

'If it's what Melissa wants then let Melissa organise it.'

'She'll never get it sorted in time.'

'Makes her sound incapable though she's a barrister with a thriving criminal practice.'

Roisin believed everyone except Roisin was basically incapable. 'When she's working she just zones out everything else.'

'Whereas you can hold the entire universe in your hand.'

'Yes. So you'll meet me Saturday?'

'I can't this weekend.'

'Off down to Dormouth? How come she never comes here? It's not like she's working.'

'She's freelance,' said Jim. 'And she works in the woolshop.'

'Oh aye,' said Roisin, 'I forgot the little part-time job.'

'It's the opening of Elizabeth's exhibition.'

'Right,' said Roisin. 'How much is she getting paid for that?'

He didn't answer that. It wasn't meant to be answered. To Roisin, work was stuff you got paid for. Anything else was just a hobby. Except – she worked hard, obsessively. Far harder than she needed to for her pay.

She was trying to dismiss Elizabeth as if paid work was the source of liberation. He thought of his mum, who had given up teaching when she married dad and had never gone back to work. She'd always been busy with something, the garden, photography, joinery. Later Edie got involved in drama and dance so Mum spent a lot of time making costumes and stage sets and was always running from one event to the next.

It had never once occurred to him that she would be more fulfilled if she was trapped in a basement poring over data.

'Sounds like you two are getting on well,' said Roisin, furiously.

'And I'm glad you two are happy. Ready to make a commitment.'

'She cops it there's a straight fifty per cent split on the assets and double the ceiling on inheritance tax. You don't think I'm bothered about that other shit, do you?'

'For a minute I was worried you were going soft.'

'Anyway, what about my flowers? And the photographer – oh, wait Joolz is taking care of that – And what the hell are you going to wear? '

'I'm doing my best,' said Jim. But you can't expect me to be best man, maid of honour and mother of the bride.'

'No,' said Roisin, looking almost subdued.

Jim would have kicked himself if there wasn't a meathead on a fairy-stool to do it for him.

'They haven't shifted?' he asked.

'No. I mean, I always knew my parents would flip but now my sisters are too scared to come near me. I'm sick of their cowardice, almost as much as my parents' fucked-up fucking fundamentalism.'

She spoke at her usual volume, oblivious of the fact that her words had bounced up to the ceiling and back down and that half the restaurant was pretending not to have heard her.

A woman in a headscarf turned and looked up

at Roisin. Stood up. She approached diffidently but with determination.

'Please,' she said quietly. 'Don't speak that way about your family.'

'This is a private conversation,' said Roisin. It might have been, thought Jim, if we were in the Italian. Even the rugby players had paused in their braying and were looking on, amused.

Roisin turned away from the woman and focused on her phone. She carried on eating too. Under such scrutiny, Jim's ability to use chopsticks would have crumbled.

The woman stood her ground. Jim, despite his discomfort, was impressed by her quiet dignity. 'Sister, don't disrespect our culture, there are too many other people to do that for us.'

'I'm talking about fucking Catholics,' snarled Roisin.

'Oh,' said the woman. She lowered her head and walked away.

'It's the same fucking God,' Roisin called after her. 'We're all people of the book. Christ.' The sound reverberated off the opposite wall and a small child began to cry. 'Anyone else want a go? Any nuns spoiling for a fight?'

'No, just you,' said Jim.

Twenty-five

Robbie spilt tea when he put the mugs down on the coffee table. He almost stepped on Prince, who wasn't exactly easy to miss. Then he sat on the sofa and jumped up again.

'What the hell's that?' He pulled a bag out from between the cushions.

'It's Paula's knitting.'

Paula had decided that she wanted to knit as well. She had a pattern for an angora shrug, which she said would be a key piece for autumn. She kept her knitting in a little plastic bag, blue with pink strawberries, said it looked like Cath Kidston though it was actually from a place that did discount linens and remnants in Exeter.

The shrug looked tiny, like a doll's cardigan. Paula's tension was all wrong. She gripped her needles like she thought they wanted to run away and start a new life.

'Why can't she leave it at home?'

Brenda didn't answer.

'She's always here lately.'

Was she? There was her regular Thursday night, when Callum went out with his mates. Then she sometimes popped over at the weekend. Maybe she'd been over one or two more nights in the week. Callum sometimes did extra work, he had a friend with his own business who catered upmarket dinner parties or something.

Brenda didn't always listen when Paula was speaking. She had such a lot to say you had to let some of it flow over you. While with Robbie, every word he said was precious and was turned over in her mind.

Robbie leant back cautiously, then said, 'I've seen a house.'

'Oh,' she said.

'Tony's been helping me.'

'Oh.' What was he trying to tell her? He'd found a house? He was moving in with Tony? Nothing would surprise her any more.

'I was thinking we – we could buy it together.'

So this was it. Paula's taunts about him never having a girlfriend weren't so empty after all. She thought again of those almost-matching shirts, of the way Tony's eyes had lingered on Robbie's cold-pressed pants. She imagined them, in long, happy silence, by lamplight, staring into a real fire. She didn't know why she imagined a real fire, rather than living flame. But that wasn't what bothered her.

'How's he going to pay a share?'

'What?'

'You've got a van and a decent little business and what's he got?'

'Not me and Tony!'

She didn't understand.

'I've been talking to Dad. You're gonna have to sell whatever happens.' The words came out slower and deeper as he went on, and his head sunk further and he looked at the floor.

'So you know,' she said. 'He's told you.'

He. Him. His dad. Bob. She was relieved. She was too ashamed to speak. Brenda, who hated debt, who'd scraped and fought to pay the mortgage, who always said no when Bob said they should be trading up, buy a place, do it up, move on, get a buy-to-let or a holiday home, she, Brenda, had a loan secured against the house. A loan for a hundred thousand pounds. A loan that was now two months in arrears. And she hadn't said a word.

'I don't want to know what's gone on,' he said quietly.

'Good,' she said. She could feel the pins and needles, the lightness in her head. Breathe, she thought. That day, when he took her to the hospital, she'd thought she was dying. Maybe she almost wished she could feel like that now. Because then she wouldn't have to face him.

'When you sell, you'll have some money. But not enough to buy a place of your own.'

'I know,' she said softly.

He talked then. Robbie, who even under torture from the Gestapo would not have told them what he had for tea, was talking and talking. He'd got it all worked out. He knew roughly what she'd have when the house sold. Not enough to buy a place outright, but a reasonable deposit. Only she'd never get a mortgage, with her wages. While Robbie had no deposit but a good income.

Andy Farrell was selling a terraced house, right in the town. It needed work but that was what was so good. Robbie could do a lot of it himself, and where he couldn't he knew who to ask. Tony was good for some of it. He was a time-served electrician as well as a general builder.

'But things will change, Robbie. One day you'll meet someone, you might want to live together.'

'That's okay. I'll have some leverage. Our house will have gained in value with the work we're doing, we'll have paid at least a bit off the mortgage, once I've got one place I can use the equity to fund another loan. Maybe even buy-to-let. And I'm trading as a limited company, so if the business goes down, they won't be able to touch my share of the house.'

'I don't know,' she said.

'It's not even on the market yet. We can see it now.'

'Why's Andy selling if it's such a great house?'

'He was going to do it up himself but the rumour is he got in over his head. They're saying he might even lose his own house if he doesn't sell soon.'

'What if it all goes wrong? If I lose my job or your work dries up and we can't make the payments?'

'Then you'll be back where you are now,' he said quietly.

She had no answer for that. But there was something else.

'What about Paula?'

Twenty-six

The rice was done to perfection and he had poured a small glass of white wine. Jim would even have sat at the dining table if he had one. Then his mobile rang.

His heart did an involuntary leap of joy. He had left a message for Elizabeth, just a short one, to say that he was looking forward to the weekend. Her phone had been off, he'd guessed, because she would be busy preparing the exhibition. No need to pick up the phone. He'd call her as soon as he'd eaten.

Then his landline rang. No one called the landline except his mum when she wanted a proper chat. Even his dad mostly sent him emails these days, albeit in flawless prose, like letters supposedly used to be.

The answerphone clicked in and Roisin began to speak. She hated answerphones. She began on a convoluted stream of consciousness where she speculated on his whereabouts and availability, gave him numerous times and methods by which he could contact her, and still she held on. He knew the tape would run out in a minute.

He picked up the phone. 'Hi, Roisin.'

'Were you there all along? Were you listening?'

As if he'd seen her naked. 'Sorry, I was just eating.'

'What?'

'It's called a meal. Proper home-cooked healthy food, which you sit down to eat. In peace. Without distractions.'

'Krish isn't coming,' she blurted.

'To the wedding?'

'The venue. They're all going to Liverpool for Philomena's first communion. It's been brought forward. He reckons Mum knows.'

'She's your mother, not the National Security Agency.'

'They'll never have the reach of the Irish diaspora,' she said with pride, as if she'd momentarily forgotten her excommunication.

'Take Melissa to the venue. It's the kind of thing you should decide together.'

'It's supposed to be a surprise. Anyhow she's away on some corporate jolly. Staying at a country house with opera in the grounds.'

'Couldn't she take you?'

'Apparently not.' Her tone was flat, without her usual defiance. 'So I really need someone to go and check it out with me.'

'I could go next week.'

'But next week's too late. They only agreed to hold it this long because the owner's a mate of Krish's.'

He felt the tug of obligation. Everyone else had

let her down. She needed him. But –

'You know I can't do it this weekend.'

'The exhibition's on for a couple of weeks, isn't it?'

'And London is full of *chichi* overpriced eateries.'

'I'm only getting married once,' she said.

He sighed. 'I promised Elizabeth.'

'Okay.'

She hung up abruptly. Jim sat for a moment, phone still to his ear, feeling oddly bereft. Wondered if she'd call back. Wondered if he should call her. He sat for so long he missed the start of the World Service documentary on epigenetics he'd been intending to listen to. The landline rang.

'Roisin?'

'It's me.' Elizabeth.

'Oh hi. Sorry. I was just expecting – well, not really expecting but – How are you?'

'Fine,' she laughed. An uncomplicated, happy laugh. He liked that, uncomplicated. Her laugh, her breath, her skin – He wished she was here now. He wished he could see her, touch her, hold her now.

But instead he said, 'It's all going to plan then, the exhibition?'

He was thinking about last weekend. How she'd determined he should have his bucket-and-spade holiday. They'd bought ice-creams and walked along the beach, away from the crowds. Scrambled across rocks still wet from the tide. Saw an oystercatcher in the distance, then another, then another. Looked into a rock pool. Each seeing another world. Not the same world, he saw an ecosystem, she saw colour and form and texture, but they both saw it, and he thought, this is what we share. This feeling doesn't need words.

She was talking about – what? Trestle tables gone astray, problems with the blog, works that didn't work. The excitement as the juxtaposition of two pieces brought something new to both of them. He heard the words but he somehow didn't feel them. He only felt, wanted to feel, her.

'What about you?' she asked.

How to say what he felt? To a phone?

'Roisin's been haranguing me. She wanted me to look at venues this weekend but of course I told her I couldn't.'

'You don't have to come,' she said quietly. Did her voice sound smaller, strained?

'Of course I do. I mean, I don't have to, I want to. I'm looking forward to it. And I know it means a lot to you.'

'I'll be busy, I won't have much time to be with you.'

'No that's fine. Unless – you don't want me to come? Will I be in the way?'

'I want you to come.'

'Good.' What to say now? 'I can't wait to see you.'

'Nor me.'

Silence. He didn't want to go, felt his words had been so inadequate in conveying what he felt, but couldn't think what else to say without sounding melodramatic or just a bit pathetic.

'See you Saturday,' he said.

There was a pause then she said, 'See you,' then she was gone.

He sat for a moment, feeling sad now she'd gone, feeling he'd got it all wrong, wanting to call her back but knowing it would be just the same if he did. If he'd been with her he could have held her. There would have been no need for words.

He was still staring at the phone, though it couldn't help.

Twenty-seven

Jim woke with his cheek feeling cool. There was such relief in that coolness that he tried to hold onto it, among the heat and the ache in his neck and the nausea. His cheek was being cooled by the floor tile. Suddenly that feeling wasn't enough. There were more urgent impulses. He got up just in time to pebbledash the toilet bowl.

Some time before that, he had projectile vomited in the lounge. He was almost impressed by the physics of it, the musculature involved, the poetry as his stomach muscles clenched and released.

So he thought later as, hollowed out and trembling, he made a pitiful attempt on hands and knees to clean the puke from the weave in the carpet. He thought about crawling back to bed but decided it was safer to stay where he was, naked, on the bathroom floor. He guessed it was about 4am. Too early to call Elizabeth.

He woke. Had he slept? The effort of getting to his phone was almost beyond imagining. A hundred years later he made it. It was just after eight. She'd be up, today. He called. Her voicemail kicked in. He left a message. His voice sounded almost human. He hoped she picked it up. He hoped she called him. He was glad she was not here, to see him brought so low. He wished she was here, to mop up his vomit and hold his hand.

He drank some water. He threw up again. His head hurt. He crawled into bed. The duvet was too heavy. Like being buried alive. Had he slept again? Woken again? He checked his phone. No messages. What time was it? He tried to sleep. He went back to the toilet. Molten lava. Back to bed.

He woke and it was dark. Reached for his phone. One message. A text from Roisin. Assorted expletives. Random punctuation. Or perhaps that was just the way it danced before his eyes. He slept again. Elizabeth was at the opening, sipping wine, surrounded by admirers. Everything was perfect. Fraser by her side.

It was just a dream, he thought, as he woke sweating and half crawled, half ran to the bathroom, getting ready to vomit, but there was nothing left.

Twenty-eight

When they walked into the Boatshed, there was a girl with her hair in plaits coiled round her ears and a tie-dye skirt, smiling and asking if they'd like to pay a pound and sign the visitors' book. Brenda felt Paula bristle like Prince when he saw that Jack Russell from across the way.

'No thank you,' said Paula without looking at her, and kept walking, striding like she did when she was going into a shop to complain. Brenda tried to laugh but it sounded high and false. She groped in her purse and found two pounds but turned her head away from the visitors' book and kept walking.

'She said you didn't have to pay,' barked Paula.

They stood in the middle of the room. Brenda didn't see anyone she recognised. The people were mostly young, but none of them looked like Paula's or Robbie's friends.

'Bohos,' sniffed Paula.

Paula was wearing culottes, which she said were on-trend since Jennifer Lawrence had worn them. Brenda knew Paula had dressed up, not because tonight meant anything to her, but so that she could show people, look, I don't even care about this, and I'm still better dressed than any of you.

She looked around for something she could hang onto. She couldn't see anything she would recognise as art. Bits of wood and metal that looked like they were left over from the days when it really was a boatshed. Bottles of wine and beer and plastic cups on a bar which was really a surfboard balanced on a decorator's platform. A wall where you could leave a note saying what you thought – not that she would dare.

There was a banner on the wall, made from appliqué that said 'Inclusive Dormouth.' Below it a fishing net with all sorts of things sticking out of it.

'Well it's certainly not *ex*clusive,' Paula said, looking round.

There was a doll dressed as a fisherman, wielding an Aran needle like a harpoon, with a knitted fish on the end of it. Brenda thought she saw the fish wriggle. Another doll looked like a mermaid, until she looked closer and saw a moustache and a bulge in the front of the tail. There was a calico whale with an embroidered face that she couldn't help thinking looked like Dora Mickelthwaite, just as Dora herself appeared.

Brenda started laughing. Paula looked bemused, then Brenda whispered, 'Look! The whale has come to life.'

'Or is it the mother of the bride?'

Dora was gliding towards them, resplendent in a full-skirted floral print dress with a lilac jacket and hat.

'Brenda,' said Dora.

'Dora,' said Brenda.

Dora nodded at Paula. 'Dost like it, lass?'

'It's not your usual thing, Dora.'

'No, but we're broadminded in Yorkshire. We've had Henry Moore for decades.'

'And I bet he's still chafing,' muttered Paula.

Dora gestured to Elizabeth across the room. She was talking to a group of people her own age in front of what looked like several bits of driftwood nailed together.

'She's been let down by her man. Well you'd know all about that, Brenda.'

Brenda waited for Dora to comment on the superiority of Yorkshire men, but for once she was silent. She only blinked rapidly and stood up straighter as she drifted away.

Brenda saw Fraser out of the corner of her eye. Blushed at the memory. How had she told him about Bob? When she hadn't told anyone else?

Elizabeth came over. She was smiling, holding a glass of wine.

'Hi,' she said. 'I'm glad you came.'

'This is my daughter Paula,' said Brenda, for lack of something to say. Paula smiled uncertainly. 'You must be really strong. Lifting all that wood.'

'The sculptures aren't mine. I wish they were.'

'Why?' asked Paula. She looked around. 'I thought it was going to be more fashion. Knitting and stuff.'

'Oh.' Elizabeth smiled. 'Sorry, no it's not fashion. How's the scarf going?' she asked Brenda.

'Finished.'

'We've got some lovely new colours in.'

'You can get it cheaper online,' muttered Paula.

'We liked the fishing net,' said Brenda.

'I was a volunteer on the project,' said Elizabeth. 'It went really well. It's even inspired one guy to knit a vegetable patch!'

Brenda knew how she'd do it too, suddenly could see herself crocheting cabbages, could feel the wool over her first finger.

Fraser walked towards her. She was dreading that he'd say something to her in front of Paula, but he didn't appear to notice them at all.

'There you are,' he said to Elizabeth. 'You really should come and speak to Charlotte before she goes.'

His eyes passed over Brenda who attempted to smile through her tension but he turned back to Elizabeth. 'She has a friend who's curating a small exhibition in Bath. With a particular interest in textiles.'

Elizabeth smiled at them. Fraser steered her away. 'The community work can wait,' he muttered. 'Do you want a career or do you want to spend your life running basket-weaving classes –'

Over the other side of the room there were dolls and toys. Brenda followed Paula who stopped in front of a knitted doll. Everything was knitted, even the dungarees she was wearing, with white stitches in them to look like paint splatters. The doll was knitting another doll, identical but smaller.

'Look Mum,' said Paula, 'they're like Russian dolls.'

And that doll was knitting a doll too. She got closer to see if that doll was knitting and then –

'She's got no face,' said Brenda.

'I guess she ran out of time,' said Paula but Brenda was already walking. She had to get out.

Through the bubble in her ears she heard Paula calling but she kept walking and as she reached the door she saw Fraser turn towards her but she didn't stop, even when she bumped into him and the red wine flew out of his glass and onto his crumpled pastel clothes.

Not going, but gone. Paula came and found her, standing by the crossing, holding onto the metal railings because if she didn't she might float away. She knew what people meant now when they said someone was grounded. Because she had no sense that she would stay here. If she let go she could end up anywhere. The terror wouldn't leave her till Paula called Robbie and he came and finally she agreed to let go long enough to get in the van.

Twenty-nine

Neil was having a great time at the opening. For a start, there were these two women who looked like they'd come to see the Westlife tribute act and had just realised they were in the wrong venue. As they stormed out the older one spilled her wine all over Fraser. Neil managed to find a full glass and raise it as Fraser caught his eye. Sweet.

And his anxiety about the painting had almost totally disappeared. Martha had taken half-finished canvases, hence the palimpsest idea. She would have said if there was a finished painting among them. They hadn't actually discussed it yet because he'd picked her up from the station and they'd come straight here but he was sure it would be cool. Fraser had nothing on him, and his boss thought he could do no wrong.

Elizabeth was surrounded by people as you'd expect, so he'd have to wait for an opportunity to get her alone and tell her how much he admired her work. For now he made do with cheesy wotsits and warm white wine in a plastic cup and mingling with Elizabeth's gorgeous young friends.

Like Adrienne, who told him her co-mothers

had named her after the poet Adrienne Rich and she'd spent her early childhood in a women-only community in West Wales, before her 'real' mother moved with her to Aberystwyth, trained as a planning officer and become vanilla and serially monogamous. There Adrienne had grown up loved and unambiguously heterosexual. He wondered if she had made a point of telling him that last bit, leaning casually against the wall, big kohled eyes staring up at him, her hair spiked and dyed black.

She was wearing a torn T-shirt and had hair under her arms and smelt of fresh sweat and stale booze. Made him think of Lisa 1 when they lived in that squat in Leeds 6. Her pointy little teeth that used to bite just enough. She'd read Adrienne Rich for a while, he remembered, then sighed. Why was he breathing in this foxy, gorgeous girl and thinking only that his ex-wife – and by implication he – was a contemporary of her mother?

Adrienne pressed her body sensuously against the wall.

'Dad, have you seen the…'

He turned to see Martha. There was a petulant look on her face. Adrienne smiled and moved away.

'Did no one ever teach you not to interrupt?'

'*You* never taught me anything. Besides, it was a rescue mission. You had her trapped. At least your breath would anaesthetise her. Anyway, you brought me here.'

'Sorry, I thought you were talking to –'

'Who? I don't know anyone.'

'You've met Elizabeth.'

'Maybe I should have asked Lisa. She likes art. Has something to say about it.'

'I like art.'

'Yeah, about as much as you like age-appropriate sexual partners.'

She looked around. Why was she giving him grief? But she did look a bit forlorn, behind her defiance. He supposed it was hard, being here. He wondered where she'd really want to be. She never mentioned boyfriends, or girlfriends. He didn't know if that was because she didn't want to tell him, or because there weren't any.

Her mother had apparently been bitterly, determinedly celibate since he left, as if to go on reproaching him forever. He hoped that hadn't affected Martha. He couldn't stand the thought of her being pawed by some spotty adolescent oaf (a girl wouldn't be so bad) but nor could he bear to think of her being poisoned by her mother's vengeful loneliness.

Martha was wearing a short strappy dress and army boots, another look that had been popular when he was a student. These young people. He felt sorry for kids now. How could she shock? His generation had already been there. Some never left.

He remembered when he'd gone home with a pierced ear and his mother had nearly eaten her apron. She used to stuff a corner in her mouth if she was about to swear or say something she'd regret. She'd kept putting more and more in her mouth, still staring at him, till he was scared she would choke. Now a kid could go home with a tattoo on his arse and his mother would pull down her pants and show him one just like it.

This was what they'd done to their kids. Out-teenaged them. Martha was oddly subdued in her eyeliner. What might she be pushed to? He felt tender for her. If only they'd left her some taboo, something they hadn't already done – and told her about – that she could try for herself.

Fraser was talking to Elizabeth who was listening intently. The wine stain on his shirt should have made him look stupid but apparently it didn't. That was more than complicated. Neil felt a little visceral jump somewhere in his chest, spreading to his throat, his belly. Was that love or angina? Which would do him the most damage?

Neil didn't like this sudden lurch into introspection. He decided instead to sidle up to Elizabeth. Surely she would want to be rescued from that arse. He stood just outside Fraser's eyeline. He seemed to be quizzing her about whether Maud had any paintings in the flat. Not mentioning one in particular but Neil of course knew which one he was looking for. Elizabeth smiled at him, charming but evasive. Said she didn't know much about Maud's work. She kept her art work in a separate room and she didn't allow anyone in there.

Neil was happy now. He didn't mind if she lied to him, as long as she lied to Fraser as well. And she hadn't actually lied, just been evasive. Shrewd that. Made him admire her all the more.

Standing as he was, he almost felt the urge to

make faces behind Fraser's back, make rabbit's ears with his fingers, like they used to when he was at school. But Elizabeth looked up and smiled at him. She had a beautiful, warm smile.

Martha was working her way through the exhibits. She quickly moved and dismissed, as if she couldn't possibly waste her valuable time, only occasionally stopping and looking more closely at something. He'd thought the exhibition would be quite exciting but of course Martha could go to stuff like this any time in London, when she wasn't slumming it at the National or the V&A.

He was talking to Elizabeth, which should be the ultimate happiness, but he couldn't help noticing that Martha had sidled along and struck up a conversation with that toad Fraser. Not that he wanted to come over all heavy dad, but Fraser didn't seem the type to indulge a giddy teenager.

Martha took her phone out and started flicking through images which she showed to Fraser who made a passably convincing show of interest. He's just winding me up, he thought, but he couldn't quite convince himself that Fraser would sink to that level of pettiness. And then Fraser looked up from the phone, over Martha's head, and caught Neil's eye, and gave a sinister grin, the sort the shrewd detective gives the villain who realises with a sickening lurch that all his schemes have come to nought, just before the final ad break before the denouement.

Elizabeth, sensitive soul that she was, began to speak to Fraser, thereby distracting him from Martha.

Martha turned to Neil. 'I've been showing Fraser some of my ideas for my project.'

'Palimpsest,' said Fraser meaningfully.

'Great exhibition,' said Martha, to Elizabeth, in an offhand adolescent way that was effusive but sounding cool concealing the fact that she really was impressed, if not overawed – Levels of meaning swam before his eyes like CGI figures in a crowd scene, there was a pattern there, a repetition, if he could just find the join.

'Thanks,' said Elizabeth. She finished her wine and Fraser handed her another.

Martha made some comments which to him sounded quite knowledgeable and made no sense whatsoever. Perhaps they were based on the exhibition notes pinned up at each corner, handwritten in coloured inks on the jauntily torn insides of cardboard boxes. So Martha had told him. The words had gone all blurry, like they were crawling away from him. But then he didn't have his reading glasses with him.

'I like those dolls,' said Neil. 'Make me think of greenfly.'

'Really?' Fraser raised one eyebrow.

'Yeah. They carry their young fully formed within them. Daughters and granddaughters all ready to go. As soon as they land on your Memorial Garden standard teas. But of course I'm just a cemetery manager, what do I know about art?'

He smiled sheepishly at Elizabeth. Self-deprecating humour, women love it. She smiled back, perhaps a moment longer than the comment deserved, or as if she was pissed and her reflexes had slowed. Interesting.

'No Jim tonight?'

'No, he couldn't make it.' Her face was revealingly inexpressive.

'Shame, I was hoping to talk to him about encouraging birds in the cemetery.' Never, ever slag off the boyfriend. 'He's a nice guy.'

She didn't answer. The silence got bigger and deeper till he thought he might drown in it. She stood, looking suddenly gawky and vulnerable. Or perhaps just unsteady on her feet.

'I expect he was busy with work, or family commitments.'

'They're like Amish dolls, aren't they?' said Martha, and he caught the tone, a little too eager to please, and felt a twinge of pity and a desire to protect. And confusion. He thought Martha didn't like Elizabeth, saw her as a threat, taking advantage of her vulnerable old dad. 'Remember Dad, we saw them at the American Museum with Lisa?'

Had Martha been there? He didn't remember. And why did she have to bring up Lisa now? He was undaunted. He finished his cup of wine.

'The Amish dolls, it's to do with graven images –' began Martha, all tipsy and wistful but he felt he was on a roll now, he was – His earnest desire to speak to Elizabeth was hindered only by his awareness of an empty plastic cup in his hand.

'Because he wouldn't want to miss this otherwise. A night like this, there will be plenty of admirers buzzing around.'

'Like greenfly?' asked Martha.

'They don't buzz,' said Fraser, looking bored.

'Maybe to other greenfly,' said Neil. Elizabeth smiled. Martha rolled her eyes and turned her attention to Fraser. Someone walked past with a bottle and Neil asked him for a top-up.

Neil carried on talking to Elizabeth, and the words flowed now, and she was smiling. Martha was talking to Fraser, something about open source blah blah relational blah blah collaborative...

'God, it's like being back at work,' muttered Fraser to Elizabeth. 'Undergraduate insights. They think they've just invented something you've heard for the ten-millionth time.'

'Yeah, well,' said Neil. 'If she has got undergraduate insights, that's pretty impressive cos she hasn't even started her 'A' Levels yet.'

Martha was looking at him in thanks, he thought, but then he realised she was actually looking at Elizabeth. Like it was her approval that mattered.

She's changed her attitude to Elizabeth, just because she likes the art, like you might fall in love with someone who's not that great looking just because they're in a band and –

'I was speaking colloquially,' said Fraser.

'I thought you being an academic, you would use more precise language.'

'At least I'm competent.'

'What does that mean?'

'Competent? Look it up. Along with theft.'

Fraser snatched Martha's phone from her and thrust it at Neil.

'You're showing me a picture of Shane MacGowan?' It was the picture that came up when Neil was calling her.

'Show me that picture again,' said Fraser to Martha.

'Tell him to fuck off,' said Neil to Martha.

He looked at Elizabeth for approval but she seemed concerned, with that half-frown. Or maybe wasted.

Martha was strangely docile as Fraser showed him a portrait of a woman. He couldn't make out much detail – the glasses again – but he could guess from Fraser's smug, punch-needing expression what it was.

Neil looked at her. 'I thought you only took unfinished paintings.'

'I thought you'd already taken everything of value.'

'I suppose I expected you to be sensible.'

'You're supposed to be the adult!'

He couldn't argue with that.

Fraser leaned in and hissed at them, 'Touching though it is to see you re-evaluate the assumptions that underlie your relationship in the light of experience – when am I going to get my fucking painting!'

'Only one thing is certain about this painting,' said Neil, 'and that is that it's not yours!'

'That's true,' said Elizabeth, with a drunken giggle.

'You're in a state,' said Fraser dismissively. 'I'm taking you home.'

'Are you?' said Elizabeth, 'really? Because I'm not sure I can remember where it is. Home, I mean.' She giggled again, an uncharacteristic high-pitched noise. Neil tried to convince himself she was still adorable. Fraser took her by the arm.

As he watched the woman of his dreams walk into the night with another man, Martha didn't even pretend not to gloat.

Thirty

Neil was wearing his pillar-of-the-community smile but it was starting to ache. His head was hurting. The sun was in his eyes and he was sweating under his dark suit jacket. Wondering how much longer he could stand here, and whether it would look disrespectful if he rested one buttock on a handy headstone.

He wasn't good at this stuff. Perhaps he should have let Teri do it but he was afraid she'd vaporise in sunlight and besides she'd frighten the children.

The museum was running an activities programme over the school holidays and had asked if they could bury a time capsule in the cemetery. The kids had been working on it all week.

The contents of the time capsule would provide an imaginative and wholly dishonest account of life in the early twenty-first century. A Prince George of Cambridge commemorative travel cushion. A Dormouth Carnival programme. A copy of the previous weekend's *Sunday Times*. A memory stick with a short film of all the kids and a recording wishing the future well. A Comic Relief red nose. A keyring from the Museum shop (chipped at the edge).

One of the kids had even added an obsolete iPhone. That had to have a street value. Perhaps if things got desperate he'd come and dig it up himself under cover of darkness. Claim it was an exhumation, they always did those at dawn.

Hardly indicative of our times. What would he put in there? A county court judgement and a seagull strangled by a plastic bag. Donkey lasagne and high heels for pre-schoolers. A selection of legal highs and a bottle of premium cider. Except he'd snaffle the Gogaine and the apple-flavoured mouthwash given the chance.

Martha had got up late on Sunday. Then they'd both had a drink to delay the inevitable. Halfway down the bottle, they had a touching bonding moment where he told her not to worry about the picture. He was her dad, he was responsible, he would make everything right.

She said she knew he was responsible. They drank some more and forgot about it. Three-quarters of the way down the bottle, she threw up. She looked fairly green this morning when he put her on the train on his way to work.

She'd said that Elizabeth hardly drank normally, which she'd got from Fraser who'd apparently known her since she was one of his students, all of which was news to Neil. How come she'd found it all out in one meeting while he'd been – well when he thought about it, he hadn't actually spoken to Elizabeth that much. At least, not the in-the-irresistible-flesh Elizabeth, as opposed to the one who haunted his dreams.

He hadn't climbed the golden stairs to her flat but had admired her when they passed in the hall, or when he glimpsed her in the Kebab and Calculator, while she was sitting with her young, gorgeous, creative friends and he was holding court with the sad, middle-aged blokes who hung around the bar (hoping to ensnare one of the young, gorgeous things when it was their round).

They were doing a little photo-op for the local paper. Dora Mickelthwaite was here, he wasn't sure in what capacity. Apparently the new Mayor and Mayor's Companion were both on holiday. And Pippa Middleton had declined the gig.

He stood holding one end of the ribbon, trying to stop his smile turning into a rictus grin, while Carol from Dormouth Museum held the other end and Dora held her speech and the silver ceremonial scissors. The kids gathered round like shepherds in a Nativity. The capsule (actually a fireproof metal safe from eBay, Carol had confided) presumably held the same symbolic properties as the baby Jesus.

The kids looked so wholesome. This was the kind of thing Lisa would probably want Tom to do in the holidays. He'd rather see him out climbing trees and building dens. Moving on later to minor skirmishes with his contemporaries and a bit of recreational shoplifting. The kind of benign neglect he'd grown up on. Not that he could recall ever having climbed a tree.

Neil had always instinctively avoided anything middlebrow and worthy. *Blue Peter*. Scouts. That wasn't what he wanted for his boy.

Colin from the paper gave him a wry smile and headed off. He'd take the piss out of him in the pub later. The cemetery staff were hovering with the digger just out of shot, waiting to do a reopener for a funeral tomorrow. Normally it would have been done by now but the grave was not far from the location of the time capsule so he'd had them hold off.

The only story the media loved more than 'Elf and safety gone mad' was 'Feckless public functionary fails to protect our kids'. The last thing he needed was little Tatiana or Tristram staring up forlornly from the gloom – although it was only a four-foot-six so it was unlikely they'd be killed.

Carol was marshalling her flock. Dora was heading straight for him. He'd told her once that he'd lived in Leeds and still had friends there. He'd asked if she got back much. She'd looked bewildered. As if she were a refugee from a long-forgotten civil war in a remote corner of the globe, keeping alive the memory of a people whose nation had long since been subsumed, and he'd just told her Easyjet did flights and you didn't even need a visa.

His phone rang.

'Sorry Dora, luv,' he said, inexplicably lapsing into a Yorkshire accent. 'It's our Martha.'

She never rang. She texted or messaged or occasionally emailed just for the hell of it but she never rang.

He walked away as he answered and an outburst began which he couldn't immediately follow but it had something of the self-justificatory tone she'd had when she raided the biscuit tin when she was seven or took pennies from his pocket to buy sweets at nine.

'I told Mum about the picture and she says it's typical of you, even though I said it wasn't your fault, and she's already called a courier and she's told them to invoice Dorbridge District Council which I'm sure they won't let her do, will they, and I really didn't want to get you into trouble.'

'Give me the name of the courier,' he said. There was no way he could pay. He was already rolling over payday loans, and regretting his blasé tone as he'd leant on the bar in the Kebab and Calculator explaining to anyone who would listen (Colin from the paper) that the AER was actually lower than an overdraft if you paid them back on time.

He might soon be resorting to shoplifting himself. How did anyone ever afford to get divorced? How could he even contemplate doing it twice? The bachelor pad lost its allure when he had to resort to own-brand lager to wash down his value baked beans.

So the challenge was, how could he get Malcolm to authorise payment for delivery of a picture which didn't exist?

Thirty-one

Paula and Callum had a day off but then Callum got called into work at the last minute. Paula hated being by herself so next thing she was on to Brenda.

'Let's go out. Do something together,' said Paula. Brenda's heart sank.

They walked along the prom, Paula's heels clicking on the pavement. Then they walked back again. Paula looked around, bewildered, as if she knew this was supposed to be fun but couldn't understand why.

Prams cutting across her. Men with their tops off pointing their big brick-red bellies at the pasty shop. Dawdling families walking six abreast, blocking their way. Paula's heels hesitating in their tapping before impatiently cutting through them.

Brenda never came this way in summer because dogs weren't allowed on the main beach. She felt hemmed in, there was a throbbing in her head. It's just the humidity. Always makes you feel like something terrible's about to happen.

'What about a cream tea?' asked Paula brightly.

What about going home? thought Brenda.

'Unless,' said Paula, moving closer, 'your stomach's playing up again.'

'It's fine,' said Brenda, then wished she'd used the excuse as Paula crossed the road and set off down a side street.

As they walked, Paula asked, 'Have you heard any more from Gemma?'

'I've signed the papers,' said Brenda. Her stomach lurched.

'That's great, Mum! I was so worried you were in denial.'

Tell her now, thought Brenda, but then Brenda also thought, wait till we're sitting down.

'What about feedback?' said Paula. 'Gemma should be getting you feedback from viewers.'

'She said she tried to call those people but she just kept getting voicemail.'

'And has she got you any more viewings?'

'Gemma said maybe we should wait till we get the crack sorted.'

'Mmm,' said Paula. 'I'll have a word with her about that.'

'A mate of Robbie's is going to sort it. Tony Goodwin.'

Paula perked up. 'It's sad about him, isn't it?' she said brightly.

'What?'

'His wife died of cancer. He had to cut down his work to nurse her through it. And now his business has gone down the pan.'

Down the pan, thought Brenda, her stomach turning over in sympathy, so she didn't immediately register what Paula was saying. So it wasn't divorce or drink.

She thought of him sitting quietly in their kitchen while she ignored him, the way he rested his hand on their wall as if for that precious moment he wasn't thinking about anything else. She wondered who did buy that shirt.

The D'Or Tearoom was busy but they found a seat near the back.

'Toilet's in the courtyard,' said Paula, nodding to the open door. 'You have to ask for the key.'

'Thanks,' said Brenda, looking around.

The café had only recently been taken over, although the decor made it look as though it had been here forever, with the display of old teapots on painted shelves and the black and white prints of Old Dormouth and the paisley wallpaper. Before this lot it had briefly been a French place and before that it was a place that did lunches for the old folks – roast dinners and cottage pies with puddings and custard.

When they were kids it was a Wimpy, Brenda remembered. Mum used to bring them here for a treat. She'd liked the ketchup bottle in the shape of a tomato. There was a mustard one as well, in the shape, presumably, of a yellow tomato.

It hadn't bothered her even though, at that time, she would have said that yellow tomatoes didn't exist. Now she had a daughter with a boyfriend who was a chef she knew they did, as did purple carrots and round courgettes.

Paula looked at the menu which was in one of those leatherette books. 'That's good, isn't it?' said

Paula approvingly.

'What's that?' said Brenda vaguely.

'A list of rules. Means everyone knows where they stand.'

Brenda looked at them. 'Mobile phones must be switched off.'

'I've got mine on vibrate,' said Paula approvingly.

'All breakages must be paid for. Please avoid spilling crumbs by using the plates provided. Our china is premium quality. Please do not give it to young children who may break it.' Brenda looked up. 'Well what are you supposed to do with a child?'

'Read on,' said Paula eagerly.

'We want our patrons to enjoy a tranquil tea or a calming coffee. Please consider whether your child's behaviour is compatible with our aim before ordering.'

'They've thought of everything,' said Paula approvingly.

They ordered from a shy young waitress.

'Me and Callum were talking about getting a café together one day. With his cooking and my customer service skills, we'd make a great team. Maybe we'd get to see each other then.'

'You've both got decent jobs,' said Brenda. 'Do you want to give that up to be self-employed?'

'It worked okay for – for dad,' she said.

Brenda didn't answer.

'Do you miss him?' asked Paula. 'Think about him all the time?'

'I see his van.'

'When I split up with Aiden I kept seeing guys in the street and thinking they were him.'

'I don't do that,' said Brenda.

'You're probably still in shock.'

By the window-seat a woman was frantically folding up a pushchair while a man who Brenda took to be the café owner stood over her like a security guard at an airport, the baby – and possibly the mother – in tears.

The waitress brought Brenda's tea in a teapot with a strainer, a pot of hot water and a milk jug. Brenda reached for the teapot but the owner looked up and dashed across the room to lay a restraining hand on the pot.

'Leave the tea to infuse for three to four minutes,' he said.

'She knows,' said Paula. 'She was just moving it, weren't you Mum?'

'I might not know much but I know how to make a bloody cup of tea,' muttered Brenda.

At least her scone was delicious, light and fluffy, neither soggy nor dry. She could almost imagine eating it.

Paula took some of Brenda's jam and put it on her cheese scone. Brenda was afraid to look in case the owner was having a panic attack of his own.

'So, have you started looking for flats?' she asked.

'Not really,' said Brenda, uncomfortably.

'Because there are some studio flats out there in your price range, even a bit below, if you want to keep some back to live on. At least you'll have your half of the house money. Say, a hundred and twenty after fees and removal costs, that's not bad.'

She didn't know then, about the debt. Bob hadn't told her.

'Robbie's seen a house,' Brenda began.

'You won't find a house on your budget –'

'I know. That's why we're going to go in together.'

'What?'

'Robbie and me. We're going to buy a house. Together,' she said again.

'Oh.'

The weather must have finally broken because a couple in wet waterproofs and walking-boots had just attempted to enter the café. The owner stood at the border, insisting they were full, although there was a small table in the corner, near the display of ceramic thimbles.

Brenda had it all planned, she was going to explain it and tell Paula she was sorry and that she knew how it must make her feel, them trying so hard to buy and all, but the words wouldn't come. Just like 'Love you' wouldn't come.

'It'll be good for Prince,' said Paula. 'Some of those flats, you're not allowed pets. Ridiculous, if you ask me. You buy it, you should be able to do what you like. Same with double glazing. You can't have it if you're in the conservation area. I mean, they've got streetlights and on-street car parking. They're not "in keeping with the period", are they?'

'I s'pose not,' said Brenda.

'I should go,' said Paula. She waved at her kindred spirit and he brought the bill.

'I'll get that,' said Brenda.

'No need,' said Paula, head down.

Was she crying? Was Paula crying? Brenda wanted to ask but again the words wouldn't come.

Paula left the right money (including tip) on the table and said, 'I'd better get back for Callum,' and before Brenda could get out of her chair she was gone.

The owner came over. He took the empty plates and dabbed around her indecisively with a cloth, like he knew it was rude not to wait until she'd gone but he couldn't help himself.

'I had no idea before we came here.' He shook his head sadly. His mournful Midlands voice swooped low. 'Jam and cream. It's a nightmare to get out. Life was easier back at the foundry.'

Thirty-two

Mum was – of course – at work in the garden when Jim arrived. He slipped in the back gate, knowing she'd be there.

She got up, went to hug him, hesitated, holding out her hands. 'I'm covered in mud.'

'Good!' he said, taking hold of her. 'I wish I was.'

This was how he always thought of her, hair slipping out of a loose ponytail, muddy garden clothes on, gardening gloves thrown aside.

'Dad's on the patio.'

'I'll say hello then dump my things.' He took the path to the small stone courtyard at the side of the house.

Dad was engrossed – of course – in a book, a straw hat shading his eyes, oblivious to the bumblebees buzzing round the passionflower on the trellis behind him.

'I hardly like to interrupt you,' Jim said.

His dad stood up, grinning, put down his book.

'So good to see you, son.'

He'd been here all his adult life, but sometimes, at moments of emotion, Jim, heard a faint

Caribbean song in his voice.

They chatted then Jim got changed and went to help his mum in the garden. This was where he wanted to be, on his knees, smelling the earth, feeling it under his fingernails, getting up close with woodlice and slugs.

They worked side by side. Light summer jobs, a bit of hand-weeding and dead-heading, the kind of jobs you could do without thinking which left you free to talk. They chatted about Mum's plans for the garden – an espalier peach tree, creeping thyme for the gaps in the path, extending the bog garden alongside the pond. Sometimes they enjoyed an easy silence.

Like the one he shared with Elizabeth at the rock pool, he thought. Maybe that was what made it feel so right. It was like his childhood. Mum in the garden, Dad with his book, each in their own world but firmly together. It was then he'd invited Elizabeth to come here. Was that only two weeks ago?

He was still feeling a little weak, perhaps, when he called her after his illness, a little light-headed, disconnected from the world, but her voice had sounded thin on the phone, like he had to strain to hear it, and the more she said it was fine, him missing the opening, the more he felt it wasn't. So although he was glad she was coming here, he just wished it wasn't this weekend, that he could have gone to Dormouth, so he could hold her and know they were alright.

A robin landed on a branch of the gnarled old apple tree. Jim had been listening to birdsong, he realised, all afternoon, teasing out the various songs. He watched the robin, charmed without feeling the need to consider the boundaries of its territory or its breeding history or its avian magnetic compass. He could just enjoy birds. It was like bumping into an ex-girlfriend and being genuinely happy to see her, and pleased that you'd both moved on.

He felt giddy with fresh air and stretching out his convalescent muscles and being here with Mum. His parents would love Elizabeth, they would love her, and he loved them all.

Dad offered to drive to the station and Jim went with him. He refused to acknowledge that there was a small grey cloud in the blue sky of his earlier euphoria.

Edie had invited herself along this weekend, and Edie's train was due into Bath just minutes before Elizabeth's, which she'd done to be helpful, but which meant he'd have no time alone with Elizabeth for hours yet.

She got off the train looking demure. Her beige jeans and white cotton shirt screamed understated. He wasn't sure if she'd changed her hair colour again. It was blond but not bleachy blond. It almost looked natural.

She had barely said hello before he headed off for Elizabeth's platform. Edie and Dad were close behind, apparently chatting easily, as if she'd only been here last weekend, not eighteen months ago. Elizabeth got off the train. He saw her and he felt his heart stop. As if he hadn't seen *her* for eighteen months, not just under a fortnight. Their eyes met. Was there some reserve in hers? He tried to think of the right words.

'Your hair's so gorgeous!' said Edie, reaching out to touch it.

'Edie!' said Dad but he was smiling.

'It looks crinkly but it feels so soft. You're like a storybook princess,' she said, hands all over Elizabeth like a two-year-old.

'Edie,' said Jim, but quietly.

'It's okay,' said Elizabeth. She was laughing. She was charmed. Jim accepted defeat. He was going to have to compete with his own sister.

Jim was nervous. Why was he nervous? When all was flowing? Elizabeth was all flow, he thought, smooth and shapely, from the way her hair fell long down her back to the gentle curve of her arm.

Of course he'd wanted Elizabeth to meet Edie. He'd imagined them in London, at a pop-up gallery, or an eccentric tea house, or a bar where a band had played before they were famous, the kind of places Edie always knew about and Elizabeth would love. He wanted her to meet all his family. Just not all at the same time.

The talk at the kitchen table was amiable and undemanding. Dad had a store of funny stories which he told well, playing each part as he told them, from the garrulous woman in the village shop to a cheeky ex-pupil. Jim wondered if he missed teaching, the constant stimulus of other people, the opportunity to perform.

Jim complimented Mum on the food. Elizabeth

admired the salad, brightly coloured with marigold petals and peppered with nasturtium leaves.

'The colours are so beautiful,' Edie enthused and then laughed and said, 'Jim, why aren't you breathing?'

Elizabeth laughed too. 'You looked so deep in thought.'

He thought, I must pay attention. Must work harder at looking relaxed.

Elizabeth and Mum had talked a little about the garden and were now onto chutney-making. Elizabeth said she also made blackberry jam, picking blackberries from the local hedgerows while he remembered to breathe and to ease out the knot in the small of his back and to listen. Tried not to notice that Edie was looking bored, and wonder what the consequences might be.

At least she kept a smile plastered on her face. Roisin would be asking what was the point, when you could buy something twice as good for half the cost? Or that her ancestors had toiled the land so that her family could get an education and not have to.

What else would Roisin do if she were here? She'd charm Dad, for a start. He could imagine her. 'So, Mr J, Jim told me how you used to wake them in the school holidays by declaiming from *Huckleberry Finn*.'

And Dad would smile, and allow himself to be persuaded to stand and do his party piece. And Mum? She probably wouldn't know what to say to Mum. It occurred to him that, just as Roisin at her most menacing still could charm, Roisin being charming might appear to some a little menacing.

That reassured him, somehow. Knowing that Mum might not like Roisin as much as she liked Elizabeth (though of course she'd always be pleasant to his friends for his sake).

There was a pause in the conversation and Dad asked Edie how work was going.

'Great,' she said.

'What do you do?' asked Elizabeth.

'PR. In the past I've been a corporate whore. But this is different. It's for a mental health charity. So I actually believe in what I'm doing. I've been lucky. With my history –'

'And it's such a competitive field,' said Dad. 'And how's your job-hunting going?' he asked Jim.

Elizabeth looked surprised but didn't say anything. Edie looked like she knew a secret but definitely wasn't going to tell. Mum looked sorry for someone, but who?

'There's nothing,' said Jim, trying not to be terse. It hurt him enough, but knowing his dad was disappointed somehow added to the burden. Dad loved learning. Jim guessed he would have been an academic if he'd had the chance. The fact that Jim had made it meant a lot to him. Except that I didn't after all, thought Jim.

The truth was, the longer he was out of academia, the harder it would be to get back in. There were armies of people coming up behind him, younger, brighter, closer. But he wasn't yet ready to give up and take another direction. So he was still working for Roisin, telling himself it was only temporary.

Dad asked Edie if she had any time left to read. She reeled off a list of recent American novels she'd enjoyed and a couple she'd hated. They got into a passionate but amiable debate. They could talk all night about books.

Edie got on well with everyone, could talk about anything, it was no surprise that she would make a friend of Elizabeth. Now she was talking about an exhibition she'd seen at the V&A and Elizabeth was saying she wanted to go and Jim thought, she didn't mention it to me.

'I'm so glad you two got together. Jim thought it was just a one-night stand but I told him to get back in touch.'

Elizabeth blushed. 'Well –'

Mum started conspicuously clearing their plates. Dad grinned and helped her.

'While Roisin tried to talk him out of it. She never does like to share. How do you guys get on?'

'We haven't actually met yet.'

'Probably just as well.' She turned to Jim. 'How are the plans for the civil partnership?'

Roisin hadn't got the venue so she'd been pissed off with him all week. He'd told her about the norovirus but she looked as though she didn't believe it. Without actually saying so, which made it impossible to refute.

'Coming along,' he said blandly.

'How was the opening?' Edie asked. He'd been waiting till they were alone to ask Elizabeth about it. Now it looked like Edie was more interested than he was.

'Good. A few people actually looked at the art. Plenty more came to drink and flirt and fight, but that's normal.'

'Who was fighting?' Jim asked.

'There was some sort of confrontation between Fraser and Neil. I think Fraser was condescending to Neil's daughter.'

'Really?' He wasn't very good at sarcasm.

'Fraser ended up wearing someone's wine, if that makes you feel any better,' said Elizabeth.

'Was that a conceptual piece?' asked Edie and they both laughed.

Dad brought in a summer pudding and double cream. It was his party piece, his home-made summer pudding. He began to serve up ridiculously large portions.

'So why don't you like Fraser?' Edie asked Jim. 'Does he have the hots for your girlfriend?'

'Could you pass me the wine?' Mum asked Jim. She took the bottle from him and poured a drop in his glass although it was nearly full, and put the bottle in front of her.

'It's okay, Mum,' said Edie. 'I'm not going to drink it.' She smiled at Elizabeth. 'I don't drink because it only gets me into trouble but they're worried I'll do it anyway. They used to only have water at the table but I said it was silly, don't they think I go to pubs and know people who drink and do drugs so if I can be sensible with them I certainly can here. Not that I've always been sensible, they know that, but I am now.'

She paused for breath. Jim tried to think of something to say, to draw her back, to break the silence, to stop his mum from tapping at her wine glass with her fingernail.

'Edie, I'll show you the new pond tomorrow. We've got frogs already.'

'Great.' She sat up straighter and smiled, preparing for the challenge of small talk. 'And you've been decorating? The hall and Jim's bedroom?'

'It's not Jim's room,' said their dad. 'It's for whoever wants it. We just thought that it made sense to give it to Jim and Elizabeth tonight.'

'I know, I didn't mean it like that, I wasn't complaining, after all he's here a lot more than me and –'

She stroked her eyebrow with her finger. Her secret signal to Jim. I'm out of synch. She'd explained it to him once. In her head she heard the right words, made the right gestures, had just the right facial expression, but when she spoke it came out all wrong, too loud, too fast.

'So how's the flat?' asked Dad. 'Managed to get the boiler sorted?'

Jim launched seamlessly into a tedious account of the difficulty of finding skilled tradesmen willing to do small jobs in London, wondering how many people were being bored by this precise conversation at this precise moment, thinking, why am I so good at saying nothing, filling the pauses, is it all these years of practice?

'I might buy a flat one day,' said Edie, smiling. She was still holding her fork, twirling it round in the air. 'My job's going okay, I know it's only a short-term contract, and the funding runs out in

March and the charity sector's in meltdown but I'm doing well, they really like me, and I think it would help me. A home. Stability. I know you won't give me money for it like you did Jim, but still...'

She looked around, smiled placidly, apparently oblivious.

Mum spoke slowly, her voice tight and low. 'Edie, you know why we can't give you the money.'

'Course I do and I'm not asking for it. Of course he deserves it and he's worked so hard and one day he might even have grandchildren while I only ever have abortions.'

'Edie –' said Dad, 'you know you've had a lot of help. And your brother's had nothing –'

'You should never have paid that credit card. Since I've been going to the support group I've found out all about the law on mental capacity and the obligations of banks. They knew I had a fluctuating condition and yet they didn't put a stop on my card. I mean who spends twelve thousand pounds in a day on throws and cushions! We should have taken the case. That would have stuffed them. Even if we'd lost it would have sent a really powerful message to the banks.'

Dad spoke quietly. 'Edie, you were in hospital. You weighed six stone. There was no way you could even have thought about a court case.'

'No but if you'd held them off – Or I could have gone bankrupt. Then they'd have got nothing. And you'd still have your money.'

'We did what we thought was best for you,' said Dad.

'I know you did. And I'm grateful. I'm sorry you and Mum had to move here when you really wanted to be in the Cotswolds. And that you had to cancel your trip to San Francisco. I'm glad Jim's got the flat and Elizabeth, and a proper job, even if it's not the job he wants. I was just saying it would be nice if one day I could have just one of those things. And maybe start to pay you all back. Those are the things that spin round my head but I suppose they're just dreams and they get broken up and strange when I try to say them. I'll go to my room. I'm not being funny. Just timeout.'

She made the 'T' sign with her hands, something she'd learnt at one or other of the treatment programmes she'd been on. Looked at Mum.

Then she spoke more softly. 'I know this would all be bearable if you could just love me.'

Edie got up and left the table. Dad followed. Elizabeth sat quietly. Jim should say something but he didn't know what.

Mum was shaking. Jim went to sit beside her, took her hand. Felt the callouses on it from the garden.

'I'm so sorry,' said Mum, looking at Elizabeth, though he felt she was speaking to him. She got up and left the room.

'Edie's in the garden. She won't come in till they've gone to bed.' Jim sighed. At the old house she used to sit on the swing. Just sit, for hours.

'She'd seemed okay for a while. Sparky but not too much.'

'She's got such energy,' said Elizabeth, sitting back on the bed. Mum and Dad had gone to their room too, but he knew none of them would be sleeping.

'She's getting high. You can see it, can't you?'

Elizabeth looked thoughtful. 'I don't know. She seemed happy at first. But also tense.'

'Happy is dangerous for Edie. Happy can tip over into – but then of course tension is dangerous for Edie too, and sadness.'

'Happy is dangerous? That's sad.'

'I don't mean happy exactly.' He closed his eyes and lay beside her. 'This is why I didn't want her to come. Because everything becomes about Edie. She usually avoids coming home. But she couldn't bear for us to be here and not her.'

'Maybe she wanted you here because she's afraid to come on her own.'

'Why would she be afraid? Mum and Dad are so supportive.' She didn't answer. 'I can't believe she said all that stuff. In front of you. Well, you've seen us tear each other apart. I guess that means you're truly one of the family.'

'Your mum seemed quite tense around Edie.'

'Mum's really placid.'

'Is she?'

Is she? he thought.

'It seemed like you changed the subject whenever Edie touched on anything remotely serious. When she had something she wanted to say.'

'It may seem uptight and repressed but we've been bitten too many times.' He sighed. 'We didn't used to be like this. We had such a happy childhood.'

She said, 'Maybe some things just need to be said. Even if the other person doesn't want to hear them.'

She was close to him, holding his hand. He could hear her breath, sense the beating of her heart.

'I'd better go outside. Make sure she's not chewing the heads off Mum's dahlias or something.'

He sat with his arm around Edie, in the dark, not speaking. Her breathing was spiky and irregular. Her muscles were tense, she was restless. It was as if not only her mind was jagged and troublesome but her body too. Too much energy, pulling her in every direction. He didn't speak. He knew that speaking would only stimulate her more, that sometimes it was better to say nothing. He just sat, thinking of Elizabeth, alone in a strange house.

Thirty-three

Teri was leaning over the jammed shredder, prodding it with a pen, with the power still on, her hair hanging seductively over the metal blades. He'd warned her, he didn't know how many times. No more than six sheets. If you have to do anything at all to it, whether empty it, unjam it, or even smile at it, then turn it off at the wall. Unplug it for good measure, why not?

There was something fascinating about the way her tresses hung, just out of reach. Like a horror film before the scary man in a wig with a knife appears. All he needed was some ominous music. He began to hum to himself while meditating on Teri being eaten alive by the machine.

Malcolm walked in. Malcolm? Neil quickly took his feet from the desk and assumed an upright posture. He realised it might have seemed as though he was staring at Teri's arse while she bent over the shredder, rather than contemplating her impending evisceration which would clearly have been more acceptable.

'Malcolm,' he said, playing for time. Teri stood up and rearranged her blouse to show more cleavage and unconsciously put a hand to her lower back. He'd told her that high-heeled mules, as well as being unsuitable wear for their working environment, and frankly hideous, would knacker her back but she'd just laughed at his naivety when he'd suggested flats.

The universe had shifted. A meteorite had landed in the sea and displaced a pod of dolphins. A virus had jumped from a bat to a camel and was waiting to infect a human and begin a global pandemic. A manager had come to the office of a menial.

'What brings you here?' asked Neil with false bonhomie.

Malcolm was confounded by the question. He looked at the ground. 'I – walked,' he said.

Neil contemplated his many misdemeanours. Teri, who complained that she had to walk the ten yards from the car park to the chapel every day, and presumably thought a parking bay should be made available next to the kettle, almost cracked her foundation. Only Maud in her urn remained impassive.

'I'll make tea,' said Teri, rallying. 'You do drink tea, don't you Malcolm?' she asked doubtfully.

'Tea. Yes,' said Malcolm. 'But no milk.'

Teri made a face that said that was no surprise, and busied herself with the kettle.

'So,' said Neil. 'How can I help you, Malcolm?'

'Help me?'

'What brings you here?'

'I thought – I need to keep on top of what's happening. Yes. I do.'

'That sounds very sensible,' said Neil.

'This invoice. It's for a – large amount.'

'I believe my ex-wife might have been a little over-zealous in choosing the premium overnight service from the courier. But she appreciated the importance of the discovery.'

'Discovery?'

'Of the Hugh Bonnington painting. Quite a story for a small authority such as ours, isn't it? I believe we can get some very positive coverage out of this.'

'But why was it in London?'

'Indeed,' said Neil.

'Yeah,' said Teri. 'Indeed.'

She gave Malcolm his tea. She dumped Neil's on his desk, where it splashed his copy of *Funeral Service Times*.

'I said my daughter could take some old canvases that were left in the flat.'

'Should they not have gone to the auction house?' asked Malcolm, perplexedly.

'They said they had no resale value.'

Teri's face was a study in ambiguity. On the one hand she was desperate to drop him in it by exposing him as a liar, on the other she was bound by the deep and ancient conviction that it was wrong to grass. She remained silent.

'So it was a great surprise to my daughter to realise that a finished canvas was hidden among the works.'

'Hidden?' asked Malcolm.

'*Hidden*?' said Teri.

'We were very fortunate,' said Neil. 'My daughter is studying Art and she immediately appreciated the significance of the work. A less qualified person –'

'Like a cemetery manager,' muttered Teri.

' – might have missed it.'

'And has it been valued – authenticated – by the auctioneers?'

'That lot?' scoffed Teri, flashing her eyes passionately at Macolm. 'They couldn't authenticate their granny's armchair. Which wouldn't stop them selling it. With the poor mite still in it.'

'Of course it is strictly now a matter for the heirs,' said Neil.

'But in the interests of an orderly handover,' said Malcolm. 'So that we can show that nothing has been missed.'

'What about Dr McKendrie?' said Teri. 'Isn't he a specialist on Hugh Bonnington's work?'

'So he claims,' said Neil.

'You said he's all over Wikipedia,' said Teri.

'And we have a means of contacting this man?' asked Malcolm.

'He'll be here like a shot,' said Teri, jiggling her cleavage in triumph. 'And I know Neil can't wait to tell him the good news.'

Thirty-four

Brenda had started doing hats for the hospice stall at the fete. They used to collect bric-a-brac and mildewed paperbacks but a few years back someone had hit on the idea that it would be better to sell hand-knitted new goods. It was round about the time Dora Mickelthwaite joined the committee. It had stuck.

Knit seven, knit two together. BBC News was on in the background. She liked the way they had the same few stories on over and over again. Like a kid's bedtime story.

It was the weather. She watched a cloud move across the map. The temperature was a degree lower than an hour ago, but the weatherman was as sure and smiling as he had been then. Where had that one degree gone? Was he lying then or now? Prince rolled over on his side and she wished she could do the same, drift like high cloud, go to the same place as that one degree...

The front door was flung open. Brenda froze. She tried to move but couldn't, just like in the water in her dreams. Later she couldn't say what she'd thought, a burglar or Bob coming back? She hadn't thought at all.

Prince was wagging his tail. She could hear it on the hall carpet. Then she heard Paula baby-talking Prince. It was only Paula. Breathe.

She walked into the hall. Just act normal, she thought. 'We've had an offer –'

Paula put her hand up. 'I know, Gemma told me.'

'Is she allowed to do that?' Then Brenda noticed Paula's cerise-print wheeled suitcase.

'I'm staying for a bit,' said Paula. 'You may be selling but it's still my bedroom and Robbie's got his own room.'

Prince was licking Paula's hand. Was Brenda meant to offer the same welcome?

'It's only an offer,' she said. 'Gemma says we should hold out for more.'

'I can't stay with Callum when he's being such a selfish pig.'

Brenda went back into the living room. Paula followed her, stood over Brenda as Prince went and sat at Brenda's feet.

Paula continued arguing with herself. 'Why does he always work Sundays when he knows it's my only day off?'

Brenda picked up her knitting. Knit five, knit two together. But hadn't they agreed they would work all the hours they could? So they could get a deposit together for a house. Then have two children (a boy and a girl, in that order). Later they would get married, but only when the boy and girl were old enough to act as page boy and flower girl.

Paula ran from the room. Brenda looked out of the window at the marigolds. The ones she'd always thought of as weeds. Their daisy flowers danced in a light breeze, caught in the last sliver of evening sun. The marigolds would go on dancing, but she wouldn't be here to see them.

Paula came back. They both stared at the news. They had cut away from the studio, the fifteen-minute loop that had been so calming. Now they were showing pictures of a building. They were waiting for someone to go in. Or maybe someone to come out.

Purl row. Brenda looked across at Paula. She noticed that although she was still in her work clothes, her nail varnish matched her suitcase.

'Alright?' she asked, finally.

Paula sank further into the sofa. 'It's nothing,' she said. 'Just irritable bowel.'

Thirty-five

Waking to the searing afternoon heat in Elizabeth's attic. When it's too hot to touch but unbearable not to, kissing Elizabeth gently awake, thinking of earlier when she'd been on top of him, leaning forward to kiss him and for a moment her hair had enclosed them, like they were in a forest glade, in another world where there was only sex and him and her –

And now they had to go and meet Edie.

Jim and Elizabeth sat at a table outside the café where they'd arranged to meet. Last time they came it was the afternoon. He'd enjoyed the busy atmosphere, watching the world go by while tucking into a cream tea. Now the sea was a particularly fine blue green, the streets still warm from the heat of the day, the perfect continental scene. Except the only passersby were the occasional dog walker and all the cafés on the front shut at seven.

How had this happened? Last weekend, somewhere between waking up late and leaving early for her train, Edie had suggested visiting for the weekend on her way to Cornwall, saying she really wanted to see Elizabeth's exhibition. And maybe Elizabeth had been too polite to say no, or maybe he'd thought that if he spent some time with Edie he could talk her round. Or maybe he thought if he acted normal (normally, Dad would say) the world would be normal.

There'd been no tension between Mum and Edie anyway, because they hadn't been in the room at the same time, not even when Edie left in the car with Dad.

Edie spurned all his offers of advice and found her own B&B. She said she didn't need picking up at the station but would meet him at six – just name the place. She didn't mention Mum. And Edie being Edie, if she was on her mind she'd have said so. While he was thinking about the rift all the time, but saying nothing at all. And Mum was saying nothing.

'She's late,' he said as a waiter half-heartedly swept round them with one hand and picked a spot with the other.

Elizabeth looked past him. 'Not she. They.'

Edie was wearing her favourite vintage tea-dress with giant Jackie O glasses – at five past seven at night! Roisin was wearing what she'd described to him when she bought it as a classic shift.

He forgot the name of the designer, in fact she probably had too, so taken up was she with the fact that she'd got a two-hundred-pound dress for fifty-nine quid online. She'd told the story as if it were a matter of her own cunning and guile, rather than a matter of pressing a button and entering her credit card details. They were contrasting and stunning, though even he thought that Edie's glasses would go better with Roisin's dress.

He knew what he was doing, distracting himself with musings on their clothes, because he didn't care about their clothes. *They* didn't make him angry.

Edie – well he was already angry with Edie. But what was wrong with Roisin? She was like a child who couldn't bear to be left out of the gang. But even the thought made it hard for him to stay angry. That was exactly what she was. He sighed. Took Elizabeth's hand under the table.

'You're late,' said Jim as Roisin and Edie stood over them. 'And there are twice as many of you as we were expecting.'

'Listen to Victorian Dad,' said Edie.

'We tried to call but we just got voicemail,' said Roisin. 'Can you get a signal round here or do you have to rely on pigeons?'

'He doesn't like surprises,' said Edie matter-of-factly to Elizabeth, as if she were the voice of reason here. Then she turned to Jim, smiling as if at a pedantic headmaster. 'I was in a faff looking for my train ticket and I'm not meeting my friends till Sunday so Roisin offered to drive me down and see the place. And it took so long we thought it made sense for her to stay.'

Roisin took the afternoon off? She'd played hell when he asked for a day's leave, said they were already short-staffed.

'You didn't tell me about the fucking M5!' growled Roisin, flinging herself into a chair. The waiter, leaning on his brush, broke off from texting long enough to glare. For a moment, Jim felt personally responsible but Edie cut in, 'Come on Roisin, everyone knows about the M5. Even I know about the M5 and I'm not allowed to drive!'

'Shall we take a walk?' asked Elizabeth. 'There's a nice pub or –'

Edie jumped to her feet. 'Let's go before that stary young man outgrows puberty.'

They walked on. Jim pointed out the view. Edie glanced at it, said it was stunning and carried on chatting. Roisin grunted.

They turned in, past the fishermen's cottages, some with flaking paint, some bright and new with tubs of bedding bursting out. The main road was a little livelier than the front, families heading back from an early tea, older couples and groups on their way out.

Roisin growled. 'What is it with this place? Is everyone fucking staring? Have they never seen people like us before?'

A man turned to look at them, then pulled his young son closer, as if to block his ears.

Elizabeth said, 'I suppose it is very white here –'

'I was talking about people under seventy.'

Edie laughed. 'Roisin, you almost had me there, with your implausible conversion to Black consciousness.'

Jim felt bad, because Roisin had put Elizabeth on the spot, as if she had to defend Dormouth, and annoyed with himself, because he too had laughed for a moment.

'We are a rainbow coalition of sorts, aren't we?' Edie said, linking arms with Roisin on one side, Jim on the other. He went to put his other arm around Elizabeth but she was just out of reach.

They passed a fish and chip shop with seating inside – laminate tables and bolted-down chairs. Edie said it would be fun to go in. Elizabeth said the food at the pub was better. Roisin said they had to have fish and chips at the seaside. Jim went along with Edie and Roisin, then realised after they'd sat down that maybe Elizabeth had wanted to go to the pub because her friends would be there.

Their builders' tea arrived and Edie regaled them with tales of the B&B.

'The owner's got the worst bleach job ever and it looks like she tried to do her own eyebrows and singed them. And the shower's just a cubicle in a cupboard. No window, no extractor, nothing! That's got to be illegal, right!'

'And when we got there she started blushing and trying to be all reasonable, asking us if we'd like a double or a twin. So I drew myself up to my full height and said, "*I'm* not a dyke," all offended. It was hilarious.'

'Of course you're not,' said Roisin. 'If you were you'd have slept with me by now.'

'You should have asked us. Elizabeth could have recommended somewhere,' he said to Edie as Roisin went off to the toilet in the courtyard, muttering something about whether indoor plumbing was too much to ask.

Edie leaned forward and said to them in a stage

whisper, 'I couldn't leave her, she was too upset.'

'Upset?'

'Krish has decided not to go to the wedding. And Melissa's going to some black-tie event and she's taking someone else as her plus one.'

'So maybe she's not out at work,' said Jim.

'Her plus one is another woman,' said Edie. 'Someone she went to school with. But don't say anything about it. Or Melissa. Just be sensitive.'

Roisin came and sat down.

'Roisin's getting married,' said Edie to Elizabeth.

Very sensitive, thought Jim.

'It's not a marriage, it's a civil partnership,' said Roisin.

'Why don't you wait and do it properly,' said Edie with a twinkle, so Jim knew she was winding her up, but he worried that Elizabeth wouldn't.

'I'm not colluding with all that shite. Church, state and patriarchy. No offence, like.' She nodded to Elizabeth. She sounded more Scouse than ever. Elizabeth gave her a small, confused smile.

'Are you religious?' asked Edie.

'Well,' said Elizabeth. 'I don't think I believe in organised religion, though I go to church with my parents when I'm at home. I do believe there's an energy when people come together. I think if there is a God it's not a man with a white beard. It's more of a presence, a feminine –'

'There is a God and *he's* a bastard!' growled Roisin.

There was a moment's silence. Elizabeth lowered her eyes.

Edie exchanged looks with Jim. Jim wondered if he should make the 'T' sign. Time out. But Edie came to his rescue. 'I think marriage sounds great. Making a public commitment before friends and family and society.'

She looked dreamy for a moment, and Jim felt dreamy too, knowing that this was what he thought. He was grateful to Edie and briefly forgot to be angry with her. Then he felt alarmed. Was Edie seeing someone? Had she already run off and got married in Vegas and not told him?

'What about you guys?' She was looking at Elizabeth. Elizabeth looked flustered. She was blushing. The blush ran all the way down to the neckline of her dress.

'We're not there yet,' he said, trying to take the heat away from Elizabeth, but the 'yet' seemed to hang ominously in the air, and Elizabeth looked even more uncomfortable.

Thirty-six

'Hideous, isn't it?' Neil said amiably to the woman standing by the Hugh Bonnington memorial.

'Gorgeously hideous,' she agreed. She had bright eyes and a captivating smile. And she's your target age, he heard Martha mutter in his mind.

'His wife commissioned it,' he said. 'You probably know his famous painting of her, nicknamed *The Mermaid*. Sea wall, long hair, skirt trailing. Of course, Hugh never called it that. They say he found it insulting.'

They stood side by side for a moment, looking at the monstrosity in marble, the kind of thing you would get in a garden centre with water coming out of the mermaid's mouth – or worse – but, to be fair to the poor guy who'd landed the commission, he'd perfectly captured the young Olive's face. Sort of Marilyn Monroe meets Margaret Thatcher.

'It's like something from a wedding cake,' she said. 'Wedding cake is much on our minds at the moment.'

Our? 'You're getting married?' he asked.

'No but my twin's boss is. He's here somewhere, said he was looking for woodpeckers.'

Neil rapidly computed the odds of spotting two black birdwatchers here in a single season. 'Jim?' he said.

She smiled. 'You must be psychic. Or else you hear dead people.'

He lowered his voice. 'How did you guess?'

'Oh, I do too,' she said casually.

'And Roisin's with you?'

'She's got to catch up on some work. She's back at the B&B, juggling her laptop and her phone, pretending not to be impressed by the speed of their wifi.'

Jim walked towards them, smiling distractedly, less interested in them than in the nesting box behind them.

Neil said. 'Have you seen the badger sett? I can show you if you want.'

Jim looked at his sister. 'Edie?'

'Oh yes!' said Edie. 'I love badgers!'

Neil didn't want to discourage her by telling her they were nocturnal. They set off walking, Neil and Jim striding manfully, Edie dropping back to read the headstones.

'So sad!' or, 'That's lovely!' she exclaimed from time to time.

Jim seemed distracted, head slightly to one side as if he too had voices in his head who demanded his full attention. Or perhaps he was just listening for birdsong.

'I didn't realise you were still around,' said Neil,

when she was sufficiently far away. 'When you didn't come to the opening.'

'I was ill,' Jim said. He'd said it so many times to people who didn't believe him he'd even begun to doubt himself.

'I'm glad. Elizabeth's a nice girl. And that Fraser's a shifty character.'

He let the words sink in, waited until Jim looked really disconcerted before continuing. 'I'm sure he only took her home because you weren't there. Although she could have walked back with my daughter and me.'

'Took her home?' said Jim.

'From my point of view, I was quite relieved. He'd been taking an interest in Martha and you know how impressionable kids can be around lecturers. You knew he was a lecturer?'

'Yes,' said Jim.

'Course you did,' said Neil. 'After all, that's how Elizabeth knows him.'

'I think they met through Maud,' said Jim, frowning.

Neil remained strategically silent.

'Took her home?' said Jim again, like he was shell-shocked, just as his sister caught up with them.

'I'll be off,' said Neil. 'Just fancied a walk. No kids this weekend.' Did the sad divorced dad look but Edie seemed unmoved. He'd have to think of a different approach if he saw her again.

'Maybe I'll see you in the Kebab – The White Horse later?'

'Maybe,' she said.

Jim was staring into the canopy of an oak tree and didn't speak.

Neil set off, whistling to himself. He liked Jim, he did. And he hadn't said anything that wasn't true.

He'd light a celebratory cigarette as soon as he got to the gates.

Thirty-seven

'So what's the plan?' asked Roisin on Saturday night. They were sitting at a picnic bench by the crazy golf. Jim was next to Elizabeth. He held her hand, too exhausted to answer. He felt like he'd been entertaining two demanding toddlers. Elizabeth had been lucky, she'd only had to go to work all day.

'Well, we thought we'd go to the White Horse, the food's not bad and Elizabeth knows everyone there –'

'They do great wood-fired pizzas,' said Elizabeth.

'They've got wood-fired ovens here? It's only a matter of time before they get electricity,' said Roisin.

'I hope you're not going to say "no offence" again,' said Edie.

'Why don't we go to Michael Caine's in Exeter?' said Roisin. 'I've heard it's the only place worth eating round here. Michelin-starred, right by the cathedral –'

'Sounds great!' said Edie.

'We hadn't really thought of going that far,' said Jim.

Roisin looked at Elizabeth. 'It's alright, we'll pay, you being the struggling artist and all.'

'I can pay,' said Elizabeth quietly.

'You'll have to drive,' said Jim.

'I don't mind,' said Roisin.

Edie mock-spluttered her drink everywhere. 'You always say a meal out without a drink is like sex without a partner.'

'Exactly. It has its place from time to time,' said Roisin primly.

Jim chose not to notice that there was a battle going on between these three women, and that he was the prize. A passerby would see only a group of friends exchanging repartee and sharing laugher. It could be a scene from a romcom, a kind of offbeat cut-price Britflick take on *Sex and the City*, with Elizabeth's pale unworldliness, Roisin with her sleek black hair and tailoring as sharp as her wit, Edie with her flamboyant movement and effusive frocks.

Not that he'd seen a lot of romcoms, but his last girlfriend Annika had a secret weakness for them so he'd seen the occasional one with her. It had conflicted with all his ideas about Sweden and about Annika. She'd been androgynous, wholesome and forthright, a successful scientist in a primarily male department. Perhaps this had been the little corner of herself she'd had to hide.

Everyone would have their favourite, like the Spice Girls. Of course he knew which was his.

But somehow, as he was looking at Roisin, she caught his eye and he saw that look, the look he had noticed on the face of the woman in the sandwich shop near the office and on the new member of the Urban Wildlife Group who had green eyes and a particular interest in lichens. It was the look that you never got when you were celibate, but as soon as you met someone, it greeted you everywhere. And now Roisin? Now?

Elizabeth was still smiling, but it was a polite, obliging kind of a smile. Roisin phoned Michael Caine's and established that there was no way they were getting a table. He thought the fact that it fully booked on a Saturday night at the height of the season should not have come as a total surprise to her. They set off for the pub. He took Elizabeth's hand again, as if she could shield him from the power of Roisin.

Somehow Edie, Roisin and a bottle of wine had invited themselves back to Elizabeth's flat. He wanted them to go, wanted to be alone with Elizabeth so they could tear each other's clothes off. Then he'd start a row about Fraser which went on till dawn and ended in frenetic making-up sex.

Or alternatively he wanted them to go so he could fall into an alcohol-fuddled sleep while concluding that now was not the time to have a rational discussion of a loaded subject.

They'd drunk too much in the pub. Neil was trying to charm Elizabeth and Edie. He'd bought a round of celebratory drinks when he saw Roisin. They spoke regularly on the phone but had only met once. He talked again in glowing terms of when Roisin took him out to lunch on expenses, an event so rare in public sector life, it seemed, that it was seared into his memory.

They'd only shaken him off when he'd been invited by some guy called Colin to go back to his house and play poker. Jim thought that only happened in gangster movies but apparently not.

Edie was busy planning Roisin's wedding. 'I think Roisin should do the suit and Melissa the meringue like Ellen and Portia – Or no, better, you in something classic and severe and very Audrey Hepburn, and Melissa more classical and statuesque, maybe draped ivory silk? You in black, her in white. You could make it a two-tone themed wedding – I'm so excited –'

'You've never even met Melissa,' growled Roisin.

'No but I can picture her. Tall, blond, athletic – I can't wait to see you together. Of course, if I'm invited, I wouldn't assume. But you'll have no trouble getting something to wear from Krish, even if he's not coming –'

'I'll leave him out of it,' said Roisin, her eyes meeting Jim's for a moment.

So much for Edie being tactful, thought Jim.

'And of course you're invited,' said Roisin. 'Just don't go doing any of that mad stuff. At least not till the reception.'

'Or do barristers get married in uniform, like soldiers? Will Melissa wear her wig and gown? Or if not maybe she'll do it for the honeymoon. You could pretend you're down in the cells and you're her client. I could lend you handcuffs –'

'They've already done that,' said Jim.

'We're not wearing meringues. Or bondage.'

'You could design something, couldn't you?' Edie said to Elizabeth. 'Jim said you make your own clothes and sofas and things.'

'I bet you made that dress, didn't you?' said Roisin, with only the slightest curl of her lip, so he wasn't even sure it was there.

'So what *are* you wearing?' said Edie, oblivious.

'I'm not telling you.'

'Is it vintage?'

'You think I'm wearing secondhand?'

'Something old –'

'I did look for some antique jewellery. But then it's just too – old-fashioned.'

'What are you after?' asked Elizabeth.

'How about jet? Would go with Edie's black and white theme.'

'Traditional Victorian funeral wear,' said Edie. 'Sounds ideal.'

'Okay, well maybe white gold or –'

'I might have something,' said Elizabeth. 'My friend's a jewellery designer. She takes old silver and refashions it. Just give me a minute.'

She came back and held up a necklace. To Jim it looked like an old fashioned locket on a short, metal rope, but Edie said, 'I love it.'

'It looks like cable,' said Roisin. 'The stuff you get on gate locks.'

'Industrial chic. Anyway, a lock is kind of appropriate, isn't it? I bet these sell for a fortune,' Edie continued undeterred. 'And you can put a lock of Melissa's hair in the locket. Or your stash, whichever you prefer.'

'It sounds like a right dog's breakfast. I don't mean that it is, I just mean that's how she makes it sound.' Roisin gestured at Edie.

'A blend of diverse cultural influences which has produced something beautiful and unique,' said Edie. 'Just like you.'

Roisin had barely looked at it. Or Elizabeth. She left it on the table. Roisin and Edie continued the double act. He was tired, Roisin was drunk, he was drunk, Edie sounded as if she were drunk. Jim tuned out. He usually did. But even then he couldn't miss the discordant note.

Finally they got up to go. Edie said, 'Don't forget the necklace.'

'It's okay,' said Elizabeth, 'it's fine if you don't like it.' She bent to pick it up and Roisin snatched it away.

'I'll maybe take it, see if it goes with anything.'

Thirty-eight

It was her favourite picture of them. At that restaurant out towards Chudleigh. All smiling, raising a glass to the camera. The waiter took it for them. Brenda, Bob, Robbie and Paula.

There was a ghostly space between Bob and Paula that was once filled by Aiden, the lad Paula was seeing before Callum. Paula had made her take it down when they split up. She'd got one of the lads at work to photoshop Aiden out, and then the picture went back up.

Robbie said since she was rewriting history, she might as well slot Callum in. Paula said the place was already taken by Robbie's imaginary girlfriend.

It was a special night. A celebration of the day they'd been working towards all these years. The day they paid off their mortgage.

She'd put it away because Paula said she should 'depersonalise the space'. That viewers needed to be able to imagine themselves living in the house, and they couldn't do that if it was too obviously yours.

Now though, she could put it back. They had

accepted the offer from the brother and sister. Still, the offer was subject to them getting the crack repaired as well as all the usual conditions. Saying she was selling the house felt about as real to Brenda as saying she would die one day. She knew it was true, but she didn't actually feel it would happen.

Paula came in from somewhere, twirling her car keys. Threw herself onto the sofa, arranged Prince by her feet and picked up the remote. She flicked through the channels, scowling at each one. Where had she been on a Sunday morning? Too early for shopping. To see Callum? Her dad?

On Sundays Brenda used to go to see her mum at the home. The atmosphere there was different at the weekend. There was less coming and going than on a weekday. No podiatrist or hairdresser or social worker. No doctor unless it was an emergency. More families came. There was even the odd one would take their relative to church. She wondered if the residents could tell the difference or if it was just a different wall of faces talking at them.

'I thought I'd put it back, for now.'

'That's fine,' barked Paula. Prince's ears pricked up. She threw down the remote and went out to the kitchen. She came back with a bag of pickled-onion crisps and a low-fat yogurt.

She dipped a crisp into the yogurt. 'It's probiotic,' she said furiously. Prince sat up expectantly, although he knew he didn't get fed when they were eating, which made Brenda think that Paula did feed him when she wasn't looking, which made her annoyed. Our house, our rules, they used to tell the kids, but of course it wouldn't be for much longer.

'So what are you doing with yourself? Taken up bingo?'

Brenda frowned at her.

'Or drink?'

'No.'

'Just knitting. Spoken to Dad yet?'

'No. But you have.'

She'd always been close to her dad, for all her shouting and carrying on about his going. She must have been there, been round to his place in Starcross. What would they have done? Probably Paula would have made him a cup of tea and done all the cleaning. She could picture that, but not him. His face. So she knows about the money. She's waiting for me to tell her. But I can't. I just can't.

She didn't know when it was that Paula had become the one in charge. Like she was the mother and Brenda the daughter. She'd been through it with her own mum, of course. But not at this age.

'I don't understand.' Paula sounded like a child again but then snapped out of it. 'You never spend anything on yourself.' She made it sound like an insult.

She stroked Prince, didn't look at Brenda. 'You been to see Robbie's house yet?'

'No.' Robbie kept asking her.

'You should talk to Dad,' said Paula, flatly.

'I've tried!' Brenda heard someone shout, then

realised it was her. At least she thought it was her, but there was an emotion in that voice she didn't recognise. She couldn't remember the last time she had shouted at anyone.

'He says you won't talk to him. He said you never do. Just walk away and sulk.'

She didn't sulk. When things got heated she went away to try and think it out. Because otherwise things came out wrong. Shouted.

'This is why I didn't talk to you about it. You get caught in the middle.'

Paula sighed. She went back to flicking the channels. There was still nothing on that was good enough.

'You spoken to Callum yet?'

'He knows where I am.'

Poor Callum. He worked sixty hours a week basic, more when he could get the hours. But none of it was enough. Because it still wasn't enough to buy a house.

'You'll have to go home some time,' said Brenda.

'I always call this home,' said Paula. 'He moans about it.'

Home. The home. Her mum unravelling like an old jumper. Not even knowing Brenda's face. Olive Bonnington's eyes lighting up as she said, 'Well at least I've got my memories.'

Olive Bonnington who lived in the luxury wing of the home where the residents each had their own kitchenette and landline phone. Not like her mum's little room on the north-facing side with barely room for a bed in it. How long would it take Olive to get through a hundred thousand pounds?

Prince was resting his head on Paula's black cropped pants. Brenda thought it was lucky that before storming out on Callum she'd found time to put a lint roller in her case.

'The one who's in the wrong has to make the first move,' said Paula, like she was reading a procedure from the office manual at work. Or like a child in primary school who's been turned on by her best friend.

'It's not about winning,' said Brenda. 'It's about working things out. For both of you.'

Paula glared at her then gave Prince the empty yogurt carton to lick out.

Thirty-nine

Roisin offered to drop Edie at the station and Jim went with them. Elizabeth said she had things to do.

He sat in the back seat so they could continue their conversation, sideways because his legs were too long. They were talking about some friend of Roisin's brother who did stop-motion animation. Edie had a friend who was looking for just that kind of thing for a viral campaign. Jim thought grumpily that it couldn't be 'just' *and* 'that kind of thing'.

'Dolls and puppets, like yer woman does,' said Roisin.

He had taken Roisin and Edie round Elizabeth's exhibition while she was at work. They had looked around in a subdued, attentive manner, like actors pretending to be absorbed gallery-goers. He had been so relieved Elizabeth wasn't there.

'I bet Elizabeth would love it. She'll meet him at the wedding,' said Edie. 'In fact aren't we all on the same table?'

'We've made some changes,' said Roisin.

'Melissa wants a top table. So Jim will be with us.'

'But Elizabeth will still be with me,' said Edie.

'I thought you'd go better with Joolz and the wanky new-media crowd. Elizabeth can sit with Melissa's cousins.'

'Not the Gloucestershire Rimmington-Spiffingtons? You are joking, aren't you darling?'

'What do you mean?'

'The Jilly Cooper set? What's Elizabeth supposed to say to them?'

'I don't want to sit at the top table,' said Jim. 'You agreed from the start I could be with Elizabeth.' His voice squeaked a little, he wondered if he was making an issue unnecessarily.

'We need you at the top table,' said Roisin. 'It's traditional.'

'Right,' said Edie. 'The civil partnership. A proud tradition that goes all the way back to 2005.'

'You're the one who wanted a meringue.'

'You're the one who insisted it's not a wedding.'

'We're here, said Roisin. 'Sling your hook.'

Edie laughed and kissed her.

'Come with me Henny,' she said. 'You know I'll never find the right platform.'

'There are only two platforms. Up and down.'

'Don't you mean left and right? And you know I could never get them. Or tie my shoelaces. He did them for me for years.'

'Glad to see you've moved on,' said Roisin.

Jim got out of the car and waited for Edie. Why couldn't he just laugh it off like Edie did? She knew how to handle Roisin.

He put his head in the window. 'I'll walk back to Elizabeth's,' he said coldly.

'Sure, I'll get on the road,' she said amiably, apparently missing his tone.

He took Edie's case and headed for the other platform. She followed, almost skipping to keep up with him. People passed them on the steps so they had to walk in single file and couldn't speak.

There was a group of foreign students on the platform, probably heading back to Torquay, chatting animatedly in their accented, oddly grammatical English.

He checked the screen. 'It's on time,' he said.

Edie looked like she was about to burst. 'Just tell her!'

'What?'

'If you don't want her to split you up from Elizabeth –'

'What?'

'This top table thing.'

'Oh.' He looked at the board again, was momentarily panicked when he couldn't see Edie's train, realised it had flicked to arrivals. The train had come all the way from Edinburgh. Destination Penzance. It was almost unimaginable.

'Brides do this kind of thing, don't they?' He'd read something on the Tube over someone's shoulder. Bridezillas and their mothers. Funny how things you'd never normally bother reading become fascinating when glimpsed over someone's shoulder.

'Listen,' said Edie. 'I love her. But there's a great big need-shaped hole in Roisin that will suck in everything in its path. She can't help it.'

Don't you start lecturing me, he thought. Not after all the damage you've done.

'Elizabeth is great. And she's not a control freak. But she's not a doormat either.'

Edie's face visibly shifted into a sad but wise expression. She was probably mimicking one of her many former counsellors. 'It's Roisin's wedding but it's your life. Stop bottling everything up. Just be honest with yourself about how this makes you feel. And then tell her. If you do want to be with Elizabeth.'

'Train's coming,' he said, stepping forward with the case.

Forty

Neil waited for Fraser outside the auction house, doggedly finishing a roll-up, resisting the temptation to chip it and put it in his pocket for later, after Tom had found one and almost eaten it. He hadn't explained to Lisa that it was his attempt at an economy drive. She already hated him smoking and measured his habit in terms of what might have been. Tom on a golden beach, smiling in a snorkel mask, if only Dad hadn't blown the holiday budget on fags. We've got a beach, had always been his retort. He'd come here, hadn't he? Left London, comprehensive network coverage, decent gigs?

Fraser turned up and asked Neil why he had to be there at all.

'I'm not going to steal it,' Fraser said. He was nervous, thought Neil. Like a bridegroom outside the church. Neil the unreliable best man who'd forgotten the ring. He guessed that was how it worked. It was a scene he'd seen in countless sitcoms and soaps, though both his own weddings had only involved a casual saunter up to the register office.

Lisa 1 didn't believe in marriage but said she'd done it to provide legal protection for Martha. She'd gone through the vows in a furious monotone. And Lisa 2 – he didn't even know what Lisa 2 thought, only that somehow they'd found themselves there and had done it.

Why had Fraser said that? I'm not going to steal it? Because it had crossed his mind? He did have that look of desperate longing you might see in stalkers or people who kidnap their own children.

Neil had to be here to ensure the chain of custody of the painting (he imagined an incredulous snort from Fraser if he said that, and that even his snorts would sound posh). Alternatively, he had to see his own humiliation through all the way to the end.

Fraser was pacing now. Neil realised that he'd rolled and lit another cigarette, all unconsciously. Like sleepwalking. Just like the other day he'd found himself unconsciously ogling the discarded butts outside the pub, thinking how many fags he could make from them if he swept them up and took them home. But it hadn't come to that. Yet.

Fraser was now the dad outside the maternity ward (another TV staple). Neil decided to spin it out just to ratchet up the tension.

'So what is it about this Hugh guy?'

'Are you really interested or are you just making small talk?'

Neil thought about it, puffed reflectively. 'I think I'm really interested.'

'He came here, he painted ordinary people, but he made them extraordinary. He had this amazing empathy, this ability to engage with their most intense feelings and recreate them on canvas. He was able to see beyond the banality of life.'

'And you can't,' said Neil. 'See beyond the banality of life.'

'That's why we need artists,' said Fraser.

Neil wasn't sure about that. Art was okay, he loved a bit of telly or music. But for him life was too much excitement. Art was a chance to get off the rollercoaster. Preferring it to life was like preferring pornography to sex.

'So we need artists to tell us plebs what matters.'

'Hugh Bonnington was a *pleb* if you want to put it like that. It was the war that helped him escape.'

'The working-class hero? Hardly your scene, I would have thought.'

'And you'd know?'

'Tell me then.'

'I'm from an army family. That's how I got my public school education. My dad was posted in Germany.'

Neil could see it all. They were about the same age, after all. He went to public school, the only kid who wasn't posh, then he went to university in the Eighties, when everyone was claiming to be working class. Felt alienated from all of them. Instead of trying to fit in, he decided to deal with it by pissing everyone off. Play the oik at school, the young fogey at uni. Neil had met people like that before. That was the problem with getting to his age, you'd seen everything before.

He threw his fag butt away and said, 'Let's go and see her.'

'Aren't you going to pick that up,' said Fraser, but he didn't stop, and Neil could see the eagerness in his eyes.

They went in. Andrew Bufton-Tattersall (that wasn't his real name but it was as near as Neil could recall) greeted them. He had ruddy skin, reddish hair, and somehow thought he would suit a pink shirt and cravat. Although Neil suspected that Mr Bufton-Tattersall, like most of what he sold, wasn't the genuine article.

'This is Fraser McKendrie,' he said, grudgingly as he introduced them.

'So pleased to meet you, Dr McKendrie,' said Andrew.

'He's not a heart surgeon,' muttered Neil.

Andrew led them into the showroom.

As he walked he pointed out an oil painting which to Neil's untrained eye looked like a terrible maudlin piece. An old woman at a spinning wheel with the lady of the manor showing charity. Big gilt frame. The sort of thing his mum would have thought looked classy. Fraser's look was so withering that Andrew didn't even bother to speak.

'Such a tragic death,' said Andrew.

'Yes,' said Fraser.

'Good for the book though,' said Neil. 'As Maud leaves the stage, the painting appears.'

'A tired conceit,' said Fraser. 'Walking into the sea.'

'Bit Reggie Perrin,' agreed Neil.

'I was thinking more of Evelyn Waugh,' said Fraser.

'Didn't he write that thing on the telly? *Brideshead*. Anthony Andrews with the ridiculous floppy hair and the teddy and those awful tweedy clothes –'

He felt two pairs of incredulous eyes on him.

'Of course,' said Andrew, practically rubbing his hands, 'it would be wonderful to have the opinion of an expert such as yourself. Perhaps the family could be persuaded to pay for an authentication –'

'Not from me,' said Fraser.

They walked past all the dodgy bits of furniture, the tables laden with vases and jewellery and leather-bound books – the kind of thing faux traditional pubs buy by the yard. He probably sold horse-brasses by the pound as well. Andrew stopped before an easel covered with a red velvet cloth and theatrically whipped it away.

Fraser laughed.

'What?' asked Neil.

'The pose. It's the same as the picture Maud painted of Olive. Hugh's little joke. I didn't know that. It's not in any of the sources.'

Neil wasn't exactly losing control of his bladder and his sides remained resolutely unsplit but Fraser seemed so genuinely joyful that he began to relent and think of him as human after all. He tried to concentrate and apply himself to the picture.

Even he could tell it was something a bit special.

Maud stared out at him, unmoved. Except he had trouble connecting the vital yet earnest young woman in the image with the doughty old lady of his imagination. The background was abstract, geometric blocks of bright colour where the Olive picture had a hearth, pots and pans hanging from the wall, an everyday working kitchen.

The paints and brushes on the table looked like they were coming to life, like they were going to dance away. She looked slightly flat against that background, like it was a montage and she'd been glued on. Or like an icon. Perhaps that was the message. Maud and Olive, Madonna and whore.

Except – there was that hint of wickedness around the eyes. Like she knew a secret which she might tell you, but only if she thought you deserved it.

He'd only seen the Olive picture online but even then she had looked so full and ripe in her picture. And the dough rising in the bowl on the table – all that sub-Freudian shenanigans. Maud didn't have that sensuality but there was a fascinating look in those eyes. Cool yet playful, promising and yet –

Celibacy was destroying him. He was fantasising about a picture.

Fraser was transfixed, it seemed, standing back, and then moving in close. So close that Andrew had stepped forward protectively. The emotion, the joy, the –

'It's a fake,' said Fraser, turning away in disgust. 'It's a fucking joke.'

'What?' said Neil. 'I mean, shouldn't we get an expert?'

Fraser gave him a withering look.

'I mean, a technical person. A chemist. Someone who can take samples and all that.' He'd seen it on the telly.

'You don't need a technical expert for this. The paint's barely dry.'

Forty-one

When Brenda and Prince got back from their walk, Tony was outside, sitting in a van, drinking tea from one of those stainless steel mugs.

She went round to the window and he lowered it. 'Did you knock? Paula should have let you in.' What was Paula playing at now?

'I'm early,' he said. 'Thought I'd just have my coffee.'

'Come in and I'll make you a proper one,' she said. Then she thought, now I'll have to sit with him, on my own in the kitchen. And maybe he'd have been happier in the van, reading his paper or playing on his phone. Although he hadn't been doing either of those things, just sitting with his drink.

They sat in the kitchen. She noticed Prince sat quietly under the table, as if he was used to Tony being around.

'Robbie's probably left by now,' she said, just to break the silence.

'Yes?' he said.

She went to sip her tea but it was still too hot. 'So you've got a van,' she said.

'Borrowed,' he said. 'A mate who's on holiday. I'm doing a couple of jobs for him as well.'

She thought perhaps she should ask him about the jobs but then she'd thought too long so they both sat a bit longer, saying nothing.

He looked out again at the marigolds, as if they might join in the conversation.

'Did your wife like gardening?' she asked, and then thought, why did she say that, where did that come from?

'No,' he said. His smile was sad but for the first time he looked at her when he spoke and she thought he was about to say more when Paula stomped in.

She was wearing a nightie with pink teddy bears on it, showing her fake-tanned legs and painted toes. Like a child dressed as a grown-up but the other way round. She had no make-up on and Brenda thought she looked younger without it. Prettier too. She could almost see the child who had looked up to Brenda. Not for long though. Paula scowled.

'Paula, this is Tony. Come to fix the crack.'

'Uh-huh.'

She threw a Tupperware on the table and took out a mini samosa.

'We had a webinar and buffet lunch yesterday,' she said. 'Help yourself.' Brenda shook her head. Tony looked amused.

Paula had torn open the samosa and was taking the filling out with her fingers, putting tiny pieces of potato in her mouth one at a time, placing the peas on the table.

'Me and Callum were texting in the night. I'm going back home.'

'That's good,' said Brenda. Brenda didn't know why Paula was so angry.

She glared at Brenda. 'I told you he'd back down.'

Brenda couldn't breathe. Brenda could see that, knew that, like she was watching someone else. She'd seen Paula's painted toes as she flounced out. Wondered where were the bunny-rabbit slippers? Already packed? But they stay here. Except nothing's staying here, the house is going. Then there was just her chest and her ears and her churning belly, everything beating beating beating. Beating her.

'It's okay.'

A hand on the back of her neck, she wanted to say, take it away, she was too hot already, this was making her hotter but as she thought of the hand everything else eased away.

Tony. She'd forgotten about Tony.

'You're okay,' he said. He took his hand away. She closed her eyes. She could hear him putting the kettle on. People always do that, put the kettle on.

He made her tea without sugar. He must have noticed that was what she made before. He sat back at the table. He'd made himself coffee in his stainless-steel mug. Maybe it was just habit. Making two cups.

He sat. Not speaking. That was alright. She didn't want to speak either. Just breathe. She suddenly realised she was breathing now, it was all slowing down. It had all slowed down while she was watching Tony and had stopped watching Brenda.

No need to speak, and yet Brenda said, 'She's spoken to her dad. Now she blames me for everything.'

'Kids do that.'

'You've got kids?'

'One daughter. Grown up now. Like yours,' he said, sounding surprised, and she was thinking the same. So they both laughed.

'She must miss her mum,' said Brenda.

'She's angry.'

Angry, thought Brenda. She understood that. And maybe she understood Tony. He looked sturdy. Like he wouldn't fall over if you pushed him. But there were things you couldn't see from the outside.

Debt and death.

'I'll get out of your way,' she said.

Forty-two

Everything was getting a bit intense. Neil had tried to make a joke about the fact it was the Dormouth Transition Town Campaign's summer family barbecue, said he was going to put Tom and Martha on to roast, but Tom had started crying. He thought boys laughed at that kind of thing. *Horrible Histories* and all that.

'What is a transition town anyway?' Martha had asked on the way up here.

'It's an admission of failure from people who thought they were living the dream and have just woken up.'

'Huh?'

'Well, they move to Dormouth because it's an old-fashioned town, a bit kitsch, a bit shabby. But then they think, it's so parochial, so undiverse, so reactionary. If only it were more vibrant and cosmopolitan and generally less like Dormouth and more like the place I've just moved here to escape from.'

'Oh.'

'Charlotte and her chums think that if they ban carrier bags and introduce the Dormouth pound it will suddenly be transformed into a utopia for cultural entrepreneurs, hip artisans and superannuated dope smokers.'

'No one calls it dope any more.'

'*They* do.'

'But getting rid of carriers is a good thing.'

'Of course it is.' He himself owned several 'bags for life'. Roughly one for each time he'd been to the shops. And he suspected that at some point today he'd be corralled into paying a pound for one that said 'I do it for Dormouth', all because of Charlotte's presumably ethical but still foxy red lipstick.

He lay back on the grass. Charlotte's grass, next to Charlotte's barn conversion with obligatory view. Even the sheep grazed in rows. The Devon dream, only a couple of miles along the green lanes from Dormouth but in another world.

The kids were off mingling somewhere. He had a halloumi and roasted veg kebab and an enormous portion of *patatas bravas* in his belly. He could still taste the chilli. Someone had brought a barrel of ale from a local microbrewery and he was savouring that. The sun was just turning from unbearably hot to pleasantly warm. There was a gentle breeze playing on his face.

He felt a movement as someone lay down beside him. A scent of perfume, something spicy yet floral, warm and seductive. Without opening his eyes, he put out a hand and found another.

'Charlotte,' he said.

'Are you sure?'

He opened his eyes. She was resting on an elbow, looking down on him. She still had that

London sheen. Her hair was cut stylishly short. She was wearing a jade and amber print dress and little button earrings in jade and a chunky necklace in shades of amber that was probably made by a collective somewhere. She was not beautiful but dressed as if she was, which made you think she must be.

She'd been in marketing at the Tate or the National or something and apparently still did similar work. She frequently mentioned words like consultant and project but never seemed to name a client. Her ex was still in London. He was the director of a small but well-regarded gallery in the East End and cropped up from time to time on *The Review Show*.

Neil wondered if Charlotte regretted her move. Who was there in Dormouth to appreciate the understated expensiveness of that dress?

'Are you looking after my mermaid?' she asked. One of her first actions on moving here was to inveigle her way into the Hugh Bonnington Trust for which she now did a lot of highly visible but unspecified – and unpaid – work.

It was an open secret that as soon as Olive was in the grave and the ownership passed to the Trust, they would ditch the mermaid and replace it with something they viewed as more in keeping. Charlotte had jokingly suggested the local museum might want to put it in their ornamental pond and they had accepted the offer.

He looked over Charlotte's shoulder and saw Martha talking intensely to a guy with a dyed-black fringe falling over his green eyes, while absentmindedly passing food to Tom to keep him quiet. Neil sighed. He remembered his own long-fringed days.

'Memorials are the responsibility of the grave owner,' he said to Charlotte in a mock-officious tone.

'Don't I know it. That woman will live forever, just to spite us.'

'Shall we plot her murder?'

She lay back. 'We should. We're in cosy crime country after all. A village garden party, rolling Devon hills –'

'An assortment of odd characters with implausible but intriguing backstories.'

'Trouble is, the motive would be all too obvious,' said Charlotte. 'Do her in before she spends it all on tat just to spite us.'

'I suppose he was her husband.'

'And marriage is a sacred vow?' She smiled at him ironically. He lay back as if impaled by that combination of pale blue eyes and full red lips. 'So tell me your implausible but intriguing backstory.'

He wondered how much was lip under that lipstick. He'd watched Martha use a pencil to make her lips look bigger. Charlotte's lips appeared fascinatingly full for a woman of her age. His age. This was what Martha wanted for him, an age-appropriate partner. Why not?

'Dad we have to go now. Tom's getting tired and I promised Lisa he'd be back by – are you still drinking?'

He looked up to see Martha silhouetted against

the evening sun, holding Tom's hand, other hand on hip, the exasperated stance she had no doubt seen Lisa 2 adopt around him.

'I've only had two pints.'

'Three,' said Tom.

'Three,' said Martha. 'And a Pimms chaser.'

'You believe a four-year-old more than me?'

'I'm nearly five,' said Tom.

'He was counting,' said Martha.

'You're checking up on me?'

'Tom's learning his numbers and he likes to count things.'

'I can say my numbers up to one thousand and the alphabet backwards!' said Tom.

Neil turned to Charlotte. 'We've got his name down for MI5.'

'You said you'd only have one with your food,' said Martha. 'I'm calling a cab. Come with us if you like.'

'You can't get a cab, it's miles. And they charge the earth around here.'

'If you haven't got the money Lisa will pay and you can sort it out later. I know she wouldn't want us getting in a car with a drink-driver.'

'You make me sound like a criminal.'

'You would be, but I'm not giving you the chance.'

'I'm afraid I've had a drink too, or I'd drive you myself,' said Charlotte. 'You're welcome to stay here. All of you. Felix is at his grandma's so there's plenty of room.'

Martha looked offhand but her eyes darted

fleetingly back to where she'd been sitting. Two eyes met hers then looked away again.

Neil sighed. At some point in Martha's future this guy, or another like him, would sweep his greasy locks aside. Their eyes would meet. They'd have intense, anguished discussions about the futility of life and frenzied, animal sex.

'Jasper wants you to stay,' said Charlotte. It dawned on him that the embryonic existentialist was her son, down from London. Charlotte was probably already planning double dates.

Martha looked fleetingly at Jasper whose attention was suddenly urgently required by a blade of grass. He saw Martha's resolve weaken.

'I'll drive you in a bit,' he said. 'The roads are quiet, I'll be careful –'

It was mid-week after all. He'd had to take time off to come here, which he suddenly found intensely irritating. Charlotte had gone native already, thinking everyone was either retired or working from home in a converted outbuilding or bespoke home office with solar panels and wifi.

Or perhaps she'd planned the whole thing around Jasper. Who had probably already exchanged contact details, if not yet bodily fluids, with his temporarily less-than-adorable daughter.

Martha took her phone out. 'I can't let Lisa down,' she said.

Why was she being so unreasonable? Sabotaging both their evenings just to prove a point.

'I said I'll drive you!'

'Bit late to assert parental authority now,' said

Martha. Charlotte giggled then suppressed it. Martha walked away, holding Tom's hand as she made the call.

Charlotte and he exchanged desultory banter until he heard the diesel engine pull up, then Charlotte noticeably relaxed.

'You can still stay if you want,' she said.

He caught the edgy jauntiness in her voice, saw the way her foundation was bleeding into the tiny wrinkles round her eyes. Thought about the pub. Elizabeth, fresh-faced and fearless.

'One more then I have to get back,' he said.

Forty-three

It was late when Jim's phone rang. It was Edie.

'Guess what, I'm in casualty!'

She sounded giddy. 'Which one?' he asked steadily.

'Our usual. But listen, it's cool –'

'I'm on my way,' he said, hanging up.

It was like he was at a particularly gruesome themed party. Drunk and drugged people struggling up like the undead from plastic bucket seats. Some bore the wounds of fights, others were about to start one. A few civilians sat quietly in corners, nursing broken bones or gripping their stomachs, like cans they'd brought themselves and couldn't afford to share.

Youthful doctors beheld the carnage with the numb terror of teenagers who'd called a party knowing their parents would be out and now wished they'd get home soon. Weary nurses yawned and scratched but couldn't quite bring themselves to leave in case something interesting happened later.

He felt disorientated and yet this was wearily

familiar to him. How many times had Edie put him through this? What had she swallowed or cut or stepped in front of this time? He preferred to be irritated by the banality of it because beneath the irritation was the terror. What if she'd been raped? What if she'd taken too many tablets too long ago?

The place smelt of piss and disinfectant. The old shabby building seemed violated by its wall-mounted TVs and CCTV cameras and aggressive signage. He glanced up at the screen. Middle Eastern corpses laid out in rows. The reassuring repetition of other people's suffering.

Routes were marked out on the floor in coloured tape. He felt for a moment that he was back in his primary school hall, with its netball markings and painted sash windows. Helpless in the crowd while Edie confidently found their place for assembly.

And there she was, taking the lead again. No obvious signs of injury. Perhaps it was an overdose then. She was dressed in loose, comfortable but still stylish clothes, no make-up. Might have been a social worker or a mental health nurse. She was talking to a woman next to her, grey-faced and weary-looking, her veined bare legs ending in shabby flip-flops. She was nodding, as if she thought Edie were one of the staff.

'It's a nightmare,' she said cheerfully. 'You know what they say, never be ill in August. All the new junior doctors come on stream and they don't have a clue what they're doing. I'm trying to help out as best I can.'

He closed his eyes for a moment. Was she

delusional, on top of everything else?

But all he could think of to say was, 'It's September.'

'Only just!'

'What is it? What's wrong with you?'

'Me?' she laughed. 'Nothing. It's Kay. She just went out to the local shop for some Skittles. I said you've got some here and she said no, they're not red ones, I only eat the red ones, so she just wastes most of the packet and I said well I'll eat these but why don't I come with you? But she said she had to go by herself and she got mugged on the way back for her phone and when she got in there was blood coming from her head.

'They hit her from behind with a bag, must have had a brick in it or something but I did everything right. Called the ambulance and the police, except maybe I was wrong and we should have got a taxi but head injuries, better to be careful, I thought, that was right wasn't it, no don't tell me, I have to stand on my own two feet. I made a decision and I think it was the right one and she's in with a doctor now.'

A group of lads came up to her. They looked fierce to Jim, in their big coats and their swagger, although their faces were young. One had blood on the front of his shirt but he was walking, just.

'Night Edie. She's sweet, man.'

'She's cool,' said another, admiringly.

'Who are they?' asked Jim.

'Oh, they couldn't find their way around. I helped them out,' she said, as if she'd been giving directions to a tour group.

'For all you know, they could be the same people who attacked Kay!'

'What are the chances of that? Anyway, they're not as scary as they look. I thought it was a stabbing when I saw the blood but it turned out he just had a nosebleed!'

She was so trusting. It frightened him and made him suddenly furious with her for doing this to him, yet again, and for no good reason!

'Oh, there's Kay.' Edie immediately fussed around her, insisted on seeing the dressing on the back of her head.

'Did they give you a brain scan?'

'They said there's no need. I just have to be careful about concussion. They gave me a card with the symptoms on it –'

'Yes, yes,' said Edie dismissively, 'I know all about that. But I'm still not sure about the brain scan. Funny things, heads.' She looked around. He had no doubt in a moment she'd be marching up to the reception and demanding to speak to 'someone in authority'. And that it would probably work.

'Edie!'

'What?' She looked at him. 'You look like you want to hit *me* round the head with a brick.'

'We've got to go.'

'Why are you here?' asked Kay, as if she'd just noticed him.

'Yes, why are you here,' said Edie quietly.

'You phoned me!'

'Yes but –'

'Because I'm always here. Like Mum's always here. Not the lady in the bucket seat, not the amusing would-be gangsters. Why do you care about everyone except the people who you should be caring about? Why do you just take, take, take?'

She didn't speak. He knew why. She was counting to ten. It was another of her techniques. One she didn't often use. While he spent his whole life counting to ten. Not thinking, acting, because he was always thinking about the consequences for everyone else. Well not this time.

'I've had enough,' he said. 'I can't give any more.'

'Any more what?' asked Kay, perplexed.

'Oh Henny!' Edie was laughing. 'You've gone all country and western!'

'I mean it. Don't call me again.'

Forty-four

Someone was calling his name. Someone was calling a name. Was it his? He wasn't sure. He tried to open his eyes but couldn't. Everything hurt. Something was wrong, terribly wrong. He'd been dreaming, hadn't he? Something peaceful and far away. How long had he been out for? It seemed like forever but dreams did that to you sometimes.

That voice again. There was something wrong about that voice. Like he had slipped through time. He'd got in the car, hadn't he? Then the pub. But there was no one there. Not even Colin from the paper. That voice...Came home, finished off the whisky. Too late for the Inconvenience Store. Took Maud's tablets. That must be it. He was off his face. But if he was going to hallucinate, he'd rather it was –

He opened his eyes, painfully, as if something was tearing. He was seeing double. He immediately closed his eyes again. A nightmare beyond his worst fears. Two Lisas were staring down at him.

Forty-five

Jim couldn't sleep. He'd have paced if he had the room to do it. He kept seeing Edie's face, hearing over and over her words and his words...He woke up. On the sofa. One arm hanging on the floor. It was asleep even if he wasn't. He moved gingerly. Gingerly, why did no one use that word any more when it was perfect, not since children's stories Dad had read to him and Edie. Edie.

Then the whole thing started again, her words, his words but worst, her face as he delivered his less-than-killer blow and walked away.

He went to rub life back into his arm and as he did so cricked his neck. It was twenty past five. Decided to get a shower and walk to work. It would only take about – Simple arithmetic failed him. Blanket himself in routine. Hide in the database.

It was before seven when he got there but Roisin was already in. Not that she was a morning person. She forced herself to get in early and then made everyone else suffer.

Her office door was open as he walked past. Her eyes registered surprise when she saw him but she quickly looked back at her monitor. This was how it had been since that weekend. Sometimes he thought he'd imagined the whole thing, the look. But then she'd been so scrupulously normal that he knew something had to be up.

He took her in a coffee. She looked terrible.

'Here,' he said.

'I'm always suspicious when employees come bearing gifts,' she said.

Employees. The word hung between them.

'I read in *Metro* that caffeine's good for puffy eyes.'

'Are you going to throw it in my face?'

He tried to think of an apt response but hesitated a moment too long. Normally he could do banter with Roisin on autopilot. It was like flying a jumbo jet only slightly more challenging.

'It's pollen,' she said, violating the silence.

It's Melissa, he thought, but he played along. 'When did you ever breathe in fresh air?'

'Cut flowers.'

But cut flowers brought them back to the wedding and Melissa too.

'I'm sorry Krish isn't coming to the wedding,' he said, but that brought him back to Edie.

She shrugged. 'I knew he'd bottle it.'

'You okay?'

'I'm fine. But you look shite yourself.'

'I need to get away for a while,' he said. 'We had this terrible argument. I said things I never thought I'd say –'

'Take the rest of the week,' she said.

'What?'

'The office is quiet. Deaths have dropped off since the heatwave.' She looked pensive for a moment, as if blissfully contemplating a flu pandemic or a sustained freeze, then recalled herself. 'Go and see your family. Or wander round on the moors with your binoculars doing whatever it is you do out there. Recharge.'

'Thanks. I'll stay late tonight to make sure everything's covered. María José can do the stuff that won't wait. She's already better at my job than I am.'

'And to think she only came in as a temp.'

'Like me,' he smiled. While a voice inside him insisted, I'm still a temp. This is not my life.

'Melissa okay?' he asked.

'Sure. But you won't want to hear about us now.'

'What do you mean?'

'After the row. Have you split up? I mean no one would blame you, it's always hard, the long-distance thing.' He couldn't help noticing that Roisin sat forward eagerly.

'I was talking about Edie.'

'Oh.' She sat back, reassessed. He should get out before she reversed her generous offer of leave. She was looking dangerously like her old self. 'Well she had it coming.'

'She did?'

'All that with your mam. And you let her walk all over you. I love that mad bitch but you've got to live your own life. So you'll be heading down to Dormouth?'

'Yes.'

Roisin opened her mouth as if to speak but then didn't.

He went to go.

'What do you think about favours?' she asked.

'It's good to help each other out.'

'I mean wedding favours. Bits of overpriced shite you put on the tables that just get thrown away with the leftover spuds. I think they're a waste of time but –'

'But Melissa thinks –' He smiled and kept walking.

Forty-six

Neil kept thinking he was in an airport. Thank you for flying PFI. That almost made him smile. There were signs pointing in every direction, but for now he was staying put, clutching his tepid americano in a paper cup.

People moved around him, the frequent flyers with eyes fixed firmly in front of them, impatient of the others stopping to read the signs. Staff in their colour-coded uniforms glided through. Cleaners buffed the floors, wiping out the steps of those who had gone before. The franchises sold books and nuts and snacks but instead of cameras and perfume and giant blocks of Toblerone, they had small blocks of Toblerone and cheap slippers and deodorant. And no drugs. He'd tried to buy some aspirin for his head but they said they weren't allowed to stock any.

Lisa 1 sat staring straight ahead. Lisa 2 had left them in the car park, saying she had to go and sign some forms. No, she didn't want him with her. There was nothing he could do for Tom now.

Then she had exchanged a complicit look with Lisa 1. These two were now allies and he was their hostage. Their solemnity unnerved him and made him want to giggle but he sensed this wouldn't go down well. Instead he sat and was aware of the smell of his own boozy sweat.

He went to the toilet. The world fell out of his bottom. Maybe Maud's tablets had been laxatives after all. Walked back to his seat, feeling the ache in his muscles, the throbbing in his head.

Lisa 1 got to her feet as if they'd just been called for boarding. He stayed where he was, bemused. She looked at him contemptuously.

A doctor was walking towards them.

He felt like he was in an episode of *Holby City*. A nice set piece. Girl in a hospital bed, divorced parents either side trying to maintain a united front. And not doing particularly well. He preferred *House* where everything was gleaming and high tech, more like a spaceship than a hospital.

Here the decor was tired. The nurses looked pasty-faced and exhausted. Even the machines seemed to bleep half-heartedly. He was waiting for Lisa to run her fingers along the surface and check for dust.

Was that really Martha in the bed? It looked a bit like her but Martha was somewhere else, staying out all night in eyeliner and not much else with Charlotte's oily offspring. To think that had been his worst fear.

She opened her eyes. Lisa moved into range and took her hand. He shuffled forward self-consciously, unsure of his lines.

'Where's Tom?' asked Martha.

'He's okay,' said Lisa. 'He's on his way home with his mum.'

'I can't feel anything.'

Jesus, he wished he couldn't!

Lisa's eyes darted at Neil then away again. 'That's the drugs,' she said.

Lisa 1 was messing with the script, confusing Neil. She was the one who always insisted on telling the truth. He was the one who would comfort with an easy lie.

He was about to say something but the close-up on Lisa's eyes showed she was pleading with him. He didn't think Lisa could do pleading. Demanding was about as close as he'd known her to get. But she was definitely pleading. Those eyes were saying, not yet.

'What happened?' asked Martha.

'You were in an accident,' said Lisa. 'Someone drove into the taxi.'

Martha's eyes closed again.

'Don't you have anything to say?' Lisa hissed at him.

He looked at her. 'She should have come with me.'

Forty-seven

He had a key but still it was her place so Jim knocked before letting himself in. Fraser was there, sitting on the sofa while Elizabeth sat on the edge of the bed. But there was nowhere else to sit, of course, would he have preferred it if she was on the sofa beside Fraser?

She looked surprised to see Jim, as if her mind had been profoundly elsewhere, as it had been when he saw her sketching, but her smile was genuinely warm. He wanted to kiss her. He didn't want to kiss her. Not in front of Fraser. He wanted Fraser to go. But he couldn't say so. That would be impolite.

He sat beside Fraser on the sofa. Elizabeth was looking at her feet, or perhaps the rag rug she had made herself. Fraser had a tight, fixed smile on his face which made Jim want to punch him. He suppressed the thought.

'How's the book going?' he asked, for lack of something to say, then realised it was the worst thing possible, to ask someone in the midst of a major project, that demanded all their commitment and energy, to give a flip summary in general conversation. He was starting to feel better.

Fraser looked at Elizabeth but said nothing. He apparently didn't feel obliged to maintain a facade of politeness as Jim did. She looked back. He sensed tension, but also complicity. This wasn't quite the welcome he'd been hoping for.

Then Elizabeth smiled at Fraser. The warmest, kindest smile you could imagine. A smile that would have left Jim breathless. If it had been directed at him.

Elizabeth stood up. 'Thanks so much for coming, Fraser. I realise how busy you are so I won't keep you any longer.'

Fraser stood up in a trance and walked out without saying another word.

Jim watched him go then turned to Elizabeth. 'How did you do that? Did you lay a spell on him?'

She laughed. 'That's my mum's minister technique. She always has to be able to move people on without hurting their feelings.'

'I didn't know you and Fraser were friends.'

'Oh we're not friends,' she said.

'Then why was he here?'

'He's still upset about Maud. He thinks if he'd spoken to her he might have learnt something vital. But he wouldn't have. Fraser has an endless gift for self-sabotage.' He was still trying to make sense of that when she continued, 'Never mind that, why are you here? I wasn't expecting you till tonight.'

It could have sounded like a rebuke, but she looked delighted.

'I got an earlier train.' Roisin's goodwill didn't extend to letting him take the pool car. 'I just wanted to get here. But if it's too early, if you've got plans –'

She kissed him. A light kiss. Just enough to say, it's okay.

'What are *your* plans?' she asked.

'I have to work out this family stuff.'

'You do,' she said. Or perhaps she said, 'You do?' He couldn't tell whether she'd been hoping he'd say something else because now he was being dazzled by her smile. He hoped she wasn't using the minister technique on him.

'And you and Fraser, do you have things to work out?'

She had that faraway look again. Was it thoughtful or evasive?

'I didn't want to involve you in this,' she said, finally. Jim swallowed hard. He waited.

'I want to be involved,' he said, thinking, do I? Do I need another fascinating but complicated woman in my life? Hadn't he thought, hoped, that this would be simple?

'He thinks I copied a painting.'

'Oh.' He rallied. 'Well, there's nothing wrong with that, is there? You explained. It's an established learning technique –'

'Well, not just any painting. A painting that hasn't been seen for sixty years.'

He thought for a moment. 'Not the famous burnt offering?'

'It seems,' she said airily, 'that a painting has

emerged, that resembles the description given in the diary of the art dealer who intended to buy the painting Hugh did of Maud, that apparently precipitated the departure of Maud from Hugh's life, and his destruction of the painting, the supposed turning point in his artistic career, not to mention a handy hook for Fraser's biography.'

'But that doesn't necessarily mean it's a copy, does it? I mean, lots of people know the story.'

'I pointed out to him that the description in the diary is not specific. That it's quite possible that anyone with an interest in the subject might also have read it, and might have decided to create a painting based on what they knew of Hugh Bonnington's technique, of the model herself, of the period.'

'Perhaps someone with an interest in the nature of the collaboration between artist and model, someone who had given a great deal of thought to the idea of model as muse.'

'Indeed,' said Elizabeth.

'And did he believe that?'

'About as much as you did.' She sighed. 'If he hadn't tried to bully me, I might have told him.'

'Told him what?'

She smiled mischievously.

'So if it is a copy, where's the original?'

'That would be in my studio.'

'Why didn't you tell me?'

'I don't have to tell you everything,' she said.

'Shit. I told Roisin there wasn't a conflict of interest and now I find out you're holding a significant chunk of Maud's estate, if it is even Maud's – I mean –'

Why was he thinking about Roisin now?

'She gave it to me,' said Elizabeth. 'And I'm going to give it to the Trust. Once things have settled a bit.'

'You can't just – I mean, was it even Maud's to start with? How did she come into it? Did she steal it from Hugh?' He tried to work it out. 'That would make it his, which would mean it would now be Olive's, or possibly the Trust's, while if it was Maud's, and she gave it to you, then it would be yours, but then Maud's heir would probably dispute it, if there's only your word to go on, they might even accuse you of exploiting a vulnerable old woman or theft or –'

'Like Picasso's electrician,' she said.

'Yes,' he said. 'And I don't want you accused because I know it's not true, but other people might not –'

And the heirs are our clients, he didn't say. But he thought it. He was identifying his interests with his employer. Not Sebastian, who had briefly wafted around the office before disappearing to a yoga retreat in Pushkar. But with Roisin.

'I have to do what Maud wanted,' said Elizabeth.

'And what did she want?' he said, trying not to sound weary, but thinking that Elizabeth's unworldliness, which he normally found so endearing and charming, could, in a certain context, for someone who wasn't overwhelmingly in love with her, be a little irritating.

'I don't know,' said Elizabeth.

'Maud never explicitly told me who she was but we arrived at an understanding. It wasn't hard for me to guess. I'd studied their work, the local connection with Hugh Bonnington is inescapable. And Maud isn't a particularly common name, even in that age group.

'And then one day she looked at my copy of *Woman Baking Bread* and I knew. It's hard to look at your own work. That's why I don't have any of mine here apart from that one. It's a copy so it doesn't really seem like me. But when she looked at it, although she didn't actually paint that copy, it was like she got a shock. She couldn't take her eyes off it.

'And she was full of questions. So we talked about copying. What it involves. I said I thought it was about more than technique. It was about trying to feel what the artist felt, see what they saw, to –'

She unconsciously raised her hand, as if she was trying to draw the thought, as if that would force it into words, then the spell broke. 'A while after that she came and said she wanted to offer me a commission. She had a painting she wanted me to copy. And then she showed it to me.'

'And you still didn't talk about it?' Jim was incredulous.

'There are some things you don't say to people because you know they need to keep up a facade. You know that they know what you want to say, but you still can't say it. Like you won't tell Roisin what you really think about her wedding.'

How did she know that? When he hadn't said anything? Because she was perceptive, shrewd, intuitive. And he was an idiot. He wondered, what couldn't Elizabeth say to him?

'Of course, that's another reason why Fraser's angry with me. Because I knew Maud was here, but didn't tell him.'

'You knew him before the funeral?' asked Jim innocently.

'He was my lecturer. Did I not tell you?'

'I don't think so,' he said. She was looking at him askance. Now instead of being annoyed that she hadn't told him about Fraser, he was feeling guilty that he was pretending that Neil hadn't already told him.

He decided to move back onto safer ground. 'I can see why Maud wanted you to know about the painting. But why copy it?'

'She said she didn't know who the woman in the painting was. She wanted me to paint her. She wanted to know what I saw, what I felt. I think she'd been trying to paint it herself. She had canvases and sketches in her flat, all unfinished.

'There was something haunting about those half-finished sketches. Like they were ghosts. But ghosts of someone who didn't yet exist. That doesn't make sense, does it? I wonder if she kept painting, when she was married. Certainly she never sold or exhibited. That's what I'd have asked her, if I felt I could. Not about Hugh.'

'And what did you feel? When you did the painting?'

'Confused. There seemed to be some conflict in it. Paint seemed to be applied boldly and then softened. The stance of the model was not quite static, not quite moving. Hugh's known for the boldness of his work, slapping on the paint, working it crudely. Earthy and vital. But this was tentative. It would be great to X-ray it.'

She frowned a little as she remembered. 'I'm sure that she was originally standing quite differently. And yet the face is really strong. Resolute. Painted with a very clear, sharp technique. Painted fast, and yet precise. It's as if when he painted the body she was changing, or at least his perception of her, as he worked. But when he came to the face he was sure of what he saw.'

'Or as if he knew she was about to leg it.'

'Perhaps. Maybe he sensed it, even if he didn't consciously know.'

'And you told Maud all this?'

'I would have done, but she didn't ask. When I showed it to her, she said she understood now.'

'Understood what?'

'I don't know. Then she said she liked mine better than hers, and why didn't we swap? I said we couldn't do that, but she said she thought I should have hers. She said she could see I would know what to do with it.'

'That's quite a responsibility she put on you.'

'I know. I wish I knew what I'd done that pleased her so much,' said Elizabeth. 'Then I'd do it for all my commissions.'

Forty-eight

When Brenda came out of work, Robbie was waiting to pick her up. She got in the car and he started driving the wrong way. At least it was the wrong way when she left home this morning.

He stopped and parked in a street near the seafront. Not near enough to have a view, but near enough to get the noise from the pub and the smell of the chip shop.

'This is it,' he said.

'What?'

'The house. Andy's given me the keys.'

'I told you. Just go ahead.'

'You can't buy a house without looking at it.'

She didn't answer.

'The way you've been lately – I just need to know what you want.'

'I just want things to stay the same,' she said.

He didn't answer.

She looked out of the window. The street wasn't so different from the one she'd lived in when she was a kid. After it all went wrong. Forty-odd years on and she was back where she'd started. What was it all for? Like walking Prince. You went for miles but you still had to do it again tomorrow.

'Is it Tony?' he asked.

'What?'

'I can get someone else to help me with the work. If that's the problem.'

'What do you mean?'

'Just – he thought you didn't like having him around. When he was doing the kitchen.'

'No one likes having builders in their kitchen,' she said.

'He says he gets it all the time, since his wife died. People avoiding him.'

She couldn't imagine Tony and Robbie having any kind of conversation, let alone this one. And she couldn't have the conversation with him either. She couldn't explain that she wasn't afraid of Tony. She was afraid of bringing what she'd got down on him.

She looked at the house again. She got out of the car. She would keep breathing. After all, she had been here before.

Forty-nine

Olive was in the same chair in the conservatory as last time Jim had seen her, in another suit, immaculately made-up, looking out towards the garden.

'Is she expecting someone?' he asked the carer who was showing them in. She had a local accent, a warm smile and plum-coloured hair showing grey at the roots.

'She dresses up every day, thinking someone might come. But they hardly ever do. She's got no friends or family and everyone who does come wants to talk about her husband. Poor mite.'

'We don't,' said Elizabeth. So now he knew why they weren't here, at least. Elizabeth had got up this morning and announced that Olive was the key to their problem. But when he asked how, she'd just shrugged and said she had a feeling about it.

As they got closer, he thought he saw sadness in Olive's eyes as she looked at a woman slumped in a chair nearby. The woman was wearing a dowdy dress that hung off her and a cheap cardigan, quite at odds with Olive's appearance.

'Her kidneys are going,' Olive said with savage glee. 'My specialist says I've got the kidneys of a woman half my age.' She gave her hand to Jim. 'I remember you. The sweet young boy from Trinidad.'

Olive turned to Elizabeth. 'You're one of the feminists. She's got nice hair for a feminist,' she said grudgingly to Jim. 'Not as nice as mine was at her age but –'

'We thought you might be able to help us,' said Elizabeth.

'She wanted to know about me being a model,' Olive said to Jim. 'She's right, it's not something anyone can do. It's a talent. Hugh always said I was his greatest inspiration.'

'What about Maud?' asked Elizabeth.

'She's dead to me,' said Olive.

'She'd dead to everyone,' said Elizabeth.

'I know, it's just habit.' She looked sharply at Elizabeth. 'Maud? Maud was never any good at modelling.'

'I think Maud was a great model.'

Olive looked at her suspiciously. 'No one will ever know.'

Elizabeth's pale skin was flushed around her neck, her chin was jutting out, just a little, but then she softened.

'We need your help.'

'What do you want?' asked Olive.

'I want to know what to do with this.'

Elizabeth took her iPad from her bag and showed Olive the screen. Olive started then recomposed her features.

'It's just a copy,' said Olive, but she couldn't take her eyes off it.

'I've got the original,' whispered Elizabeth.

'Clever girl,' said Olive. 'So what are you going to do? Expose the great Hugh Bonnington to the world as a liar? Or lay it all at the door of his scheming wife? Because I won't give into blackmail.'

'We don't want to harm you,' said Jim.

'But I think Maud wanted it to be seen,' said Elizabeth.

Olive looked at the screen again. 'He captured her perfectly,' she said. 'He was good for something, anyway.' Then her face hardened. 'Keep it till I'm dead. Then you can do what you want.'

'But there's still the problem of provenance,' said Elizabeth. 'People would question how I came to have it –'

'I know what provenance means,' said Olive irritably.

'Supposing it was yours,' said Elizabeth thoughtfully, 'then on your death it would go to the Trust.'

'It can't suddenly turn up here. Or at the house. The Trust have got a key and they've been all over it.'

'You don't have a convenient priest's hole?' asked Jim.

Olive frowned. 'You could put it in storage.'

'I don't have the money for proper fine art storage,' said Elizabeth.

'I do,' said Olive. 'A few of Hugh's works are in storage.'

'But they must be catalogued,' said Elizabeth, 'so if this painting suddenly appeared it would raise questions.'

'What you need is a time capsule,' said Olive.

'What?'

'I saw it in the *Dormouth Informer*. They buried one in the cemetery. That waste of space who runs the place was grinning out from the front page.'

'Not ideal storage conditions for a painting,' said Elizabeth.

Jim felt the stirrings of inspiration. 'How about we make a switch? Olive buys the copy, then puts it into storage, except she doesn't, she puts the real one in. And Elizabeth keeps her copy. Then in due course –'

'When I'm croaked, he means,' said Olive.

'The real painting will be revealed, and Elizabeth can take credit for the copy. Perfect.'

'And you expect me to pay for this?'

'Of course,' said Elizabeth. 'Your tribute to Maud.'

'And,' said Jim, 'it resolves any question regarding ownership. Either Hugh gave Maud the painting, in which case it was legitimately hers, and you bought it from her estate, or she stole it, in which case it always did belong to Hugh and so would have passed on his death to you and then the Trust.'

'And when the time comes,' said Elizabeth, 'it will be exhibited and studied and appreciated, as it should.'

'That will be a story,' said Jim. 'Maybe you'll get your own biography. Step out from the great man's shadow.'

'It'll be bad for Fraser,' said Elizabeth. 'It will look like he got it wrong.'

'That man!' said Olive. Jim smiled in solidarity. 'Okay, I'm in. How much do you think you'll need?'

'The Trust don't have the money to bid,' said Elizabeth. And I'm not sure who else would be interested. Without an original, it's just a curiosity. And no one except us has any reason to believe there's an original.'

'Only Fraser,' said Jim. 'Or, at least, he has his suspicions.'

'People like him don't buy,' said Olive. 'People like him never buy. They don't want to join the dance. They just want to stand on the sidelines and criticise everyone else's moves.'

Jim almost felt sorry for Fraser.

'But you're willing to dance?' asked Jim.

'Of course.'

'When shall we bring the picture?' asked Elizabeth.

'I don't need to see it. I'll give you the name of the company. You can sort the details out with them.'

'You don't want to?'

'What's the point?' Her face crumpled suddenly. 'Why didn't Maud come? When she was so close?'

'I think she would have done,' said Elizabeth. 'She just needed time.'

'Time?' Olive laughed. 'I've got so few years and so many hours.' She shook her head. 'I think about Maud and me, when I'm sat here. How we were. Both young, both beautiful – me more so of course –' she cocked an eyebrow in Jim's direction - 'and in one way I'm actually there, and in another I'm longing to go back. Maybe she had that longing too. But you can't go back, can you?'

'I thought you were bitter rivals,' said Jim.

'I loved that girl,' said Olive, taking out a handkerchief. 'Oh, not like that. We just had such fun. I never found women easy.'

'Then why did you and Hugh –' asked Jim.

'Oh, he was a man. There were always men. But Maud was my friend. That's why I told her to go. To make a life for herself. To take the painting, so Hugh couldn't take her spirit like he did mine.' She dabbed at her eyes theatrically.

Elizabeth raised an eyebrow but said nothing.

'Come and visit me, won't you dear,' Olive said to her. 'I'll tell you all my secrets.'

'You didn't tell me anything before!'

'I will now.'

'I'll come. We can talk about Maud.'

'Of course,' Olive went on, 'all this won't do your career any harm. And I've no way of knowing what you'll say when I'm dead.'

'You'll have to trust me,' said Elizabeth. She got up and kissed Olive's cheek. 'None of us can control what happens when we're dead.'

'So Maud hasn't haunted you?' She sounded triumphant. 'I will.'

'I think you might,' said Elizabeth.

As they walked home, Jim asked, 'Did you mean what you said about Maud's feelings or were you playing her?'

'What would you prefer to believe?'

Her eyes were sparkling.

'I don't know,' he said. And maybe that was the best way to be.

Fifty

Lisa 1 was in his flat. They were alone. For the first time in – he couldn't even imagine how long. Of course they'd been together at the hospital, as day became night and night became day, but always surrounded by people in uniforms who guided them effortlessly through the required procedures. Still like an airport, but airside now. When you know you don't have to do anything but what you're told.

He sighed. He had that weary sensation you get at the end of a long journey. Numb with boredom, skin grimy, lungs full of stale air, but suddenly reluctant to get off the conveyor belt and resume responsibility for your life.

She still had that stunning white-blond hair. All natural. Back when people in their crowd were sporting Mohicans or dyeing one side green or cultivating dreads she used to go as a model to Vidal Sassoon. He imagined her one day with true white hair, ice-blue eyes and great cheekbones and that image somehow merged with the one he'd had of Maud.

She was angry now but in a cold, contained

kind of way. She'd always been angry about something. He'd loved her fierceness. Whether it was McDonald's or Nicaragua or Clause 28. He remembered once when she'd dragged him out with the hunt saboteurs and he sat hunched up in the back of a van sharing cold samosas and mushroom pâté sandwiches. They were stopped by the police who were ready for a confrontation, till they saw that the driver was a slender blonde with immaculate hair who coolly asked them how could she help?

Another time she faced up to a National Front demo, going up to them and staring them straight in the face, almost as if she wanted to be punched.

Why hadn't she met someone else? It wasn't his fault, was it? It was years ago. Why was she still so angry with him? It seemed she hated him more than Pinochet and Thatcher and Bernard Matthews combined.

She tried to smile. He noticed her teeth were not the bright white they used to be. And sharp. She used to coil herself around him, bite his neck, moan obscenities in his ear. Yet so cool by day.

Should he have stayed? He couldn't even remember how they'd finally parted, only that Lisa was sure he was entirely to blame. Could they have worked it out? Grown older together? It was true he'd never felt quite the same for anyone else, he finally acknowledged. His wife was right. She really was poor old Lisa 2.

Lisa 1 was never one for small talk. 'We have to do what's best for Martha now. You'll have to move back to London.'

'What?' He felt a chill. It was as if in an unguarded moment he'd wished for something, and was now to be presented with the nightmare of the wish fulfilled.

Maybe she was not only angry and bitter, but also still in love with him? 'But –'

'How are you going to visit her from here?'

He was suddenly pulled back to the present. Martha was to be transported by ambulance to The London Spinal Injuries Centre. She would even have a police escort to ensure that the ambulance could travel at a stable speed. No swerves or abrupt stops. The police were no longer the enemy, the pigs, they had become our friends. No one could say yet how long she'd be in there. There'd be the acute phase, then rehab, then they'd have to assess whether the paralysis in her legs was permanent and total –

'This was not my fault! I told her not to go.'

'She did the right thing. No one could have foreseen this.'

The funny thing was, and it was kind of funny, he hadn't driven home anyway. Once Charlotte had realised he wasn't going to stay, she'd arranged a lift for him. He couldn't remember much about it, just bumping along a green lane in a people carrier next to a toddler in a car seat.

'You let them go and you didn't even have your phone on!'

'It was on vibrate!' he said. Lisa 2 was always complaining if he left his phone on at social events. He'd only done what she would have wanted. And during the night – he must have been too far gone to respond to it. Zonked out by those tablets. He was beginning to think Maud might have it in for him.

'Let's not argue,' said Lisa. Reasonableness, the most underhand tactic of all. 'There's nothing to gain by talking about blame. We just need to think about what's best for Martha.'

Perhaps even now she had hopes he'd come back, they could have a Charles and Camilla rapprochement, forget all their past mistakes, and be united in a soft-focus Dickensian moment over the sickbed of their crippled child.

'You can get another job. There are parks and cemeteries in London. Find somewhere near us to live.'

'I've got –'

'Another soon to be ex-wife and child. But Tom hasn't had his life destroyed by you. At least not yet.'

Fifty-one

I suppose there are some advantages to being alone, thought Jim gloomily. Like sitting in bed in his flat reading journal articles on his tablet.

His friend Günther had contributed to a paper attempting to quantify predation of garden birds by domestic cats in a suburban setting. He fired off a congratulatory email and of course refrained from mentioning his own ideas for improving the methodology of the study.

Roisin had been relatively restrained since he got back from Devon. It seemed everyone necessary to the wedding had been bullied and cajoled. She didn't exactly have an air of serenity about her but she had rattled through a morning's sales calls to solicitors with a charm that verged on saccharine.

The landline phone rang. He would have thought that there was nothing in his flat that was more than an arm's length away, but the phone was apparently it. It was probably a wrong number. His friends always called his mobile and it was late. Unless it was Elizabeth confirming the date of the auction...

It was Mum. Why was she calling at this time? She was normally in bed by ten, up early.

'What is it?' he asked.

'I just wanted to talk to you.'

'Is Dad okay?'

'He's fine.'

It must be Edie then. Of course that had been his first thought, it was always Edie, but he'd pushed it to one side and allowed himself the luxury of worrying about Dad instead. I'm not getting involved, he thought, not this time. Edie will have to dig herself out of this one.

'I've been speaking to Edie,' she said.

He pictured her holding the phone, her hands scrubbed but still that hint of earth under the nails and in the creases which was there all summer, ingrained, so that she was part of the garden and the garden was part of her.

Then he realised that his mental picture was wrong, that he was thinking of the garden of the house they grew up in, that he was seeing her standing in the hall, twirling the coil that linked the phone with its big round dial to the receiver. And although it was dark in the hall he somehow knew that the sun in the garden was shining.

He felt a longing to be back there, just for a moment, to see that old house, to feel how he'd felt then. And he thought, maybe that was all Maud wanted. It didn't have to be about regret or unhappiness, it could just be a wish, for a moment, to experience again another time, another part of your life that was gone forever.

Of course Mum was at the cottage, perhaps

sitting in her favourite chair by the stone fireplace. But for this call, no. She would be in the kitchen, the door closed, sitting at the big table. While he sat in his cell, all thoughts of sunshine banished from his mind.

'Jim? Are you still there?'

'You were talking to Edie.' Without me, he thought. How had that happened?

'We've talked a lot over the last couple of weeks, and she came down last weekend –'

They didn't invite me, he thought.

'And we've resolved a lot of things we should have sorted out years ago. And now I hope you two can make things up as well.'

The words were pouring out, as if pre-rehearsed. Which of course they were. He knew she would have been turning the thoughts over in her head because that was exactly what he would have done. It was Dad who revelled in improvisation, who could always find the right word to carry a crowd, whether the crowd was thirty reluctant pupils or a family dinner. And of course Edie could charm anyone.

'Has she apologised?'

'Jim, it was me who needed to apologise.'

'She was the one who –'

'She was the one who told the truth,' said Mum.

There was a silence where at some point he realised he was supposed to insert a suitable response but his mouth was dry, his hand was trembling so instead he closed his eyes. He heard a car drive past and then there was quiet.

'I suppose I didn't – bond – with her like I did with you. She was so demanding, even before she became ill. Or perhaps it was always there, just undiagnosed. It wasn't her fault, she didn't do anything wrong. I suppose – I sometimes thought, she was loud, we were quiet. Maybe it was as simple as that.'

'I always thought she was your favourite,' he said, in a choked whisper. 'Growing up. She took up all your time.'

'I tried to be fair,' said Mum. 'Perhaps I tried too hard.'

'But things are different now?'

Mum appeared to miss her cue as there was another long silence, punctuated only by the ticking of the clock next to the phone in the hall which now existed only in his imagination.

'Yes,' said Mum, cautiously, like the word was a stepping stone she was testing to see if it could take her weight.

So that was it. Everything was fine. Edie had been an adult, managed without him. Mum was happy. He was free.

'I've got to go,' he said, and put the phone down before she could respond.

He had to call Elizabeth.

'I suppose I was waiting for her to tell me Edie was wrong,' he said.

'Don't be angry with her.'

'Edie?'

'Your mum. Both of them.'

'I'm not angry,' he said. Jim knew he wasn't an angry kind of person. He was amiable and obliging and got out of the way without resentment. Okay, he felt outrage at the mismanagement of the world's resources and devastation at the closed doors of academia and something approaching terror when he considered the size of his mortgage – but no, Jim was never angry.

'When I was a kid, I was jealous of Edie. I felt like she got most of the attention. When she got ill and ended up in hospital, suddenly I had Mum and Dad to myself. It was like I'd wished it on her.'

'And you've been making up for it ever since.'

'I don't think I've ever lost my temper with Edie before. Not through all the stress and fear and exhaustion she's put me through.' Sitting up all night in a police station the night before his viva, missing a holiday because he had to pick her up from some squat turned crack house she'd found her way to with an aristo poverty tourist she'd met at a PR launch for a champagne bar. Cleaning up blood because she'd decided to slash her wrists in his bathroom rather than waiting till she got home.

'I suppose it's because it's safe to do it now.'

'So that's good, isn't it,' he said glumly.

He sighed. He surrendered to self pity. He felt a wave of tenderness for the eager little boy who had been such a trier. A sense of betrayal because all the time he'd been trying to win his mother's love had been for nothing. He'd already won.

'I thought she liked Edie best,' were the only words he could find to express the welling in his chest (although he could hear Dad's voice quietly chiding that it should be 'better').

'I like you best,' she said, which threw his mental compass into further disarray. How had he won this prize when he hadn't even had to try?

Fifty-two

Brenda came back from walking Prince, just at the point where it wasn't day or night but something else. Like there was a gap and she could fall through it.

The house was quiet. Robbie had got a job on site and had been sent on a two-day health and safety course in Bristol. Brenda was going to sleep alone in the house. When was the last time she'd done that?

She was still standing in the hall. She didn't walk into the kitchen. The kitchen where everything was smooth now. No sign that there had ever been a crack. She put the hall light on, picked up her post from the side, went to sit in the living room. Turned the TV on, just to have some noise.

Paula had been taking the bills. Bob was paying them still, or perhaps he wasn't. No one had asked Brenda for money, that was all she knew. But here was a letter with her name on it so it must be for her.

She opened the letter. Read the letter. She didn't understand. It was from the bank, the bank where she had the loan. Responding to her telephone request for a quote to settle the loan in full. They were pleased to inform her there were no early repayment penalties.

The redemption sum was £87,234.47. That made it seem real. One hundred thousand pounds was so round and smooth it didn't seem like it could touch you. It was like the billions on the TV news, beyond imagining. But those jagged little digits cut and pulled at her like stones in the shallows, clung to her like seaweed round her legs, the more she kicked the worse it felt.

She thought of times when she was younger and she'd been pulled under by the surf. Bob laughing. You were supposed to dive under a big wave, but she'd always been frightened at the thought of being beneath it, had tried to jump. Sometimes you couldn't jump high enough and it pulled you down.

That terror as you lost control and you thought you might be swept away. Coming up gasping just as another wave approached and took you down again. That moment when there was nothing but you and the wave.

Then it was over and you staggered through the current to the shallows, the water there hot like bath water when on the way in it had felt so cold.

It was over because Bob pulled her out. But Bob wasn't here.

She would call him. She wouldn't hang up. But his phone rang and rang. Not even voicemail. Not even a chance to leave a message in a small voice that sounded nervous and young and not like her own. No one to speak to. No way to know she was still here.

She had to get under. Let the waves pass. But if she went under, could she come back up?

Fifty-three

What did she want? Neil had traipsed round to the marital home at Lisa's request and found Tom in bed, the lamp on, no telly. Okay, the curtains were open and it wasn't quite Barry White on the stereo but still...

What was she playing? Indie elevator music. Or call centre. Please continue to hold. Perhaps he should have known from the start. At least Lisa 1 and he had the same taste in music. Thought of Lisa 1 at gigs, pushing to the front, throwing herself into the moshing, almost eager to get hurt.

Lisa 2 was sitting on the sofa, two glasses and a bottle of red on the coffee table. Should he sit beside her? He stood in the middle of the room, undecided.

'Those compilations from the adverts are really good value,' he said.

'We're a bit old for "Teenage Kicks",' she said, but there was no force in the words. This verbal ping-pong was a game they could keep up all day, without conscious thought. He sat beside her, then immediately wished he'd taken one of the armchairs. He'd slept in a funny position after one too many shandies (at least he'd made it into the bed this time) and had a crick in his neck.

In the subdued lighting he could almost see the young Lisa. Back from when life was fun. Of course, if he leaned in closer – which he had no intention of doing – he would see that she had changed. And that she would blame him for that. Her body torn in two by childbirth when she hadn't even wanted – No, that was wrong. It was Lisa 1 who hadn't wanted children. That was part of the resentment maybe, that he had convinced her to have a child for his sake, and then upped and left anyway.

He'd forgotten that. But of course, she wouldn't want to be without Martha now, none of us could bear to be without Martha –

He blinked hard. 'Are you okay?' said Lisa. 'There's no need to feel guilty –'

Guilty? He hadn't even slept with anyone yet. But fine to let her think he had, if this was the result.

'It was a terrible thing,' she went on. 'The taxi driver hadn't slept for over twenty-four hours, he pulled out at a junction when he shouldn't –'

He could try for the pity shag. Let a tear flow, let her take him in her arms. The great sex, the terrible recriminations, the sneaking out before Tom wakes up so he doesn't get confused – Like a window-cleaner with a faulty harness falling from the forty-third floor of a sheer glass skyscraper onto a lorry carrying a consignment of upright pointed cast-iron gateposts, his life flashed before him. Because that was all his life was, he thought, a series of more or less regrettable but fleetingly unforgettable sexual encounters, interspersed by periods of boredom.

Like a dog between walks. There was only sex. There used to be sex and gigs but he was too ridiculous to be bouncing up and down among strangers – there was a gag in there somewhere. And telly. Although telly wasn't as good as a walk. Telly was more like the toy you give the dog to keep it amused when you know you're going to be out for a long time.

'You're thoughtful,' she said. The CD came to an end. He got to his feet before she could. Put REM on. The compromise candidate.

'Martha's doing well,' she said. 'She's strong.'

He didn't want Martha to be strong. He didn't want her battling adversity, excelling in physio, training for wheelchair marathons with amputee veterans. He wanted her texting him from the station because she couldn't be arsed with the three-minute walk to the house. Going to bed in her make-up and refusing to get up before midday. Throwing herself into the mosh pit like her mother.

'You haven't been to London yet,' Lisa said.

'It's difficult, you know, travelling at the weekend in the season, and then I'd have to find somewhere to stay –'

The dog ate my homework, he thought. This is the bit where she looks deeply at me and talks about denial and tells me there is help out there. He knew she'd be loving this. Her chance to shine. She was probably on the phone constantly talking to Lisa 1 about aids and adaptations, poring over catalogues of wet rooms and grab handles the way interior designers swoon over swatches.

'You do need to face up to what's happened. Things are going to be very different for Martha. She's going to need support –'

So this was what she wanted. To tell him they were going to have to stay together for the children.

'I wanted to tell you we can get a divorce.'

He felt a visceral pain in his chest. Again. He'd really have to get that checked out.

'Then you can have your share of the equity, it won't be much but you can find a place to rent in London, somewhere accessible, and we'll manage somehow, I might take in a lodger, maybe someone at the hospital –'

She was crying. Then they were in each other's arms. Kissing, hungrily. Clothes pulled and torn. Her astride him on the sofa, lips clenched shut so she wouldn't cry out. Him wanting it to last. Wanting it to be over in case Tom got up. Wanting to bury his face in her still-clothed breasts. Wanting to kiss her slender neck in a tender, post-orgasmic glow.

Wanting to get out of there so he could work out what the hell this all meant.

Fifty-four

When she opened her front door, Roisin was wearing cargo shorts and a baggy T-shirt and no make-up.

'You've come to this party dressed as me,' Jim said. He didn't exactly look like her but he was wearing clothes that she'd chosen for him. One lunchtime about a year ago when she'd convinced him it would be fun to go shopping.

'You're still wearing those old things,' she said.

'They've hardly been worn.'

She let him in. 'It's actually a sort-of compliment letting you see me in this state.'

'It's okay. I know you'll be ready in two hours. Can I have a bag of crisps while I wait?'

'Let's stay in,' she said.

'But it's supposed to be your not-a-hen night!' She'd already done the raucous girl's night out thing. This was supposed to be a quiet, civilised meal in a restaurant.

'Let's slob out here.'

'I could go and get a bottle of wine,' he said.

'Forget it, we'll raid Melissa's wine fridge.'

It sounded fun. Much more than the restaurant. Jim was feeling playful too. Life was suddenly brighter and better. He was glorying in his new status of favoured child. He might have stopped to think this was petty, or to feel sorry for Edie, but how could he?

All these years he'd felt he wasn't as clever, or as funny, that he had to be good and conscientious because he wasn't anything else. Now he didn't need to. He even felt now he could be magnanimous to Edie. He would call her. He hadn't yet. But he would.

They went into the living room. Last time Jim had been here it had been a weird mixture of shabby-chic and squalor. Melissa's sports bag thrown on a spindly-legged chair. Coffee cups everywhere. Roisin's make-up mirror perched on a pile of investment paperwork, which she was reviewing because she said Melissa had been a fool to trust that shithead financial adviser. It had looked like it would if a group of squatters had taken over a stately home.

Now it was transformed. Two cream sofas faced each other, immaculately accessorised with rugs and occasional tables and pictures on the wall and –

'It looks like something from a magazine,' said Jim.

'It pretty much is. She went to some place on the Fulham Road and ordered the room set. A wedding present from her parents. Just as well my lot aren't coming. Argos vouchers wouldn't quite cut it.'

Jim could now answer Edie's question about who spent twelve thousand pounds in a day on cushions.

He'd no sooner sat down than Roisin said, 'Let's see what's in the kitchen.'

She went to the wine fridge first. 'Champagne, I think. Open it for me.'

'Are you sure? This isn't the supermarket stuff.'

'I'm getting married, aren't I? I'll just shove something in the microwave and we can go and watch telly.'

'What are we watching?'

'Something trashy. One of those shows where a woman finds self-worth when she changes into support pants.'

'You mean *Wonderwoman*?'

'Would Wonderwoman let some gay guy cop a feel of her tits?'

He sipped his champagne. It tasted good but maybe that was just because he knew it was expensive.

'Where's Melissa?'

'Off on some sports-related shindig in Cheltenham with most of the touch rugby team. They're staying over. I'm surprised they've found a hotel that will take them. Perhaps because it's a mixed group they don't realise that it's stag-and-hen Armageddon they've let themselves in for. Grab your dinner.'

He hadn't realised that 'the telly' was now in the bedroom. He stood aloof for a moment, but what did it mean, really? During his student days – which made up most of his adult life – he'd happily lolled platonically on the beds of female friends and colleagues. And from what Roisin told him, most of their sex didn't happen in bed anyway.

'Climb aboard,' said Roisin as she got onto the big, high bed with chintzy coverings. More cushions and fancy throws. He thought people only put them on when they were selling. How were you actually supposed to get into the thing with all this stuff on it? Not that he would be. Getting in.

'I'm worried about spilling my champagne,' he said.

'If you do we'll get the maid to change the sheets.'

He wasn't sure if she was joking.

'You phoned your mad bitch sister yet?'

'Not yet.'

He waited for a response but Roisin was transfixed by the screen. She maintained an iron grip on the remote and kept up a running commentary on the programmes they watched, flicking between channels as soon as she got bored. He ate his wild mushroom risotto – if that was what it was – and enjoyed the champagne. Roisin didn't seem to have time to eat though she found opportunities to drink. When the bottle ran out she sent him to the kitchen for another.

He clambered back onto the bed. He felt euphoric. He felt like he was in a really high-end hotel and it was all on expenses. He suspected that Roisin felt the same way.

Roisin was still talking. He didn't have to listen to the words to laugh. He just knew it was funny because it was Roisin.

'You're so funny,' he said.

'I fucking know,' she said, frowning, which made them laugh more. This was how they'd been when he started work, when he was on his own, and she had barely met Melissa.

'You helped me so much,' he said, 'when we first met.'

'I know, I was your fucking guardian angel.'

'I didn't know what to do. I had no job, I'd broken up with Annika...'

'We had some great times, didn't we?'

'And I couldn't have bought my flat without this job. Not that it's a patch on yours. I bet my whole flat would fit in this bedroom.'

'In the en suite –'

'In this bed –'

'In this glass –'

'Do you want to know a secret?'

'Course I fecking do. Then I can hold it against you forever. What is it?'

Jim looked thoughtful. 'When I was first working with you, I got offered a six-month research contract. I turned it down. I wanted the mortgage.'

'So? I bet the money was shite.'

'I'm a fraud. I've told everyone that my career was what mattered, more than anything, but when it came to it, the flat, the security mattered more.'

'It's hardly *Sophie's* fucking *Choice* is it? There'll be other jobs.'

'That's what I thought at the time. But there haven't been.'

'So you made a mistake. You'll have other chances. And meanwhile you can work for us.'

She flicked the channels again and he caught a glimpse of a sparrowhawk.

'Go back!' he said but she was already moving onto a show about spying on your probably unfaithful boyfriend and then crying about it on air when you find out that he's doing what you already thought he was doing anyway. Or something.

Roisin was saying she had finally met Melissa's parents. She said that she'd thought Melissa was afraid they'd make her call the whole thing off. She tried to make it sound like she was joking. She was saying that Melissa's parents wanted to give them 'a little money' (which apparently meant that the pounds were measured only in tens of thousands) so they could move out of London. Somewhere leafy but commutable.

The boyfriend was crying too now. It had only happened the once. He wouldn't do it again. The girlfriend seemed inclined to believe him, which probably meant she wouldn't, because that was how it always worked on these programmes.

'He's my best friend,' she said, smudging her mascara with one finger.

'Another one with the best friend shite,' said Roisin. 'If you want a friend, get a friend. If you want someone hot to jump your bones, do that.'

'What about all *your* friends, your social life? You'll get home knackered from the commute. By the time you've walked the gun-dogs it'll be time for bed.'

'I'm getting a bit old for nightlife,' said Roisin, who only the previous weekend had been out in Soho with Joolz till four.

Maybe she would take him back after all. Her mascara was running and her botox meant her expression was unreadable (or perhaps the botox-gone-wrong show was on another channel, he'd lost track). Whereas his was transparent, or at least would be if she'd watched the show about the body-language expert with the secret to hide.

If Roisin moved out to the sticks she might work from home, or start her own company. Then the one thing that made working at Generation bearable would no longer apply.

'You've made me too comfortable,' he said mournfully.

'Why's it bad to be comfortable? You're earning, you've got your wee flat, what's the problem?'

He felt comfortable now. He laid his head back. The room was spinning, but only lightly. Why not be comfortable? Why make life harder than it had to be?

'Put the sparrowhawk on,' he said, reaching for the remote. 'Why do you always get to choose what we watch?'

She snatched it away, held it out of reach. He still reached for it, tipping his champagne on her in the process. She shrieked and grabbed the bottle and began to shake it up. He made another lunge for the remote. He ended up sprawled across her chest, where he could see she wasn't wearing anything under the scruffy T-shirt. He caught her eye and thought he saw that look again. Wondered what would happen next.

A phone rang. His phone. He sat up and reached for it in his pocket. 'It's Elizabeth,' he said. He tried to calm his beating heart before answering. Wondered what he'd say.

'I'll get it,' said Roisin, snatching the phone from him. 'I'll just tell her that you're in bed with me, soaked in champagne.'

'No,' said Jim, reaching to get it back.

'Why not?' She danced across the room.

He chased her. She was ducking and weaving. He lunged for her. She laughed, bit him on the neck. The phone stopped ringing.

She threw it at him, went and sat demurely on the bed. He wondered if the bite would leave a mark.

'Come back to bed.'

'You would have said it, wouldn't you?'

'Said what? The truth?'

He was still standing. 'You don't want me to be happy.'

'I do,' she said quietly.

'Because you're not,' he persisted.

'I am,' she said. 'You may not like it, but I am.'

He sat back on the bed, pushing a bank of cushions between them, looking resolutely at the screen and not at her, although he couldn't have said what was on it.

'You don't have to stay with her.' He froze. The words were so near to what he was thinking that for a moment he thought he had said them. It was like coming up to the surface, the shock of air after water, realising that it was actually Roisin who had spoken.

'You don't like Elizabeth.'

'It doesn't matter. You think that just because you like lots of different people, they all have to like each other. They don't.'

'She's my girlfriend. And you're my – You're very important to me.'

'You don't like Melissa.'

'Nor do you.'

'I like this.' Roisin waved her arm.

'There's more to life than cushions,' he said.

'Yes. Like property. Security. You said it yourself.'

'But not at the cost of –'

'What? Love? You've sacrificed your career for a basement. At least I'm getting a townhouse apartment.'

He knew it wasn't true. What Roisin craved from Melissa wasn't material. It was Melissa's sense of belonging.

She was deeply embedded in her family, her profession, her team, her school, even the nation's minor aristocracy. She belonged everywhere, because it never occurred to her not to. While Roisin was forever cursed – wanting to be embraced by the group, but refusing to bend or change to fit in.

And what Roisin wanted from him had nothing to do with sex. She wanted him to be her best friend.

'I'd better go,' he said.

'Go then,' she said. She didn't look at him, just frowned intently at the screen. She looked suddenly very small in that sea of cushions. She flicked channels again till she found the sparrowhawk. It was in a suburban garden plucking at the breast of a blue tit. A sonorous voiceover intoned that we shouldn't judge it, it was only doing what it had evolved to do.

He thought of what Elizabeth had said, that he'd fallen out with Edie because it was safe to do so.

'I'll make coffee,' he said.

Fifty-five

Neil woke up in the foetal position, naked and sweating whisky, wondering for a moment if he'd been kidnapped and beaten and left tied up in a sack. No. He was back at Maud's, in the built-in cupboard he used as a wardrobe. Those aches in his abdomen and groin were a protest from his sadly-neglected shagging muscles. And that was his limp, sticky penis cleaving to his thigh.

Somewhere between putting her knickers on and tidying up the CD case he'd left on the floor Lisa had mumbled something about checking on Tom and had disappeared upstairs. He sat and waited but she didn't come back down. Was he supposed to follow her up there? Or did she want him to leave? It hadn't even occurred to him to consider what *he* wanted.

When he fantasised about Elizabeth, his body was as young and lithe and responsive as hers. But in reality he had a tired fortyish, okay, nearly fiftyish body. He didn't know that he had the energy to start again. And there would be a certain comfort in going back to Lisa, who didn't expect – or particularly want – athleticism and passion, who wouldn't mind – or even notice – the additional inch on his belly.

He thought it was like being on holiday and you're offered an upgrade to a better room but you can't be bothered packing up all your stuff and getting your suitcases and the kids and the bags of manky beachtowels and sticky pop bottles into the lift.

A voice that might have been Maud pointed out that he hadn't actually been offered the upgrade. Elizabeth seemed to be getting on okay with Jim. Before he could digest that she asked archly why they would offer you an upgrade halfway through the holiday?

I don't know. Maybe someone's turned up who was in your room on their honeymoon and they want it again. Or maybe someone wants two rooms next door. Maybe when you first arrived you reported the poor quality of tiling and lack of water pressure in the shower but now you've pretty much got used to them.

He used to like hiding out in the wardrobe when he was a kid. Practising for a coffin perhaps. He'd found his vocation without even knowing it. Mum used to go mad, said it was dangerous.

Wrapping himself in the floor-length skirt of Mum's best dress. She wore it to Dad's works' dinner dance. Her perfume, slightly stale, the softness of it on his face. What was it? Surely not silk – probably one of those synthetic materials which were the latest thing then. The dress was still there long after Dad had done a runner.

Maud laughed. Not the Stephanie Cole Maud

but the Maud in the picture who had put down her paints and was looking at him.

You haven't even tried! It would be just like you to let inertia stop you having the room you always wanted. It might have had a jacuzzi!

Fifty-six

She was getting in, into the water, swimming out, swimming further, not stopping. There were waves, big waves. It was better to get under. It was quiet under the water. Like crawling under a big duvet. No waves, movement, nothing hitting you. No sound. She came up. Waves breaking over her head. Breathe! But water filled her mouth as she reached out.

Fifty-seven

His head was in her lap. She could see his face.

'Oh it's you,' said Fraser between gasps. Brenda had half-dragged, half-floated him onto the beach. 'Last time I saw you I got wet too.'

'What?'

'At the opening.'

'Oh,' she said. 'I didn't think you recognised me.'

She thought how normal this all seemed, even though Prince was shaking himself dry and panting next to them and he wasn't the wettest or the one who was panting most of the three of them.

'Are you okay?' she asked.

'Yes, fucking marvellous. At least I was until you and Lassie showed up.'

'You were trying to kill yourself,' she said.

'Well, I wasn't trying to perfect my butterfly stroke.'

Brenda moved away from him and threw up. Except it wasn't really vomit. Just salty water. The whole of her felt salty, inside her nose, her throat, her lungs, in her head. A burning sensation. A tingling. Like she was in the sea and the sea was in her. She was alive!

'Sorry,' she said.

'You're more ill than me,' he said sulkily, lifting his head from the sand. His fringe was matted rather than floppy. Paula had told her that you could buy a spray now, to make your hair look like you'd been in the sea.

'I swam till I was beyond the waves,' he said. 'Then I stopped. I thought, you can't stop. You either keep going or you swim back. But I couldn't decide. It was like tossing a coin. I just thought I'd wait and see what happened.' He sighed. 'The smallest decisions are always the hardest to make.'

She looked out at the horizon. It was just getting light so the sea and the sky were the same soft grey.

'You were going under,' she said. 'I couldn't let that happen again.'

'You're very phlegmatic.'

'I haven't got a tissue. I'll call an ambulance.' She knew how this worked, she'd done it before. She looked for her jacket, which was further up the beach where she'd thrown it before going in.

'Don't. They'll put me in a psychiatric ward. Have you seen those people?'

He smiled. She thought it was a joke of some kind. She put on the jacket and her sandals.

'If you won't have an ambulance then you'll have to come home with me,' she said. She waited for him to argue but he said nothing. He just stood up.

They walked from the beach and turned up the main road. There was no one around so Brenda left Prince off the lead. Fraser kept pace with her at first, then dropped back.

'Is it far to the car?'

'We're walking,' she said.

'Walking? Do people still do that? My car's in the car park.'

Brenda was suddenly anxious. 'You'll get a fine if you leave it.'

'Don't worry, I'm paid up till midday.'

'Why –' she began, but there was no point in going further. She just laughed, and when she looked, he was laughing too. Or maybe choking or bringing up brine. It didn't matter, she laughed anyway.

'People like you, you're sort of like dogs,' said Fraser, between mouthfuls of toast. She'd offered him jam and he'd asked for marmalade before finally settling on butter.

'Oh,' said Brenda. She'd talked to him, coming up the hill, to fill the early morning silence. Talked about Bob, because that was the only bit of what she'd been thinking she could explain. Not Bob so much as the lack of Bob. He didn't seem to be listening but that made it easier to talk.

'You're lucky. You see the world in black and white.'

'I used to think things were simple,' Brenda agreed.

'No!' he said impatiently. 'I'm not speaking

metaphorically. I mean monochrome, or maybe greyscale. You've no sense of beauty or passion. Even your tragedies are banal. They run along the same, well-worn narrative path. Meanwhile you worry about what to have for tea or look forward to what's on TV. That's your entire emotional range.'

'Well,' said Brenda.

'But it's not a bad thing!' said Fraser. 'I envy you your little life. I mean, you're not the one who's just tried to kill yourself.'

'No.'

'But perhaps that's because you've never been truly alive.'

They were both silent for a while.

'It's not true,' said Brenda finally. 'That dogs can only see in black and white.' Paula read it in a magazine. They can see blue and yellow. And yet most dog toys you bought were red or orange.

He was wearing some of Bob's old clothes which she'd made him put on after a shower. She hadn't had one yet, just changed into her spare dog-walking kit while he was in the bathroom. Still salty, but she hadn't wanted to leave him. Salt coming out of every pore, it seemed, like her body was working to push it all out, keeping her alive.

'Whereas Maud must have felt regret. To be part of this world of art, to give it up to be –'

'Ordinary,' said Brenda.

'I've always been successful,' he said sadly. 'Academically, socially...Women always want to have sex with me, even though I ignore them and make them feel like nothing – in fact *because* I ignore them and make them feel like nothing. I even won trophies for swimming at school.'

'Perhaps you'd have been better cutting your wrists,' said Brenda.

'None of it was enough. Because I couldn't be an artist. The best I could manage was to hang around true artists. But then I'm the one who's being ignored and made to feel like nothing. And I'm the one who can't walk away.'

Brenda guessed that now would not be a good time to say, it's only a picture.

'Of course, finding the long-lost Bonnington wouldn't make me an artist, but it would make me part of his story. Not just an outsider looking in.'

'It's only a picture,' she said.

'I envy you,' he said. 'You're nobody. But you don't even care. You don't want to achieve anything, do you? You're like a cow chewing the cud. You don't think or do. You just are.'

Perhaps he was right. She didn't want to do things or get things. She just lived in fear of losing what she had.

'You have no concept of the scope of history. You live in the moment.'

She was trapped in the moment. She had to expand to fill a moment, she had to be a moment, knowing that there was another and another and another moment to follow and no way to escape.

Was her mum in the moment? Was she forever in another moment, one long forgotten by everyone else, but happening like new to her? Like Brenda. Over and over she'd walked up the hill, opened the door, and seen Bob was gone. Then over and over she'd opened that letter. Words swimming before her eyes, apart from one line that stood apart from the rest. 'Redemption sum: £87,234.47.'

'I owe a lot of money,' she told Fraser.

'Doesn't everyone?' He yawned and belched salt. Or perhaps it was the smell of her own skin, glowing. She was nothing to him, she realised. Her life, her feelings, her pins and needles were nothing. And then they were nothing to her. Her head felt light, free. She could breathe.

She laughed and he looked at her, smiling now. 'So, what did you spend it on? Clearly not plastic surgery. I can't see you drinking or keeping a toy boy. Perhaps you have hidden depths after all.'

There was a shape outside the window, caught in the corner of her eye, so quick that when she turned her head it was gone. Prince was at the door, whining and rolling on his back. Brenda heard a scratching sound and Prince pissed into the air.

'It's Bob,' she said.

Fifty-eight

Brenda unlocked the door.

She faced Bob across a fountain of urine. Prince's tail was thrashing. He got up and jumped at Bob, tail still going, whining in a frenzy. She turned and went to sit back at the table.

'Mind you don't slip in that piss,' were her first words to him.

Bob stood and stared straight ahead, as if he couldn't look her in the eye and was trying to find the right words to –

'He hasn't done a bad job I suppose. Tony. Although there was nothing wrong with it in the first place.'

Of course. Builders talk. Not Robbie or Tony, obviously, but the rest of them, at the Dormouse Café at lunchtime, or in Dormouth Building Supplies in the morning where they supposedly went because they'd run out of decorator's caulk or raised-head screws but really they just wanted to know who was up to what.

'I couldn't get my key to work.' He was shaking his head, as if this were more important than anything else that had happened.

She'd left her key in the lock overnight. Paula said it would make it harder for someone to break in. She didn't bother to tell him. Let him think it was like the front door lock, which he'd kept saying he'd fix but never did, which Robbie had finally done when he was gone.

She was on one side of the room with Fraser and the man who looked like Bob was on the other. She liked that Fraser was still here, beside her, as if they were the jury on *X Factor* and Bob was auditioning.

Bob had torn his eyes away from the wall now and turned them on Fraser.

'Bit early for visitors,' he said.

'Yes it *is*, rather,' said Fraser.

Bob shifted from foot to foot. 'I'm working just down the road. I've got a job on for Richard Connell. He's extending again.'

Bob stroked Prince. She wondered what he was waiting for. She felt calm suddenly, totally unbothered by what was happening in front of her. She watched Bob's face get redder. Then he gave a little exclamation of outrage. 'He's wearing my clothes!'

'I'd hardly have chosen them myself,' said Fraser.

I bought those clothes, thought Brenda.

Fraser got up. 'I'll return them. Freshly laundered, of course. Now, if you'll excuse me, it appears I have a life to lead.'

As he headed for the door he stopped in front of Bob. 'It *is* quite an unmemorable face, isn't it?'

When he'd gone, Bob said, 'Who does he think he is?'

She was going to explain, was going to begin, he's not himself, but then she thought, what does that mean? Perhaps he's more himself now than he's ever been. Whereas I – am I more or less myself than when I lay side by side in bed with Bob, in the home that I thought was ours forever?

She didn't even know what she wanted to say. Her right temple was throbbing and she wanted to go to the toilet. She wanted to tell him to come back later, when she was ready for this, but she thought if she said that he might not come back at all.

'I'll make tea,' she said.

'I'm alright,' he said.

'I'm not.' She put the kettle on. He wandered into the living room, Prince following. The calm of a few moments ago had left her, as if Fraser had taken it with her. Fraser who had just been trying to drown himself had sauntered out of the room while she –

She had to sit down. Going. As if she was melting away, so she no longer knew what was her and what was the house. Was that what drowning was like? Paula said we were seventy per cent water. That was why she always carried a bottle with her. Water inside, water outside, floating all at once -

'What's wrong with you?'

She'd been dreaming. For such a long time, she thought. Prince nuzzled her. Bob stared.

She thought he was going to shake her. He wasn't concerned, he was angry. It was always like this. Just as well she was hardly ever ill because the odd time she'd had the flu it was like she'd done it to spite him.

Just as suddenly, her head cleared. She sat up straight in the chair. She'd been lying with her head on the table. 'I might have fainted. I do that sometimes.'

She was pleased with the way she'd said it. This is my life, that you know nothing about. I might wear lipstick (she didn't) or go to bars (she hadn't) or sometimes I might pass out and what's it to you?

He sat down beside her. 'I suppose we've both been through it, haven't we?'

'All the times I tried to call you. You ignored me. Like I didn't exist –'

But he had something he wanted to say. 'I should have told you about it, I see that now. I've been miserable, I can tell you. But I've come to tell you, it's all worked out.'

'The loan.' The loan he took out in her name. Without telling her.

'That's what I'm saying, everything's sorted.'

'Sorted?' She didn't understand.

'John Hannam had a chance to buy a bit of land. A great prospect, he said. But I couldn't get a business loan and the bank wanted security.'

'So you used our house.'

'I knew I could pay the loan, so it wasn't a problem.'

She'd found the letter one night when she was tidying. He hadn't hidden it very well. She should have asked him, argued with him but she couldn't do it. The words wouldn't come. When she tried to say them, even think what she would say, she felt like she was being choked.

She put the letter with his flask so he'd know she'd seen it. She lay awake all night while he slept. She got up early and walked Prince. Then she found the woman and came rushing home. She wanted to be with someone, someone alive. She'd forgotten about the letter. Till she found he'd gone.

'Then we didn't get planning permission, and business was quieter than I'd hoped and so I borrowed a bit on credit cards to make the payments.'

'More debt,' she said.

'I did it so I could pay *your* loan,' he said.

'How can it be my loan?'

'It doesn't matter now,' he said. He sounded impatient. 'The point is, John made some changes to the planning application and the council passed it. It's politics he reckons, they're under pressure to build more homes. He's offered to buy out my share. To be honest, with all the interest and the legal costs, I'll barely break even, I'd be better off hanging onto it, but if it's what you want I'll do it. I'll come back, then we'll pay off the loan and go back to how we were.'

She could go back to being Brenda. Predictable, reliable Brenda. You'd find her on the checkout, or in the aisles if they were quiet, Tuesday, Thursday and Saturday. Pretty much always, because she didn't like to swap her shifts. She might do it as a favour if you pushed her, but she liked a bit of notice. She didn't like surprises.

'Wait a minute. Are you saying you'll only sell the land if we get back together?'

'Well – yes.' He took her hand. 'Bren. You know it was always my dream to be a developer. But I'll give it up for you, if that's what you want.'

He looked her in the eye then, and for a moment she saw her husband, the man who saved her from the waves, who took her in his arms. Then he was gone.

He let go of her hand. 'But if I can't have you, I've no reason to give up the land as well.'

'How will you pay the loan? It's already in arrears and –'

'The loan will be paid when we sell the house. You can't expect me to keep paying for this place if we're not together. You have to be reasonable.'

'Reasonable! You stole from me!'

'Don't be daft! We're married.'

'You acted like I wasn't there.'

'Like you've done to me all these years. Every time I had an idea you didn't want to take the risk. Play it safe. Never mind me.'

Was that true? It couldn't be. Everything she'd done had been for the family. For the house.

'For once I could be someone,' he said, like he was pleading.

She thought about the future for the first time. She was afraid of losing her home. She was afraid of being poor. She was afraid of so many things.

But Fraser had paid her a strange sort of compliment. She saw it now. She'd got something he hadn't. She wanted to live her ordinary life.

'I'll pay off the loan,' she said. 'When I sell the house.'

Fifty-nine

Teri was packing away her Best Mum in the World mug (Neil suspected she'd bought it herself) and the mug with a picture of her husband on it which she kept hidden in her bottom drawer in case anyone eligible walked in (the fact that much of their passing trade consisted of recently bereaved septuagenarians being no barrier) and her hand cream and spare lipstick and low-calorie hot-chocolate sachets and cute cat pictures and body spray and wipes and an unopened box of green tea and sundry pink plastic items with no discernible function other than to look sweet and make a middle-aged woman in her workplace think she was a pre-teen girl in her bedroom 'personalising her space' and a couple of rolls of office sellotape and a handful of window envelopes.

No doubt she felt they owed her but as theft from employer went it was a pretty weak attempt. A mate of his had once made off with a whole pallet of toilet rolls when he was doing a summer job in a warehouse. Kept his shared house in Leeds going for a year. And going. How they'd laughed!

Her eyes were red and she was sniffling and dabbing at her nose ineffectually with a tissue. Probably weed pollen or that new mascara which she'd told her mates (several of them, at length, on the work phone) was scientifically proven to make your eyelashes grow longer and thicker.

Neil was usually a sucker for women who cried. It was Lisa 1's fierce refusal to show any weakness that had done for them. Lisa 2 would shed hot, angry tears while refusing to admit that she was doing so. It was this combination of strength and vulnerability that was irresistible to him. Teri, however, remained unappealing, with eyeliner streaked to her chin and a histrionically heaving cleavage.

Of course he knew she'd been placed 'at risk' of redundancy. It seemed everyone was at risk these days, except, strangely, him. But he'd been convinced she'd get redeployed. That she'd find herself where she'd always wanted to be, in the Drawbridge head office, slowly dessicating in the air conditioning, making her presence felt in the refreshment suite (please do not hold meetings here outside core time). She'd have been happy, entombed in plasterboard and concrete, she always felt uneasy here with the fresh air and rough stone and the whisper of slowly decaying paper.

But no, it seemed she was losing her job. And her husband was coming home from Somalia. There'd be nothing for it but to face him across the high-gloss breakfast bar. All day.

Neil supposed that to someone whose mind

was attuned to the mysteries of the infinite universe, his misdemeanours were almost invisible. That was the only explanation he had for Malcolm's intervention on his behalf. He still had his job, although he had lost responsibility for public health funerals which were going to a new interdepartmental team encompassing housing and environmental health. To compensate for this reduced workload they had had to identify savings in staff costs.

Teri opened another drawer of delights. Her face crumpled, as if overwhelmed, turning from its trademark burnt orange to the colour of an out-of-date strawberry smoothie.

'I've got a bag for life, if that helps,' he said. 'It's only had ashes in it.'

She glared at him but didn't answer.

He stood, wondering what he should say. Should he have organised some kind of collection? Prepared a suitable form of words? He cleared his throat but she spoke first.

'What is it about you? You always land on your feet.'

'I suppose I do,' he said, tumbling through space. 'But you always said you'd be glad to be out of here.'

'You're such a wanker!' she said.

All in all, it was a fitting end.

Given the atmosphere in the chapel, Neil decided to take a walk to Drawbridge Towers. He found himself trying to come up with a plausible excuse. (Return to work interview? Managers' meeting?)

Then he realised he didn't have to tell Teri anything any more.

In other circumstances he might have felt euphoric, but as he walked out of the chapel he noticed how the path that led to the cemetery gate was cracked and uneven, pushed up by tree roots. Someone had made a sloppy attempt at a repair which had only made matters worse.

People regularly complained that it made the path very difficult to negotiate for wheelchairs, prams and mobility scooters. He'd sympathised of course, added it to a list for discussion with Direct Works, but now he actually knew what they meant. He felt a little wave of fury run through him. This was something else he was going to have to care about.

When he stuck his head round the door of Malcolm's office, he seemed to be packing too. In Malcolm's box there was a satsuma, a paperback copy of Kierkegaard's Either/Or and a set of nail clippers. Malcolm was staring into the box, perhaps contemplating that the universe is largely made up of empty space. Or perhaps he just wished he'd brought a smaller one.

'You going too?' asked Neil. He'd understood the reorganisation of higher management was a carefully choreographed affair, designed to make the lower orders think that everyone was feeling the pain, while what was actually happening was that a couple of people were being offered lucrative early-retirement packages, while the remaining managers played musical chairs and ended up sitting in largely similar jobs with enhanced remuneration.

Malcolm sighed. 'It seems people feel my skills are more suited to a – strategic role.'

'I can see that might be the case,' said Neil. 'A man of your intellect. But I'll miss you. Who's taking your place?'

'Anne Lister.'

This was not good news for Neil. Anne was a quantity surveyor by trade, known to have a fierce eye for detail, and there was something in the set of her jaw which reminded him of Lisa 1.

'I just need to finalise my budget for this quarter. I still have some money left in a suspense account. We managed to make some efficiencies. The balance ends in a three. It seems untidy somehow. But I suppose it's for her to decide.'

'I know what you mean,' said Neil, peering over his shoulder at the digits that preceded the three. A nice five-figure sum. 'You'd want her to start with a clean desk and a clear mind.'

'But what to do?' Malcolm's eyebrows coalesced into concern.

Neil had an idea. 'What's the most complained about issue in the Public Realm remit?'

'Is this from *QI*?' asked Malcolm.

'No, it's from the Environmental Health customer service phone log.'

Malcolm still looked perplexed.

'Seagulls,' Neil said.

'Seagulls?'

'Well, actually it's potholes but they're dealt with at county level.'

'Seagulls,' said Malcolm again.

'I know of a consultant who's been working on this very issue. I'm sure this money would be sufficient to set up a project. And then, next year, if all goes well, maybe further funding can be found, perhaps at a strategic level.'

'But shouldn't the money go on something more – important? Improving the housing stock maybe?'

'Not your remit, Malcolm. Besides most people don't live in council housing. And of those that do, only a proportion have problems with damp or leaky windows. So a small number of children suffer from chest infections and asthma because of where they live. Who cares? While everyone gets pissed off with seagulls. So that's what gets in the papers and on the local news. That's what gets people ringing up or flaming the council's Facebook page. That's democracy.'

'Ah, the Athenian ideal,' said Malcolm. 'I suppose one must – he won't mind about the three?'

'I'm sure he won't,' said Neil.

Sixty

The auctioneer was young but his face was old. And his suit. Jim wasn't exactly up on fashion but even he thought it was like something Bert would pick out. Still, he was impressed by the way he held the attention of everyone in the auction room, as they bid for a pair of china figurines.

Elizabeth seemed to be watching intently so he didn't like to interrupt, even though he'd just got off the train, so he hadn't had a chance to talk. But then the words popped out, 'I'm not going to the wedding.'

'I'll have to go on my own then.'

'But you hardly know her!'

'And you hardly know me, it seems.'

Something moved in the corner of Jim's eye. Clothes too big for their inhabitant. But still, he felt a pang of recognition. After years of birdwatching, you could identify a bird by its jizz before you could make out any distinctive features. This was the same feeling.

'Oh God,' said Jim.

'What is it?'

'Fraser in loungewear.'

Elizabeth laughed. 'Surely not.' She turned. 'It is!'

'Ladies and gentlemen,' said the auctioneer. He had the round vowels and stolid servility of an under-footman in *Downton Abbey*.

'What about lords?' asked Jim.

'The next item is a painting in oil on canvas, part of the estate of the late Maud Smith, sometime associate of local artist Hugh Bonnington, unattributed by ourselves, but many of our esteemed patrons may notice distinctive features in the technique.'

'That's Dickensian for nudge-nudge, wink-wink,' said Jim.

'Concentrate,' said Elizabeth. 'But don't bid till near the end.'

'Why don't you do it?'

'Because everyone here knows I haven't got any money. It'll make them suspicious.'

'Whereas I'm a well-known connoisseur.'

'No, you're a visitor who they think they can stitch up because he doesn't know any better.'

The price was going up steadily, and then there was a pause. Surely this was the point to make his move?

'Wait,' whispered Elizabeth. 'He's taking bids off the wall.'

'What do you mean?'

'There's no one bidding. He's making up bids to get things going.'

'Did you learn that at art school?'

'No. *Homes under the Hammer*.'

'I thought you didn't watch daytime TV,' he said.

'Are you still annoyed because I said I hadn't seen *Heir Hunters*?'

'What do you mean, you *said* you hadn't?'

People were looking round the room. There was a low murmur.

'I don't have to tell you everything,' she said.

He looked at her. 'No, I suppose not.'

The auctioneer had stopped without losing his composure and started again at five hundred pounds.

'You were right,' said Jim. 'Is that even legal?'

'Apparently.'

The bidding continued with some momentum up to two thousand, ably assisted by the auctioneer. During bidding he was quite transformed, leading the crowd like the maestro of an orchestra.

The bidding slowed. Jim was getting ready for his big moment when he saw Fraser out of the corner of his eye.

Fraser was looking at them both. There was a look on his face, of realisation. He can't know, thought Jim. But he could suspect. Jim had visions of them bidding against each other to the end, till one of them fell into financial ruin. The room receded, Jim felt all eyes on him as he lifted his hand. There was a bid from someone else. Jim bid again. He looked at Fraser, a look of challenge. But Fraser just nodded vaguely. Suddenly it was all over.

Jim had got the picture for three thousand pounds, rather less than the maximum Olive had allowed. He felt like he'd just won an Oscar. Or at least a Nobel Prize.

'I suppose you have to sign something,' said Elizabeth. 'They never show this bit on TV.'

As they pushed through the crowd they passed Fraser. He seemed to have shrunk, or perhaps he was just lost in the over-large burgundy polo shirt and the navy jogging bottoms which ballooned like harem pants over a pair of highly polished tan loafers. Jim felt a moment of compassion for his old adversary, seeing him brought so low.

'Dr McKendrie,' he said.

'Dr Jackson,' Fraser said.

'I'll take good care of her,' Jim said.

Fraser nodded indifferently, then frowned and looked askance. Jim and Elizabeth walked on. Behind them, Jim could hear Fraser laughing. Hysterically. Or perhaps he was sobbing.

Sixty-one

Neil was sitting on Elizabeth's sofa while they both perched primly on the bed. They looked so good together it was making him aroused just thinking about it. Was that how he'd end up, dogging? Would that be his only relief from the joys of domestic life?

He held on fiercely to the hessian handles of his bag for life and thought wistfully about Charlotte with her London sheen which he would never now get to rub off. Lisa 2 wanted him back. Life for him from now on would be all monogamy. Wheelchair-accessible family fun.

He didn't want to let Maud go. But that was stupid. Maud's spirit wasn't in the jar, just seven pounds of ash and crushed bone.

People made much of that, the fact that the ashes of a dead person weighed approximately the same as a newborn, like you went out the way you came in, but he thought that was nonsense. Coincidence. If she'd been buried she wouldn't weigh seven pounds, or freeze-dried, or her bones pecked clean by vultures following sky burial, which was the way he'd like to go.

He'd have to ask Jim about the declining vulture populations of South Asia some time, but maybe not today.

'How's Martha?' asked Elizabeth.

'Fine,' he said, which was a stupid word to use, but there you go. He'd finally gone up in the car with Tom and Lisa 2 the weekend before.

'I've messaged her. And sent a card.'

'That's nice,' he said, 'she'll like that.' Thinking, would she? He had no idea.

They'd been on the ward when she'd glided up in a wheelchair, come from nowhere like a Bond villain. Of course it wasn't 'her' wheelchair, she hadn't yet been assessed for her own, that was all part of the rehab, along with learning to control her bladder and lifting herself in and out of bed and other things he didn't want to even imagine for his daughter, although both Lisas seemed to think it essential that he knew.

Already, there was a barrier between them. Already, she was becoming someone else, not just Martha, but Martha and wheelchair, part of a package. And she was slipping away from him. If they could have had some time alone – but she didn't have much slack in her busy schedule of physio and OT and he'd arranged to meet a mate he hadn't seen for years.

She didn't respond when he explained, or to his witty asides, not even to raise her eyes, as if he were a five-year-old saying 'fuck' and she had decided the best response was to ignore him. She had outgrown him. She was becoming a Lisa.

'I hear you bought the painting for Olive.'

'She bought it for the Trust,' said Elizabeth. 'I suppose it's just a novelty item but it might be of interest in any future gallery.'

He didn't believe a word but what did it matter now? They were all quiet. Jim and Elizabeth were waiting for him to say why he was here. Suddenly it seemed silly, grotesque even. Shouldn't he have asked first? Perhaps he could ask now, pretend he didn't have Maud with him, come back later.

But then he'd have to sit here again, perched on the edge of the sofa, while they lolled easily on the bed –

'I was wondering what to do with Maud's ashes.' It came out suddenly. 'I know her husband was cremated in Portugal. I wondered if you'd like to have them.'

'Yes,' she said.

'You're sure?'

'She scattered her husband's ashes at sea,' Elizabeth said. 'So maybe that's what we'll do.'

He was going to do his responsible cemetery manager bit and explain that they should get the permission of the landowner, but he couldn't be arsed. 'Yeah. Same sea, isn't it,' he said. 'You know, the Atlantic.'

There was a certain irony in putting her back in the place where she'd drowned. The sea had washed her up after all. Spat her out. Was it fitting or just macabre? Neil suspected that Maud would appreciate the funny side.

He supposed he should leave now, let these two get back to tearing each other's clothes off but he didn't want to go.

'There's only room for one woman in my life,' he quipped, as he took the sweet jar out of its bag. 'I'm going back to my wife. So the flat will be empty until Trevor finds some other unsuspecting victim.'

He handed the jar over. Elizabeth stepped back as she adjusted to its weight.

'It's heavier than I expected,' she said.

'About seven pounds,' he said. 'Some people say, you know, you're the same weight when you go out as when you come in.'

'There's a lovely symmetry in that,' said Elizabeth.

'Yes,' he said, and meant it, for that moment.

There seemed to be nothing else to say. He got up to go. He still hadn't mentioned seagulls. Why should he, when Jim had everything – youth, looks, wickaway technology T-shirts.

He would leave it. Go. But then he relented at the last minute.

'There might be a job going at the council soon. Habitat management. With a particular emphasis on reducing seagull populations in the town. Look out for it.'

'Thanks,' said Jim. He sounded flustered, looked at Elizabeth, who was staring rather hard at the urn. Maybe they'd be keeping their clothes on a bit longer after all.

'Good luck,' he said, as if he were leaving the country, or having a deathbed farewell, rather than moving a few hundred yards away to his own marital home. But he knew a phase of his life was over. Elizabeth was lost to him, and he was man enough to accept it.

Sixty-two

'I've never actually worked with seagulls.'

'But if you did –'

Jim didn't answer.

'I could move to London,' she said doubtfully.

'But *I* don't even want to live in London,' he said. 'And there's no room in my flat, so we'd have to rent somewhere else.'

So in one fell swoop he would be both landlord and tenant, thus becoming part of the very system he had hoped to avoid by buying the basement in the first place. His head ached at the prospect and it took him a moment to realise what Elizabeth had said.

'You'd move to be with me?'

'Of course. But I'm not going to give up on being an artist. I know one day other things might become more important but I'm not there yet.'

'I wouldn't expect you to.' Jim didn't know what she'd be doing at thirty or forty or fifty. He just knew he wanted to be around to find out.

'There will be other jobs,' he said. 'In other places. I think I've been stuck. I couldn't get the job

I really wanted, but I didn't want to admit that it was time to give up and look for something else. I think it is now.'

And of course, Roisin had made it far too easy for him to stay. Even letting him go gallivanting across the West Country in the pool car.

'I wish I could be sure like you,' he went on. 'I'm just treading water, about my career, about Roisin –'

'I don't want you to break with Roisin because of me.'

'She behaved so badly towards you, and I should have stood up to her.'

'That's in the past. We've both done things, but they're gone.'

What things? he thought. He could ask now about Fraser or he could let it go. Now. Forever.

'I can't be a little bit friends with Roisin. It's all or nothing.'

'Look at Maud and Olive,' she said. 'Maud wanted to see her but she felt she couldn't back down, even decades later.'

'I thought you made that up,' he said.

'I'm not sure.' She looked thoughtful. 'It seems so –'

'Possible?'

'True. I know it intuitively.'

'Your intuition might be wrong.'

Elizabeth hugged Maud's jar – he might say hugged Maud herself – close.

'It's funny,' he said. 'Olive made up the story to boost Hugh's career. But it meant that Maud would always have a place in Hugh's myth. She would always be the one who broke his heart. Far more exciting than a mere wife.'

'Exactly,' said Elizabeth.

'Exactly what?'

'Why does everything have to be true or not true? There's a God, there isn't a God, Maud had regrets, she didn't have regrets, you're not speaking to your sister, you're not not speaking to your sister.'

He realised he'd been wrong all along. He'd thought that Elizabeth's serenity meant she was the safe option. But she threw all his certainties into disarray. He'd never have thought she'd lie so effortlessly to Neil. He had no idea what she was talking about that was in the past (though he could guess). He'd thought she'd want him to break with Roisin and she didn't.

She was right (or she was not, or both). He didn't know what was true and what wasn't.

The safe thing would be to keep running round after high-maintenance women. Elizabeth offered him a different challenge. She made him stop and think. And this intuition thing was nonsense, of course. But he understood now, being with Elizabeth would bring him security and not security, a bit like the basement.

His phone rang. 'You're not not psychic,' he said. 'It's Edie.'

Sixty-three

It was Thursday, Paula's night. She'd come straight from work, still in her suit. She'd been running a course for new recruits. She said she didn't want tea, she'd eaten from the buffet, a couple of tray-bake rocky roads and some spring-onion dip.

She looked tired, rings under the eyes and shoulders high, as if they had to work to hold the suit in place. She'd been planning to go through the boxes Robbie had got down from the attic but she got a cappuccino and a chocolate biscuit and sank into an armchair. Prince made a half-hearted attempt to get in her lap but when she pushed him gently away he sat quietly at her feet.

'Me and Callum,' she said, 'we've decided to try for a baby.'

'That's good news,' said Brenda, though she didn't want to think about her own daughter 'trying'. Then she did a row of rib stitch and thought about it properly. A baby?

How did anyone dare to have a baby? When she'd done it she'd been too young to know better, but now she thought of all the things that could happen to that baby. Maybe one day that baby would be walking into the sea.

'We always planned to wait until we'd got a house. But that might never happen.' Her face dropped, but maybe she was just tired.

You had a baby and you thought it was perfect, but it just grew up to be a person like all the other people. One day that baby would be as old as her and maybe it too would forget how to breathe. 'I'm glad for you,' she said.

'It hasn't happened yet!' laughed Paula. 'I'll want to keep working though. Not just for the money, but because I like it. Especially now I'm doing this training. I think I can really get on. I'm good with people.'

Changing the subject, not making a big thing of it. Well, Brenda could do that too.

'I suppose,' she said, needles still clacking in their quiet rhythm, 'the new people have to learn all about security. Like if someone rings up about their account they have to give them the right details before they'll tell them anything.'

'Of course,' said Paula.

'And if the account was in a woman's name, it would have to be a woman who rang. You wouldn't speak to a man, even if he said he was ringing for her, or had her permission.'

Paula had been sucking the chocolate from her biscuit. She put it down now, next to her cappuccino.

'I didn't want to do it. But he said if I just phoned up for the redemption figure, then he could pay the loan off.'

'Why didn't you say anything?'

'Because you never do. You don't like to talk about things, do you?'

'But I thought you were angry with me for borrowing the money!'

'I was angry because you didn't trust me,' said Paula.

'You were angry because I let him,' said Brenda. 'You think I should have gone to the police.' That was what Robbie had said when she told him. Shouted even. As if he was making up for years of silence. Only he'd said it all to her, not his dad.

Paula looked tearful. 'I know he's done wrong. I know if it was at work and someone phoned up in this situation I'd tell her exactly what to do. Report it to the police. He's used you, don't be a mug. But – but he's my dad!'

'So you couldn't have done it, but you think I should.'

'I know it doesn't make sense. But that's how I feel.'

'But what would you do? If it were Callum –'

'Oh, Callum would never do anything like that,' said Paula, picking up her biscuit. She sucked on it until it broke and crumbs went over her jacket. Brenda kept on knitting.

Sixty-four

Neil waited on the seafront, sitting on the wall. *Paseo* time. He loved that time in Spain. Thought of when they went to Málaga, the year before Tom was born. Lisa wanted to see the Picasso Museum.

Shagging and sleeping through the afternoon, getting up in the evening, the city just coming to life. Strolling along the Calle Larios, soaking up the atmosphere. People in cafés, shops, on the street. Just for the joy of being there.

There wasn't much of a *paseo* in Dormouth.

Why here? No doubt she wanted to have a talk about ground rules. Didn't want him to waltz straight in. Would lay down some conditions. Suddenly he balked at it all.

Whatever it was, he wouldn't mean it, and she would know he didn't mean it, and they would carry on the same dance as before. He thought about the flat and his packed bags and the quiet there. And the non-existent bond that Lisa was expecting him to collect.

Then he thought about Lisa in Málaga, walking along the seafront in the moonlight, her hand in his, seeming so small suddenly, and fragile, and her so trusting that he would love her and not harm her.

Lisa appeared, as if by magic, Tom running along ahead of her. He ran into Neil and hugged his legs. Neil and Lisa exchanged glances, the child of their love between them. The perfect family scene, as their eyes locked and they realised everything was going to be okay, except Lisa looked away and her eyes seemed to tear up. Probably just the bracing sea breeze.

'So,' he said. 'You wanted to talk.'

We need to talk. That was what she'd said on the phone. That staple of soap operas. It cropped up roughly once every two-and-a-half episodes. He'd done his own survey. Incredulous. Thinking, no one says that in real life. And then she had. We need to talk.

For someone who wanted to talk, she was strangely silent. He had a sense of déjà vu. Had they lived through this scene before, or was it a flashback from a long-forgotten episode of *EastEnders?* Lisa filling up, while Tom ran happy and oblivious around them, trying to pick up a scrunched-up chip paper that was caught by the breeze.

'I know we talked about it,' she said, 'but I've decided it would be a mistake. I don't want you to come home.'

He looked at her, incredulous. Maybe not as much as when he'd been watching the soaps, but still.

'I've packed,' he said. He'd even thrown out the half-empty tub of economy margarine and the out-of-date coleslaw that were the sole contents of the fridge. The margarine had toast crumbs in it and Lisa hated that.

He'd been rekindling his love affair with toast, recalling his student days and the great cultural awakening that had been university life. Where he came from, the only things you had on toast were marge and, if you were lucky, jam (maybe cheese if it was a main meal). He'd moved into an exalted social scene where he'd discovered Marmite, hummus, tahini.

He'd even tried cashew-nut butter but that was beyond his meagre budget, although thinking about it, one jar cost about as much as a pint. Now you could even get tahini in supermarkets (though not in Dormouth, you had to go the health food shop).

Her eyes were filling up. It jolted him into recalling what she'd just said. He knew he needed to concentrate, to get this right, but all he could think was that her chin was juddering a bit. She looked the way actors did in the big scenes. He always wondered how actors made the tears come. Now he was wondering why she was holding them back. He shook his head bitterly.

Chocolate and hazelnut spread, he remembered. Posh stuff from France. Not the claggy stuff you got over here that stuck to your tongue. Someone must have brought it back from holiday. He still remembered the taste. It was something to hang onto, now the ground was giving way beneath him.

'So it wasn't a pity fuck, it was a farewell fuck.'

'What?'

'I misread the signals,' he said, almost to himself, incredulous. There was a pain growing in his chest, radiating outwards. But he never misread the signals. 'I never do that,' he said. 'I have my faults but that isn't one of them.'

'You've had plenty of practice,' she said.

'So? What's changed? Since the other day?'

'You haven't taken responsibility for what happened, have you?'

'You said I shouldn't feel guilty!'

'Only because I thought you did. Anyway, responsibility and guilt are not the same thing. Responsibility means you do something about it.'

'We can get through this,' he said. One to him on the soap bingo. He was going to add, 'for the children,' but he knew he'd never keep a straight face.

'It's not me that's changed,' she said. 'It's Martha.'

He laughed. 'If you make this sacrifice, she'll walk again?'

'Who said it was a sacrifice? Who said it's *my* sacrifice?'

More ping-pong. He didn't bother responding.

'I'd have taken you back,' said Lisa. 'We'd have gone through the whole game again.'

He knew he should be listening, that this was important, that Lisa would want him to look suitably engaged and even moved, but he was intrigued by watching a woman stop and pick up her dog mess in a bag, and then leave it on the sea wall.

'What's the point of that?' he said.

'Some people do that,' said Lisa. 'Saves carrying it all along their walk. They pick it up on the way back.'

'Except they don't.' He was suddenly furious. 'I see those little bags everywhere. It's like a shit treasure hunt. At least the shit's biodegradable if you leave it. While if you bag it up and leave it, shit and bag will be there for years –'

She was speaking. She was speaking slowly and clearly, like she would to a difficult patient.

'Martha said she wouldn't have anything to do with us if I took you back.'

Sixty-five

Brenda hadn't been back to the new house since first viewing it. She'd tried not to think about it. When she'd been in before with Robbie, she'd seen only a damp old terraced house with sticky carpets and print wallpaper liked they'd had when she was a kid, the kind you saw faces in that gave you nightmares.

She'd told him it would be fine and to go ahead and put in an offer, whatever he thought was best.

Tony was waiting outside when she got there, although Robbie had given him a key. He waited while she unlocked the door and followed her in. There was a tiny kitchen off the side of the lounge which gave onto a small concrete yard. Robbie was talking about knocking the wall down so there'd be one room in an L-shape.

Tony showed her his sketch. He went outside to the concrete yard where the only thing growing was a buddleia which had forced its way out of a crack in the wall. He walked slowly round, measuring, sketching, looking back on himself. Then he came back in.

'South-facing,' he said, beaming.

He walked around eagerly, waving his tape measure like a wand, touching things, tapping on the walls, letting the floorboards take his weight. Like he was aware of every nail and plank that was there, but at the same time he could imagine a house, a home, her home, that didn't yet exist.

She'd been holding onto a world that got ever smaller. While he'd had everything taken away but could still see – what could he see?

Tony put his hand to the wall and was still, waiting for the house to tell him its secrets.

She put her hand over his.

Sixty-six

Neil's thumbs moved frantically, pausing only when he leant to pick his beer can off the floor and take a swig. Then, suddenly, he stopped. Leaned back in his chair, looked at the bare room. His bags were still packed but the holdall was spewing its contents where he'd opened it and rummaged before meeting Lisa, looking for deodorant and cleanish pants.

There was something inherently ridiculous about rowing by text. He'd seen Teri do it enough times with her beaux, nails clacking, that grim set to her mouth. Was there also something not quite sportsmanlike about having a virtual slanging match with your newly disabled daughter?

If only they could see each other, shout at each other, then laugh and get pissed and forget whatever it was they had said. Instead there were these polite electronic exchanges. He'd even tried the retro trick of phoning but it always went to voicemail. In the texts she was terse, always somehow about to eat or see the doctor or be taken for a bath.

He had a right to an explanation! She'd

sabotaged his future. Okay, she was upset now, was lashing out. Like Lisa 2 said, there were these phases she had to go through. She was at the anger stage, irrationally blaming him for her problems. He had to rise above it and show a calm detachment which she would come to respect in the end.

Then he had a flash of insight. She'd done it for him! Martha was right of course. He was so proud of her for seeing what he couldn't. He and Lisa would never make a go of it. Although she had a good heart, there was too much repression in her. He needed to soar. She would always want to keep him on the ground. If not under it, just yet.

Lisa would like that, he thought. Standing beside the grave which she would have conscientiously purchased and memorialised in accordance with his wishes (not that he'd expressed any, you could throw him in a skip for all he cared). She'd much prefer him dead, where he wouldn't, disobligingly, have thoughts that contradicted hers.

But now they'd split up, would she still feel responsible for the funeral? Who would? An unimaginably manly Tom? Presumably Martha would have come round by then and would do the necessary. Maybe not.

Maybe there would be no one and his public health funeral would be organised by an indifferent council official who would rummage through his things. The indifference would be soothing. No complicated emotion or fraught subtext.

He just hoped that this hypothetical individual would be impressed by his collection of collectible proto-punk vinyl. Maybe he'd help himself to his unopened picture disc of the New York Dolls' *Trashed in Paris '73* and end up with responsibility for memorial benches in the public realm as a penance. Neil wouldn't mind. Made the guy human.

He listened for the voices in his head, held his breath but there was only an insistent silence. He couldn't hear Martha or Lisa or his mother, not even Fraser's sneer. And Maud wasn't there. Seven-pound Maud.

Of course Maud was just a dead woman who he had never met. But he had the uneasy sensation that it wasn't so much that he no longer believed in Maud, as that she no longer believed in him.

Sixty-seven

Jim woke alone in his single bed. His monastic cell. He wished Elizabeth was here but she wasn't. He'd have to do this on his own.

He put on his suit with the narrow lapels and the slim-fit shirt. When he'd first tried it on he'd complained he couldn't move.

'You don't have to move,' said Roisin. 'You just have to stand up straight and look pretty, not build a dry-stone wall or chop down an oak tree.'

The thought made him smile and then he unsmiled. He hoped this would be the happiest day of someone's life because it certainly wouldn't be his.

When he got to Roisin's flat the door was opened by a woman in fake tan and rollers and not much else who shrieked and giggled as she showed him in. There were others running round in varying states of undress, painting toes and plucking eyebrows, kicking aside sleeping bags and airbeds, swearing and laughing in their singing Scouse tones.

In the living room he nodded at Joolz who, with

her cropped hair, skinny trousers and leather jacket, looked as bemused as he was by the perfume and preening.

Melissa wasn't there. Another of Roisin's traditions. She was spending the night with her family at their 'place in town'.

Time passed glacially. He and Joolz got coffees. She worked in the IT department of a major bank. They talked for a while about innovations in cloud-based data storage and he asked her about a smart watch he'd seen recently on a technology programme. Joolz could talk about this stuff for hours and it saved him having to think.

Finally Roisin appeared. The hens clucked and cooed. Joolz said, 'Fucking smart.' Roisin, for once, said nothing.

'Wow!' he said. 'You look amazing.' She wasn't wearing Elizabeth's necklace but it hardly mattered now.

She harrumphed and rearranged his tie. She was standing very close, a slight frown as she assessed it, then adjusted it again.

'What's up?' she asked.

'Your eyes look so big.' They were bigger and darker than he'd ever seen them. Like a frightened child.

'That'll be the make-up. You got the rings? And the speech?'

'Check,' he said, patting his pocket. She heard the rustle of paper but still opened her mouth to speak. She's going to ask to see them, he thought, and felt weak with anxiety. He'd never have made the French Resistance.

'Rosie,' screeched one of the Scousers, from outside on the street, 'your pumpkin awaits.'

Somewhere along the line they'd gone from taking the Tube to the wedding, to getting a taxi, to a chauffeur-driven Bentley. The rest of the party were to come in Joolz's car.

'Joolz,' said Roisin, 'round this lot up, or you'll be arriving after me. And tell Angie we're coming, and tell her to stop fucking shouting or we'll have the residents' association on our backs. Again.'

Joolz stuck her head out of the window and was presumably about to relay the message verbatim at volume when Jim called her back. 'It's okay, we'll catch her on the way.'

Angie was on the doorstep, in a tiny dress and towering wedges, chatting to a moustachioed old man in tweeds with a terrier on a lead. She held the door slightly ajar and kept her ciggy inside to stop smoke blowing towards him. Roisin waved her arm impatiently.

'It's supposed to be the other way round,' said Roisin.

'Well I'm an invert, aren't I,' said Angie, winking at the old man.

Why a Bentley, he thought as they drove along in silence. Roisin would never have chosen a Bentley. He hated that smell of old leather. And Roisin's perfume was making his nose hurt. Why did people think perfume was attractive?

Walking through the ground floor of a department store – not something he often chose to do, but it happened occasionally, usually around

Christmas – was like being subjected to chemical attack. That acrid taste on his tongue, the sweet-sharp-sickly smell leading to a throbbing in his head.

Elizabeth didn't wear perfume. She smelt of herself. And long summer days and hope. He tried to recapture that memory, while looking out of the window. It was actually quite a pleasant day.

If the weather had reflected his mood there would be storm clouds gathering. What did they call that, when it happened in books? Dad had told him once. The blue sky made him think of the dreamlike summer with Elizabeth. Was it over already?

He should talk to Roisin. He didn't have much longer. Their chauffeur, in his absurd uniform and peaked cap, would make a couple more turns and they would be there.

'They've forecast showers for later,' said the chauffeur gloomily. Why did he speak now, just as Jim was about to? When he'd had the whole journey to assert himself but had just sat staring straight ahead?

'It won't rain,' said Roisin. 'I've forbidden it.'

'You want the whole world to bend to your will,' said Jim. 'But life's not like that.'

'Today it is,' she declared. 'Today I am a bride.'

Jim went to open his mouth, but they'd arrived.

When there are two brides, who waits and who walks up the aisle? Roisin had thought of this, of course.

The room where they were holding the ceremony had entrances at either side. When they arrived, he was to look through their door, until he saw Melissa's father give a signal from the other. Then the two brides, on the arms of their respective escorts, would walk in and meet in the middle, where the registrar awaited.

This arrangement also meant that the seating could be set in a curve, rather than either side of an aisle, which might have led to conspicuous gaps on Roisin's side.

He looked across at the other doorway. A man who must be Melissa's dad smiled back roguishly. Jim had expected an old buffer with a shock of white hair. Instead, Melissa's dad was sharply stylish and wore an earring and no tie with his pinstriped three-piece. He gave the signal but Jim gestured to hold on.

'Are they there yet?' asked Roisin.

'Yes.'

'Then what are we waiting for? Let's get this shit over with so we can all start drinking.'

Jim looked around the room. 'Not yet,' he said, and then his heart jumped in his chest. Twice.

A voice behind him said, 'You look beautiful, Roisin. That dress!'

Jim kind of liked the dress too. It was off the shoulder and made from some iridescent greeny-purple material that made him think of mallards' heads. Not that he would share that description with Roisin.

'Thanks,' said Roisin

Edie was wearing a suit rather like his. She'd

told him androgyny was in, but the severe cut and neutral colours didn't suit her. This somehow made it even more poignant.

'I love the taffeta,' Edie continued. 'Understated but with a bit of pizzazz.'

'Krish got it for me at cost,' Roisin said. She looked close to tears, but whether at the thought of the absent Krish or the extent of the bargain, Jim wasn't sure.

'And I can't wait to finally see Melissa. I bet she's going to be beautiful.'

'She's wearing –'

Edie put her hand up and quieted Roisin, a trick Jim had never managed to pull off. 'Let me be surprised when we go in. In fact, shall we?'

Edie offered Roisin her arm. Roisin looked bewildered.

Jim went to the door and gave the signal to Melissa's father to go. Then he slipped in the door and took his place at the end of a row next to Elizabeth. The music began – something contemporary and choral which Melissa had chosen.

The cream of Gloucestershire society stood, turning its collective head from one door to the other as if watching a tennis match. He realised belatedly that it was a real choir, but he didn't have time to look properly because he turned his head to Roisin and Edie who were gliding into the room.

They looked perfect. As they got nearer he heard Edie stage-whisper, 'Don't worry, we're twins, no one will notice a thing.' Roisin's face turned to him briefly then looked forward towards her fate.

He thought of Maud in the picture. Hugh's picture. Elizabeth's picture.

'She was saying goodbye,' he whispered to Elizabeth. 'Maud was saying goodbye, and Hugh captured it.'

He understood now. Anger, betrayal, resentment were forgotten and the aching tenderness of that moment was captured forever. Maud was saying goodbye, with acceptance and goodwill.

Elizabeth took his hand. Roisin's face was nothing like that. But maybe his was.

Reviews help independent authors!

If you enjoyed this book please consider leaving a review on Amazon or Goodreads so other readers can find it.

Newsletter

Want to know more about Kate Vane's books? Sign up to her spam-free newsletter for occasional updates on new releases and offers at katevane.wordpress.com

About the Author

Kate Vane is the author of three novels, *The Former Chief Executive*, *Not the End* and *Recognition*.

She lived in Leeds for a number of years where she worked as a probation officer. She now lives in Devon.

Contact Kate

Twitter: @k8vane

Blog: katevane.wordpress.com

You can also find her on Facebook and Goodreads – just search for "Kate Vane"

Also by Kate Vane

The Former Chief Executive

Without your past, who are you?

Deborah was a respected hospital manager until a tragedy destroyed her reputation. She has lost her career, her husband and even her name.
Luca wants to stay in the moment. For the first time in his life he has hope and a home. But a fresh start is hard on a zero-hours contract, harder if old voices fill your mind.

When a garden share scheme brings them together, Deborah is beguiled by Luca's youth and grace. He makes her husband's garden live again. He helps her when she's at her lowest. But can she trust him? And when the time comes to confront her past, can she find the strength?

This sharply drawn short novel explores the distance between the generations – between health and wealth, owners and workers, guilt and blame.

The Former Chief Executive is published on 8 June 2017 in paperback and Kindle and available on Amazon.

Recognition

Nat Keane never forgot her first murder. Sandie Thurston was killed and mutilated in her own bed. Five-year-old Amy lay beside her, soaked in her mother's blood.

Nat was the first police officer on the scene. She was the family liaison officer who got close to the family. Too close. When a man was convicted, she walked away, lonely and broken.

Ten years on she has another life. She has a job she loves counselling trauma victims and a home with her partner, Dylan, a criminal lawyer. So when Martin, husband of the murdered Sandie, asks her to work with him and Amy, why does she agree to go back?

Amy's evidence was key to getting a conviction. Now the media are hinting that she got it wrong. Martin is tortured by a guilt he won't explain. At fifteen, Amy is alternately needy and hostile – a devoted daughter who deceives her father, a sheltered child who can't stop taking risks.

As Nat is drawn into the family's secrets, is she helping them find the truth or complicit in their lies? Who did kill Sandie? And why, just when Nat needs Dylan's support, is he distracted by a controversial case of his own?

Recognition is a compelling psychological thriller about grief, guilt and memory, set in and around Leeds in the early 2000s.

You can buy *Recognition* on Amazon Kindle.

Printed in Great Britain
by Amazon